CALDO LARGO

CALDO LARGO

BY
EARL THOMPSON

G.P. Putnam's Sons
New York

Copyright © 1976 by Earl Thompson
All rights reserved. This book, or parts
thereof, may not be reproduced in any form
without permission. Published simultaneously
in Canada by Longman Canada Limited, Toronto.

SBN: 399–11862–4

Library of Congress Cataloging in Publication Data

Thompson, Earl.
    Caldo Largo.

    I. Title.
PZ4.T4674CaX3 [PS3570.H598] 813'.5'4 76-22722

PRINTED IN THE UNITED STATES OF AMERICA

This one is dedicated to:
Harvey, Frank, and Jose

CALDO LARGO

CHAPTER ONE

It was hard to take the two seriously when they began to talk about revolution although they were so religiously arched about their mission you had to know they thought they were up to something. They were young, and I wondered where Lupe had found them. Also, she had to be home when her husband came off duty at midnight, so it was crazy for her to have brought them.

Both sat across the table from us in the galley, letting the coffee grow cold in the cups between their hands. They had accepted a shot of Fundador when they sat down, but they were not there to have a nice time.

After spending a lot of time explaining to me why Fidel Castro was a much better man than Fulgencio Batista—a point I would have given them going in—the one Lupe called Raimundo told me what they wanted me to do, and I told them I wasn't interested.

"There is money in it for you," he insisted.

I hadn't thought he would ask me to do it because Castro was the better man.

"How much?" I wasn't about to do it, I just wanted to hear him put a price on it.

They had only Lupe's word they could trust me, and they consulted her a moment with their eyes. "Six thousand," Raimundo said.

That surprised me. Lupe's word must be pretty good.

They were both dressed in the kind of shirts, slacks, and

shoes you can buy off the sidewalk on both sides of the river.

But Raimundo hadn't batted an eye. He was some kind of crazy, or some Raimundo.

Even Lupe seemed surprised. She whistled softly.

"If you can help us this time, maybe we can do more business," Raimundo suggested.

"Well, maybe I will think about it," I told him, thinking of what I could do with six thousand.

Though his clothes were cheap, I noticed his hands, resting so quietly on either side of his cup, were not those of one who worked with them for his living. The more I studied him, the more he looked to me like one of those intense South American students you see. The other one was rougher material. He had a broad, darker face, was probably a mulatto, and his hands were not so fine or so still. He let Raimundo do all the talking.

"We must know very soon," Raimundo said.

"Well, I would have to think about it. They have about two hundred of you people penned up at Fort Brown right now."

"That is why we need a boat that can go near Cuba in a way that causes no suspicion."

"Well, we don't normally go that far from here. Sometimes we go around Yucatan, but most of the boats that work around Cuba are out of Florida. Why don't you try to do this from there?"

The two looked at each other; then Raimundo turned back and said, "It is very difficult from Florida at this moment."

"*Impossible!*" the other one said, lifting his chin at me as if that were my fault.

"But you could go?" Raimundo asked. "There are those who do?"

"Oh, you could do it. Some boats have. Some have run in there in a storm, too. You could do it."

Since the revolution started in Cuba, there had been guys around talking about how easy it would be to run something over there. No one knew for sure if there was any money in it. But if you run a boat for a living, you always dream of how

)u might do such a thing sometime, if the money was right.
hen you shake yourself and think about those two hundred
r so would-be revolutionaries we had in the old stockade at
ort Brown who had been picked up trying to get to Cuba. A
)t of them had been pulled in off anything that would float
nd had a motor. Four had been found adrift in an open boat,
:ying to make Cuba when the outboard motor failed. A lot of
hem had been stiffed with boats that began to leak badly after
hey hit the sea and had engines that quit after a few hours'
unning time. They weren't going to sue anybody. Some were
ust bad sailors.

I did not like it that we had those people penned up at Fort
3rown. I didn't like it that some son of a bitch had stiffed
hem on a boat, knowing they would never make it out in the
Gulf and not giving a damn one way or the other.

I didn't know if Castro was any good or not, but he seemed
to be making an interesting sight, and most of the people I
know who worked for a living sort of hoped he'd win, without
thinking too much about it.

"Getting out with the stuff wouldn't be too risky," I said,
thinking aloud. "But I don't know what the situation would be
once you got there."

"Oh, that is the *easy* part," Raimundo insisted, leaning forward eagerly.

I had to laugh. *Oh, well, where is it, we can begin to load
now,* I thought. He thought I was making fun of him and sat
back. I sobered up, yet had to smile.

"Tell me about the easy part."

In Spanish he said to Lupe, "He is not serious."

"He is serious when it counts," she assured him, also in
Spanish. Then she leaned forward and touched his hand.
"Do I know what is in the heart of a man?"

I caught most of what she said and could not have missed
the touch. Sitting back she laid her hand on my thigh, dug
her nails in, then patted the place gently.

"If we do business together, we will tell you everything you
need to know. You can trust me on that. We are not kidding

around. If we can get the supplies so far, we are not going t
lose them, you can be sure of that."

"Yow, Raimundo, but how?"

"Are you interested?"

"If you can convince me about that easy part, I might be."

"He is playing with us," the dark one said and gave me
hard look.

"Mister," Raimundo said, "if there was no risk, we coul
make the trip ourselves and save the money. It is this end w
worry about. I promise you if you get to Cuba, there it will b
very simple."

"It is a lot of money, Johnny," Lupe said.

I could not figure her interest in it.

"I'll think about it."

"When can you tell us?" Raimundo asked.

"Well, we are going out in the morning. We'll probably stay
out about three weeks."

He looked at Lupe as if she had been wasting their time too.

"We are in a hurry. These things are needed."

"Then I guess I can't help you. I would have to see how the
other two who work with me felt about something like this.
This boat costs a lot more than six thousand."

"We know that," the dark one said in Spanish.

"Yow. Well, it's my home, my living," I explained. "I'm not
against you or what you're doing, and I could use the
money." I wondered where Lupe had found them. "But a
man will risk his skin a lot sooner than he will risk his living."

"Yes. That is true," Raimundo said. "I am sorry, we are in a
hurry. The things are needed."

I made an open, hopeless gesture with my hand. "OK. Sorry I can't be of more help to you."

They both got up, the dark one just a beat behind Raimundo. The dark one acted as if he were carrying a gun, though I
saw no unusual bulges on him. It all seemed funny again.

"Maybe we will speak another time," Raimundo said.
"Please do not mention this to anyone."

"I won't." I raised my hand to promise.

"Come on," he said to the dark one.

We had shaken hands when they came in, but we did not hen they went out.

Lupe told me, "One little minute, *querido mío*," and epped outside with them.

"You brought us to a fool," I heard Raimundo accuse her 1 Spanish. "He is not a serious man. You said he was serius."

"He is the most serious I know," she swore.

"Then you are wasting your time even more than ours."

"You are just angry now. I will speak with you another ime. If Castro would be so ungrateful as you, screw your revlution!" she called after them.

"Why don't you broadcast it, you dumb whore?" the dark ne shouted back.

Some revolution.

She came inside.

"So? What do you think?" she asked, flipping her hair back over one shoulder.

I laughed and put my arms around her. "I think you are some punkins."

"What is that . . . punkins?"

"Uh . . . *calabaza*." I joggled her famous buttocks with both hands.

"Oh!" She hit me twice on the chest. "Everyone knows about that. Be serious. Why were you so stupid to my friends? I built you up good to them. You embarrass me."

"Well, hell, they come in here acting like they were in a movie, Lupe, offer me six thousand to run some guns or something to Cuba for Castro, and neither one of them looks like they ever saw six thousand—Where did you meet them?"

"Oh, I met them at a party in someone's house, my girlfriend. Everybody began to talk about Castro. One thing led to another. To these boys this revolution is serious business."

"That's what's wrong with revolutions. That and the fact a lot of people get killed in them."

"Oh, most people are dead and don't know it anyway."

"So, I am the most serious man you know, hunh?"

"You understood that?"

"Sure."

"Your Spanish is getting better. Soon I will have no secre
from you."

"You have a lot of secrets, do you?"

"Um. Many. You want to hear some now or make love?
must be home when my husband comes. You must choose."

I unzipped the back of her dress and put my hands insid
on her soft warm skin.

"You never had to be home before," I reminded her.

"Tonight is different . . . . you touch me better than any
one, *querido mío.*"

She kissed me better than anyone ever had.

"We are so quick to be ready for love, you and me
Johnny."

"Yes. I feel your little motor running."

She laughed softly. "You like my little motor?"

"Beautiful little motor."

There was a quiver in her lips and mouth when she kissec
that was like the quiver in her body I felt when I was in her.

"Others do not have a little motor?" she wondered.

"None that I have known."

"Maybe there is something wrong with me."

"I don't think so."

"I don't think so, too."

I undressed and turned back the covers on the lower bunk
and got into it while she was laying her stockings over the
back of a chair.

Because I lived on the boat, I had torn out the two bunks
on the other side of the cabin and built in a desk, lots of draw-
ers, a bookrack, and a good big hanging locker.

"*Música,*" she decided, bending over the desk to turn on
the portable radio to a Mexican station. She danced a few
steps in the moonlight with her back to me, snapped her
fingers, and sang a snatch of the song. She knew she had one
of the world's great behinds. Each side of it danced solo, yet a

perfect partner for the other. Her thighs were long and meaty, her calves and feet slender. When she walked, even old men and little boys smacked their lips, whistled, rubbed themselves openly, and uttered poetic and profane vows and pledges after her. Young men followed her though they might have to reverse direction to do so.

She flipped her heavy dark-reddish hair off her neck and peered over her shoulder at me, just touching her bottom with the dancing tips of her fingers, making mouths and cat faces.

I lunged half out of the bunk, wrapped my arms around her hips and kissed her where stretch marks were like tiny silverfish across the coffee-cream skin of her bottom. I hauled her into the bunk, and she turned in my arms.

I kissed her breasts and the other little silverfish that swam upward from her wide dark bush and down into the hollows and smooth places of her thighs.

When I had asked her if she had children, she told me she had a baby born dead. Later, when we were friends, she told me she had lied. There was a baby, a boy, born such a monster it had been taken away from her and put in a state hospital. She'd had to sign a paper. She said she liked children very much, but she was afriad to have another. Even if she were not afraid, she would not have one with her husband. He was an Anglo border guard twenty-four years older than she. She said she had thrown herself at him when she was very young. Unable to believe his good luck in having so beautiful a young girl want him while he was still wounded because his wife had run away with another man, he used and abused Lupe in ways she thought then were very dirty. He beat her and called her a whore. He said she had the heart of a whore and would be a whore always. She said her father had told her the same thing and that she was afraid it could be so. Soon she was pregnant.

She said she did not know what love was for many years. "For years, I think it is something cruel and sick." she'd told me. Then, when she learned from others what love was, she

knew she did not love the one she had married. "It is the romance that is so sick," she told me. "Love is OK, but we are
infected with romance. We dream of being princesses and
princes, but it makes us into beasts. We can do anything. It is
not love."

Johnny Hand, they name you well. You touch me so wonderful, my darling," she purred. "No one touches me so wonderful as you."

"¿Es verdad?"

"Yes, it is true."

"If it wasn't, would you still say so?"

She laughed. "Sometimes, maybe . . . . Johnny, this
time let's pretend we make a baby. You and me, Johnny. I
never say this to anyone ever. Let's make love like we will
make a baby together. With much love, Johnny. With much,
much love, my darling." She touched the corners of my
mouth with trembling fingertips. "You feel good in me. Feel
my motor, Johnny?"

"Yes."

"Say you love me, Johnny. We can pretend for one time,
OK?"

"I do love you, Lupe. It is like you said about love to me
once. I understand. I love you, Lupe."

"Be slow, Johnny . . . . Yes."

We smoked a cigarette together in the bunk. She held the
ashtray on her belly. Her knees were raised together; her back
was against the bulkhead. A woman was singing an old *ranchero* on the radio, punctuated with the mournful yelps and
cries that meant so much more than our Anglo notion of pain
and heartbreak and turned the traditional romantic words of
the poet with which both he and we had been saddled into
something you could know if you hadn't word one.

I drifted my hand up and down between Lupe's silky thighs,
feeling I could touch her so aimlessly until it became more an
annoyance than a pleasure; a wanting of something more

when we had survived our satisfaction and there was nothing more yet we really wanted to do. I lay in the crook of her arm with my cheek against her breast and could glance up and see her face from below. With her lipstick kissed away, her lips did not look so wide and full. Her face looked so much younger. Beads of mascara clotted her long lashes. Her makeup extended down her neck and over the tops of her breasts where they would be visible in the opening of her dress. There was an unnatural pinkness about it in bright light, I remembered. A solitary black hair about two inches long grew from her breast near the nipple closest to my eye.

I started to pluck it out.

"*¡Ai, parate!* Leave it. I will cut it."

"You are a good lady, Lupe."

"Yes. *Shh!* I want to hear." She cocked her head toward the radio.

It sounded like a Mexican newscast in Spanish so rapid I could not follow it.

"Oh! I don't believe it! It is a lie!"

"What?"

"He said they have trapped Fidel Castro again in the mountains, and this time it is certain, this time he will be wiped out. There is a report that he is already dead or captured. Some general promises it will all be over in twenty-four hours."

"They've said that before."

"Of course! That is what makes me so mad. They will lie in your face these days and never confess the truth when the facts prove they are big liars. No, they come right back and lie to you again. They show no respect for us. Forget the truth!"

"Our assholes do the same."

"*Ha!* Your assholes invented the game. It makes me so mad sometimes I think I will never sleep with another Anglo in my life."

"You're quarter Anglo yourself," I reminded her.

"OK. I stay one-quarter of the night." She laughed.

I pulled her down in the bed and kissed her.

"There is not time, Johnny. I must go soon. I don't need something more. It was wonderful tonight. Do you need something?"

"No."

"Good. Let's talk. I feel like talking. You are nice to talk with. You understand me."

"What do you want to talk about?"

"Anything. Ask me something."

"I didn't know you were so interested in Castro."

"I am interested in many thing. I don't know, I think he is different from the others, the politicians and the generals. Many people I like say they feel this also. He is good-looking too."

"That matter?"

"Sure. I don't like pretty men, but to look at. A man can be very ugly in a way and still be good-looking."

She separated the word so the emphasis was on "good." That gave a whole new meaning to it.

"When I look at a man, if I don't listen to the bullshit he is trying to tell me and trust my feelings, it is always wonderful. I don't mean just to sleep with. To know him. But too much I will listen and trust my brain and I trick myself and then I feel bad, for it is not wonderful. I think all the time women do this. It is because you men do not know how to use your words to tell the truth about your feelings or nothing. Your words trick you as well. You men own all the words. If women made up the words from the start, maybe we would speak a true tongue. But we have only men's words to use, so many women are never able to say nothing."

"Why do you stay with your husband?"

"He needs me. He is frightened. He thinks he is getting old. He has no one else. Since she leaves and takes the children, he never hears from his wife. And there is something between us that holds me. It is not love. It is not good. It is awful. I hate it. But it holds me. He is always afraid I leave him. We don't hardly make love no more. He knows I sleep with other men. He is not jealous in a mean way now. He is a sad man. He says I should find another and be happy. I think this is my punishment."

"For what?"

"I don't know. I will think about it and try to tell you sometime. There is no love between us. Oh maybe he loves me. I don't know. He is like my father. Many times I make my luggage to go. But I think I will never leave him."

"Why can't you stay tonight?"

"I can't." She set down the ashtray and swung her legs out of the bunk. "Come on. We must go."

"Why?"

"Because tomorrow is the anniversary of our child and I don't want to be in any bed but my own."

I drove her back to town in the truck. She had come out with the two young men in their car.

Drifts of fine sand feathered down onto the edges of the black top beneath the overhang of beach grass. Hundreds of side-going little land crabs scuttled across the road in the beams of the headlights and were crunched beneath the tires. On the inlet side of the road a garfish or something that sounded like a gar croaked from the depths of a great belly. A night owl screeched. A dilapidated truck loaded with melons was broken down beside the road. A Mexican slept on top of the load to guard it.

"How serious do you think those two boys are?" I asked her.

"I think they are very serious. Don't you think so?"

"Acted liked they *thought* they were. They're pretty young."

She shrugged. "You are still pretty young yourself. I am older than you. How old were you when you went to war?"

"Seventeen."

"They are not so young."

"And you think they have that kind of money?"

"Yes. I said so."

"How did you happen to tell them about me?"

She shrugged again. "Raimundo was very open to me. He told me all about Fidel Castro and the revolution and how he needs a boat to carry some things to Cuba. A fishing boat. He said he would pay a lot of money for the right boat and man. So I think of you. You need money. I trust you. Raimundo talks to me all night about revolution—*ai!*" She laughed and rocked her head from side to side, holding it as if it hurt.

"You sleep with him?"

She looked at me. "Yes."

"How was it?"

"OK."

"You going to sleep with him again?"

"Maybe. I don't know."

She did not like the questions and lit a cigarette. The flame illuminated her face for an instant. She always pursed her lips exaggeratedly when lighting a cigarette. Now she was frowning. Sitting back, she blew smoke at the windshield. It billowed like fog in front of me.

"Why do you ask me such things?"

"I don't know."

"I don't like it. You never do something like this before. Please don't ask again, OK?"

"OK."

She scooted over, bouncing twice on the seat, and kissed the corner of my mouth.

"Don't ever be jealous, my darling," she cooed. "There is no reason. Tonight was wonderful. What is between us is wonderful and not between me and any other."

"Wouldn't it be the same the other way around?"

"If you wish." She bounced back across the seat and crossed her arms under her breasts.

I grinned and reached over and tweaked the end of her tit.

"Don't touch me!" She slapped my hand. "I don't like jealous men. If you become jealous of me, I will never see you again."

"Maybe I am a little jealous," I admitted.

"How much?" she demanded.

"About that much." I showed her a little space between my forefinger and thumb.

"Even that is too much. I am not jealous of your women. Not even of how you look at Encanta. You know how you look at her? Like this." She made a face like a lout witnessing the birth of beauty.

I laughed. "Everyone looks at her like that."

"Well, if you ever look at me like that, I would throw up." Then she changed her mind and bounced back across the seat. "No. If you look at me like that once, I will do everything for you."

"There's something you haven't done?"

She laughed. "You are a wise guy."

"Stop here," she ordered.

I pulled the old pickup over to the curb beneath a big tree. We held each other tight and kissed. I touched her breasts, hips, reached beneath her dress and touched her thighs and held her sex tight for a moment.

"I dream of how you touch me. I will dream of you tonight and all day tomorrow. I won't go to work tomorrow."

I did not ask her who she would dream of tomorrow night.

"Have a good trip, Johnny. Fish well."

"I will. You keep well."

"Of course!"

We kissed once more, and she got out of the truck.

She leaned back in the open window and said, "If you go to Cuba, take me with you. I need a vacation."

"OK. If I do." I laughed.

She blew me a kiss and went across the grass and swung away along the sidewalk.

She lived around the corner, about halfway down the block, in a neighborhood of small fake-Spanish stucco bungalows.

I started the truck and crept along until I was keeping pace with her. She glanced over, then snapped her face forward and elevated her chin.

"If you are selling that, I will give you my heart and a million dollars."

"You have no heart. Show me your money," she challenged.

"Well, I'm not rich. I'll give it to you a dollar at a time. OK?"

"Push off! You think this is Sears and Roebucks?"

"It moves as if it is hung on little springs."

"Maybe for love sometime," she said. At the corner she gave her ass a special flip and turned toward her husband's house.

There were bums sleeping along the wall of the historical building across from the courthouse too drunk to get themselves thrown into jail for the night.

Bare feet stuck out of the windows of dusty cars that hung lopsided on their tired springs along the courthouse parking. Families had come from the ends of the country with business in the courthouse which had either been held over, or they were there to get an early appointment the next morning. On a blanket spread on the grass beside the open doors of their car a man and a woman slept in each other's arms. A child snuggled against the woman's broad back.

There was no one on the road or in the port. The Mexican still slept atop his load of melons.

I felt all right, but for the first time since I got her, I was a little anxious about living alone on the boat.

I knew it was silly; still, I took the carbine from its scabbard, jacked a round into the chamber, and put it on the bunk frame against the wall where I could reach it.

I felt so ridiculous then, lying there with a loaded rifle next to me, I could not sleep, so I got up, unloaded the carbine, put it back in its case, and shut it in the locker.

I took a drink of water and went back to bed.

CHAPTER TWO

There are all kinds of things in the sea. When we tried for some whites out near the Matagorda ranges, we did not come up with enough shrimp to warrant burning the diesel to make the run. Ezequiel and Eli spilled out the try net and separated a few good fish for the pot from the trash fish, and in the bottom of the bag there was a Navy air-to-air rocket about three feet long.

Ezequiel snatched up the rocket with his good hand and a small gray shark with his left. With only thumb and pinkie on his left it was more claw than hand.

"Hey, *capitán!*"

"Get rid of that!"

"Sure. Catch him!"

He made as if to throw the rocket at me but let go of the shark.

I caught it with both hands and hung on tight. It was a very alive little shark.

A baby shark is born as complete and ready to go as it ever will be. It is just smaller. This one was two and a half feet long and was angry before it was ever tossed. Its mouth, full of real little shark's teeth, could take a finger or chunk off my hand, and its cold little eyes were seeking with that pure intent. In some sharks the killer instinct is so strong one will kill all the others in the womb before it is born.

It was a five-footer that had gotten all but the little finger and thumb of Ezequiel Cavazos' left hand; years ago, on another boat, when he was young.

So I squeezed this one tight with both hands as it squirmed strongly and tried to attack me.

Ezequiel and Eli thought it was very funny.

Holding the damned thing like a rubbery rifle with a bayonet on it, I ran at Eli, who was nearest, and let it take a snap at the back of his old Texas University athletic shorts. It got a little shorts and a little of Eli, and he jumped about three feet in the air.

"Fuck-your-mother-it-has-teeth-bastard!" he hollered in Spanish on the ascent.

When he came down, he hauled up the back of his shorts and peered over his shoulder to examine his wound.

"Look! Look! I am bleeding!" he told me in Spanish, with a hurt look on his broad young face. "I didn't throw that shark on you," he said in English. "Why don't you make it bite him?" He jerked his head at Ezequiel, who was holding his guts with both hands while laughing and dancing on the deck.

"He's *been* bit. And it would make the shark sick," I said.

"Fuck the shark! Look at this shit! My wife is going to want to know who bit my ass. You think she will believe me?"

"There are many who would not," Ezequiel informed him in Spanish.

I threw the shark back into the Gulf and watched it swim off. It still looked mad as hell. A four or five-footer could tear up a net.

"You should have killed him," Ezequiel said reprovingly. "I never let one live. One day that one can come back and eat you. I kill anything that wants to eat me." He tapped his chest with his bad hand.

"Look at me, you crazy old man, I am bleeding," Eli demanded and showed Ezequiel his wound.

"Oh, it is nothing, my son," he assured him in Spanish. In English he added, "I will kiss him and make him well." So say-

ing, he grabbed Eli and planted a kiss on his wound, which set
Eli to jumping around and complaining again.

"Now you have given me an infection, you syphilitic old
child molester!" Eli squawked in Spanish and went off to find
the first-aid kit.

Ezequiel bent him over the hatch cover and liberally
daubed his wound with Merthiolate.

"You want a dressing also, you big queer?" Ezequiel asked
in Spanish falsetto. He slapped a big Band-Aid on Eli and
stepped back to admire his work. "One inch deeper, and it
gets his brains. Go now and look at yourself. You have not so
much to lose."

"I have more to lose than you, old man, however you look
at it," Eli replied sulkily.

"I lost more when I lose my fingers than you are ever worth,
asshole." And he gave Eli a pinch on the other cheek with
that thumb and little finger which hurt as much as being bit-
ten by the little shark.

That thing was strong. The thumb had also been damaged,
so the nail grew back on the side facing the palm. It was
sharp, and Ezequiel liked to sink it in you and twist.

We cleaned up and got ready to move and try someplace
else. They hosed off the afterdeck. While Eli swept the water
away, Ezequiel gutted three nice redfish, and a Spanish
mackerel and cleaned some shrimp, rinsed them in a bucket
of sea water, and took them into the galley to divide between
those he would fry for our supper and those he would chunk
into a pot of thick soup he began as soon as we left port and
kept going until we returned. A kind of Mexican bouil-
labaisse, it was great soup. On the docks of Tampico and Ve-
racruz big pots of the soup bubbled the clock around, for
days, weeks—Ezequiel claimed, for generations.

I came through the galley just as the old man was
laying the chunks of fish gently into his soup. I dredged

up a ladleful from the depths of the pot and tasted it.
"Gets better and better," I congratulated him.
"That is its nature," he said. *"Caldo largo* is the soup of
life."
"How's that, Ezequiel?"
"It is life!" He banged the pot with a big spoon. "Here is the
world." He spooned up the thick soup and poured it back into
the pot. "Here is life *por siempre jámas*—forever and ever.
And I? I am God." He laughed at his presumption. *"¿Quién
sabe?* Who knows? Many things are possible. You think he is a
saint? Bullshit, my friend. He is always telling jokes. He is like
me. But he is more cruel. When I discover *sexo*, the business
between a man and a woman, I learn for the first time God
has a sense of humor. He is more cruel than me, but we are
much alike." He laughed again.
"I wouldn't talk like that, especially at sea," I teased him. "A
big fucking hand will reach out of the sky and pinch your
head off."
"I don't worry. That is just the Christian god who does that.
There arc others. There are many gods and many devils. The
shark that took my hand, he was a devil. I could see him when
he bite me. I pay that devil, now I am safe for these many
years. I don't even get sick for one day. For many years my
wife gives me no children. Many years. When I come with
this"—he showed me his mauled hand—"she gives me
many."
"A devil did that?"
"Sure. God-devil, they are the same. They are all liars." He
laughed. "They are better liars even than me."
"The stuff you smoke is a hell of a lot better than the stuff
Eli and I smoke," I told him.
"Yes. Because I grow it myself from seeds given me by a fa-
mous *curandea*. I grow it on what I take from my outhouse
when it is full."
"You told me."
"It is very rare. You like some?"
"Not now, thanks."

"I will give you some seeds if you like them," he offered.

"I don't have any place to plant them."

"That is true. When you get some land, I will give you some seeds."

"Guess I would need an outhouse too and many children to fill it," I joked.

"Yes. That is the best way, of course," he said.

CHAPTER THREE

We continued to have bad luck for the next two weeks. A storm drove us in behind a little island in the Laguna Madre about halfway down to Tampico, where we anchored and tied up with the trawlers of Captains Braemer and Johnson. In three days, while the storm blew, I lost a hundred and fourteen dollars to Johnson in the card games which passed the time while we were stuck in there eating and drinking up our stores, while our ice was melting and each hour was costing us money.

The last big hurricane had torn up the shrimp beds all over that part of the Gulf. I was beginning to think we were going to have to stay out for six weeks and run all the way around Yucatan to make our nut, forget making money.

I had not owned the boat long. It took all the dollars I could scrape together, and then I had to take Eli Ramirez in as a minority partner to swing it finally. He was in for two thousand at ten percent, and I had the option of buying him out at any time. We shrimped on shares, called leys. Fifty percent of the catch went to the boat and for the purchase of the thrity-two tons of shaved ice we took aboard every trip, for seven thousand gallons of fuel, nets at three hundred bucks per, and essential stores. The other half of the catch we shared out.

Though all boats are female, mine was named the *Sgt. William T. Shea.* Shea and I met at Benning and went through jump school together. We became friends, which is a hell of a lot different from being good buddies. Neither of us had any close family. I had some grandparents, but Shea had no one. He had been given the choice of joining the Army or going to a reformatory by a judge in Corpus Christi. I had been knocking cattle for a packinghouse which went out on strike, so one day I just enlisted.

Shea and I were Regular Army, with three-year hitches to serve.

Shea convinced me what we should do was save our money, work on other shrimp boats when we got out of the Army until we could try to go partners on a boat of our own. He was sure shrimping was a good way to go. Shrimp fishing had started to boom about the time the Korean War broke out.

Until 1949 shrimping was mainly a day-tripping business. Shrimpers went out and fished in the daytime for the white shrimp, oystered when shrimp were out of season, and boot-legged a little between oysters and shrimp. Some also ran in wetbacks or Chinese, I have been told. But there was rumor of mysterious huge shrimp, some of which turned up regularly in bait nets hung from the bridges between the Florida Keys and in the stomachs of fish caught out of Key West—an enormous beautiful pink shrimp. But none of these babies ever turned up in the nets of the shrimpers.

Two brothers, John and Felix Salvador, were determined to find out where those big pink shrimp came from. A Key West seafood company, Thompson Enterprises, Inc., let them have a decrepit old trawler, which they rigged with a seven-foot try net. They tried the bottom from Key West to the Dry Tortugas for two straight weeks and found nothing.

Just as they were heading back for Key West, they put down the trawl for one last run, even though the sun had set, and everyone knew shrimp went to sleep in the mud after sun-down. When they hauled the net, they found it full of the pretty pinks, jumping and snapping. The mystery was: these shrimp came out of the mud only at night. The famous Dry

Tortugas shrimp beds were born. Shrimpers hung powerful
lights on their masts and learned to sleep during the day or
slept not at all, fishing for whites or common shrimp by day
and the new pink groove-headed shrimp by night.

Back in 1940 the trawler *Neptune,* out of Port Isabel, Texas,
came into port with a strange catch of brownish shrimp which
were hard to sell because buyers used to white shrimp considered the brownies tainted. But these proved to be another
species of the groove-headed variety, and the Food and Drug
Administration said they were perfectly good to eat. To get
people to do that took a lot of good salesmanship. Some ge-
nius realized around 1948 "brown shrimp" just did not sound
right. So the next thing you knew people were buying "Gold-
en Brazilian Shrimp," and the Texas and Mexican shrimp
beds began to boom.

The annual catch of shrimp now surpasses that of tuna,
salmon, or oysters in value.

The night Shea was killed in Korea he had been talking of
the Gulf Coast sun, Mexican ports, and dark-eyed *señoritas*
with skin like butter, while we crouched in our holes in the
bone-chilling cold which all but immobilized us. Shea had
been wearing his parade scarf since Thanksgiving, which was
when MacArthur had promised we would be parading in To-
kyo. Shea had a bad cold, both his ears were blocked so he
was all but deaf, and that sky blue silk scarf was the handiest
thing on which to blow his nose.

If MacArthur was not a shithead, he was a hundred years
too late to achieve the kind of glory for which he was geared.
Around two in the morning we were attacked. The Chinese
crawled right up to our holes, crawled up closer to us than we
ever wanted to crawl up on an enemy in war again, I think.
They fought for some gut-essential purpose. We fought for
bullshit slogans about anti-Communism that had no bearing
on anything at all once we were on cold killing ground, so we
fought mainly to stay alive and go home to try to make a living
a little better than we ever had before. The difference was: I'm

sure they were in it together for some good reason, and we were just there, and no one could give us any good reasons why. I never felt more foreign or more foolish than I did the night Shea was killed.

But Shea was right, running your own boat is a pretty good way to go.

I worked on Captain Wesley Slocum's boat for a year, then captained for him on another of his boats for three years and saved my money.

I also had ten thousand dollars from Shea's insurance. He had given me a letter when we were on orders for Korea and told me to open it only in case he got killed. All it said was:

> You have been as close to a brother to me as I could ever want a brother to be.
>
> If I wasn't dead you wouldn't be reading this. That's funny. I sure wish I was with you. You tell them señoritas "hello" for me.
>
> Be sure to go and see the guy whose name and address in Corpus is at the bottom of this letter. It's important for you to do this. He can make our dream come true for you. It's been good knowing you, Johnny.
>
> I don't believe there's anything after this, as I know you don't either, but if we are wrong, I'll hold a place for you. Hell, whichever way I'll be goin you'll be goin too."

The address was a juvenile parole officer in Corpus. Shea had fixed it so his GI insurance was paid to this guy to hold for me. You could not sign your insurance to a man in your own unit not blood kin, lest he be tempted to collect. I reckoned that was also why Shea had been mysterious about it in the letter he had me hold, in case I opened it before it was time. It would be as smart a thing to do if the beneficiary was your own brother, I decided.

Then, fresh back from Korea and working on the shrimp boats, I was into another goddamned war—the great American-Mexican shrimp war. There was still a Thompson submachine gun I bought in Mexico for three hundred dollars hidden away down in the engine room and a carbine and shotgun in my locker.

Out of that war came the Mexican-American Shrimp Association and relative peace, though we were still pulled in and fined for fishing in Mexican territorial waters with some regularity. But the war was over. Over only because the United States threatened to close our markets to Mexican shrimp, which would have put their industry out of business, unless some agreements could be reached and the shooting stopped.

Anyway, I saved my money and had Shea's ten thousand, and when this boat came available, I sold my car, got all the money together, and put it down on her, though it took Eli's two thousand to close the deal and give me a little operating capital.

So her name was the *Sgt. William T. Shea.* Sometimes you just have to have it both ways or you leave out someone important. Maybe if you can't put it together both ways, whatever you do, you are bound to leave out someone somewhere you should not.

Eli and Ezequiel and I often talked of such ideas, usually after we had a lot of shrimp in the hold, had some beers, and maybe smoked a little pot.

At the moment, however, I was feeling the panic you feel when you are up to your ass in debt, maybe trying something a little over your head, when your luck seems to be running wrong, and you begin to see the faces of all those you owe, their hands out for what is due, which you can't deliver, and I was feeling mean toward Eli and Ezequiel. I found myself thinking when I saw them slouching around or grabassing: *Goddamned Mexicans don't give a fuck if school keeps or not!* It is a bitter feeling that burns you up, burns in your mind until you cannot think straight, burns in your chest. It is a hell of a way to feel about people you otherwise like a lot and have a lot of fun with when the pressure of making money is off.

"Shrimps are *locos*, Juanito," Ezequiel said, seeing how I

was feeling when he brought me a plate of his great fish soup. There were red beans and rice on the side. "Don't try to think like the shrimps; you will make yourself *loco* too. Think like a *capitán, Capitán.*"

He gave me a wrenching pinch with that goddamned claw of his that made me holler and my eyes water.

Son-of-a-bitch-it-hurt-when-he-did-that!

"Cheer up!" He commanded. "Look. I have brought you Mexican *cerveza*. No fuckin Jax tonight."

He slapped down a bottle of Dos Equis dark beer beside my plate. The malt-colored foam raised a little head in the dark brown mouth of the bottle.

"Shrimps are cockroaches of the sea," he said. "They are very old things, I think. I bet sometime some Indian was starving and he eat one against his instinct and say: 'Hey! That's not so fuckin bad. Maybe with a little *tomate* and *chiles* and honions he be OK.'"

"You think an Indian did that?"

"He could be the only one. Sure. You enjoy your food now. It is good if I do say so myself."

It was very good. The fish and shrimp, mussels and eel, and whatever else he had in there had not been cooked into an undifferentiated sludge of taste, for Ezequiel never let the pot boil. It simmered only very gently.

"Good stuff," I congratulated him. "If I weren't in love with your daughter and you were a little prettier, maybe I would marry you."

"You wouldn't get no virgin anyway," he said, sitting down with his plate and beer. "Which of my daughters is it you love?"

"María-Antoinette, Toni, of course. Everyone is in love with her."

"That's so. You can love her until you are sickening, but if you ever touch her, I will kill you, my friend. She is my salvation."

He meant it, I think.

"Soon she will marry someone."

"Yes. That is my hope. Soon she must marry. But not you."

"How old is she?"

"Ah . . . twenty-four. Not so young. But the man for her
has not come. Soon, I think, he comes. Hey, why don't you
marry one of my others? The second you are too late for. She
will soon make me a grandfather by that stupid *gringo* who
dreams he will be a great *torero*." He laughed. "He is not even
a great fool or a good mechanic. But she is no prize either or
she would not marry with him. Their baby will amount to
nothing . . . . If I did not like you, I would give you my next
one tomorrow. Though it is not so nice to say this of my wife,
I think this one is not mine. Her legs is too long, and from the
back she looks like a boy, just a bump to sit on. She will have
trouble with children if any man can get it into her. From the
front she's not so bad. But now she cuts off all her hair. And if
she gets mad, she will put a knife into you while you are sleeping . . . if she cannot do it before."

"How old is she?"

"Ah, Chelo, she is just fifteen. No one can tell her nothing.
She just runs off to Colorado to see the big mountains. *Solo.*
On *el pulgar.*" He pretended to thumb a ride. "No one knows
where she goes. In just the clothes she wears. All the way to
the mountains in Colorado with one dollar in her pocket. I
don't know where she gets that dollar. She is gone three
months, more. No one knows where she is. The police don't
care. She is a poor Mexican. Everyone thinks she is pregnant
or run off with a boy.

"Then one day she comes into my house like she had been
up to the store. Now she has good boots and a jacket. I say,
'Where you get them boots and jacket?' She says some man
with a Buick car give her a ride and buy her boots and jacket
because it is very cold with much snow there. I ask her what
she give him. She says, 'I don't give him nothing! I am not no
puta!' She is very mad with me then. She say, 'I don't give no
man nothing. One day when I see a man and I like him, I will
take what I want and give him what I want. I am not a horse
to be ridden like *la Encanta*, who must go to her bed if she

gets a little *grano* on her precious *nalgas*. No one owns me. Not even you!' I would have hit her, but I am a little afraid of her." He laughed.

"No. You must wait a couple of years. It is my next daughter that is the one for you. She is only twelve, but already she is a beauty. Not so beautiful as my first, who is every man's dream, but this one will be like my wife. My wife was very beautiful when she was younger. We still fit pretty good.

"I was working in a field in Tamaulipas for a rich man. She was bending over a little in front of me to pick cotton. She is older than me by four years. The wind blows her skirt over her back, and I see she don't wear nothing under. Nobody wears nothing under in them days. We had nothing."

Ezequiel still wore nothing under, but I did not point this out to him.

"I never seen nothing so nice. All the men say things about what we can see, and she is very embarrassed. Later I hear some others—real tough guys, bastards—they catch her in some trees and screw her. They are drunk. It happens. But I cannot stop thinking about her. I have dreams about what those guys do to her, and I am ashamed, for I wish I was one with them that night. So there is nothing I can do but tell her I wish to marry with her and take her away from that place. I tell her we will go across the river where we will be rich.

"She says to me I am too young. I tell her she will never find a man there to marry with her now so good as me. I tell her it is better one a little young than one too old with many children. She knows I tell her the truth. 'You speak well,' she tells me. 'But you are almost a little boy.' I put my hand on her and say, 'If you will permit me to do in love what others have done like beasts, I will show you something, I think.' It was not so easy. I spoke to her until my tongue is tired. I put my hands on her everywhere. When I cannot talk no more, she lays down by the road and says, 'Maybe I will go with you.' We hid and screwed many times that night, my friend. We did not sleep. The next day, when everyone is in the fields, we go back and take some things and run away."

"That's a beautiful story, Ezequiel. I didn't know you were so romantic."

"*Ai, sí, muy romántico.*" He laughed. "You know what this woman tells me? She says, 'Ezequiel, my darling, you give me back my honor and for that I will love you always, but when is it now we begin to get rich?' This is my woman," he added in Spanish.

"Well, I'll go back and let Eli come eat," I told him.

CHAPTER FOUR

We were up above Tampico near the place we call Twenty-four-ten or The Rocks. The whole long, sparsely inhabited rocky coast between Brownsville and Tampico is dangerous. The Rocks, because of the submerged rocks and reefs, is the most dangerous spot of all. It is an old wrecker's coast.

Inshore of us a light was moving slowly along; then it reversed itself and moved back the other way.

Ezequiel laughed. "Who's that *maricón* think he is fooling?"

In the old days it might have worked. Or now, if there was a captain without a fathometer or who could not read a chart, and there were still some of those, they might be fooled into thinking that light was another boat way inshore and so be lured onto the rocks where they would break up and the wild Indians along there would come and pick his boat like buzzards picking the carcass of a dead steer.

The light was a lantern hung on a horse and rider who rode along the shore hoping to be taken for a trawler.

"*Capitán*, let me take a shot at that fucker?" Ezequiel asked.

"He is too far away," I said.

"That is lucky for him. I will just scare him instead of killing him, which is what he deserves."

"OK."

Ezequiel liked to shoot the rifle. He liked to shoot the tommy gun better, but the bullets for it cost nine cents apiece. He loved to shoot sharks with the tommy gun. Now he got the carbine, settled himself on the bow railing, and took aim on the light prowling along the shore.

"What if that light is a little skiff and not a wrecker?" Eli asked.

"Ezequiel will put out its little light," I reckoned. "Whatever it is, it could lure some luckless captain onto the rocks."

The carbine cracked and flashed on our bow. There was no reaction with the light. Ezequil shot three more times. We were much too far away for the rifle to reach even halfway there. But evidently the flash and report gave the wrecker the idea someone was shooting at him and he put his light out.

"You will have to clean that thing," I told Ezequiel.

"I always do. But I will kill some sharks first."

I made a triangulation on the flat old Indian mountain north of Tampico and the lights of the city and decided to try there.

"Don't worry," Ezequiel said, sniffing the air. "I smell *camarones*."

Trust Ezequiel.

The first try proved him a prophet or the owner of a great nose. There were plenty of shrimp down there where everyone had said the hurricane had torn up the bed. And we were right in the middle of them.

"How come you never smelled shrimp for me before?" I asked the old man.

"I never smell them before."

It was that simple.

Eli and Ezequiel lowered the doors to carry the big otter trawl down to the bottom. The doors were about ten feet long, looked just like big doors or hatch covers, and were rigged on chains to hold the mouth of the net open by flying in the water the way kites fly in the air. Properly rigged, you could comb the bottom fine enough to pick up something lost on a previous run from eighteen to twenty fathoms down.

We worked in the flood of the big lamps on the uprights of the booms. Way off in the distance behind us and in front of us were five other boats working in the isolation of their own lights. It is good to see boats out there working like that.

When we brought up the bag, it was the heaviest any of us had ever hauled, and a lot of the weight was good shrimp.

Ezequiel screamed a *ranchero* yell that was half coyote and half an explosion of joy from a heart that would otherwise burst to try to contain it.

"*Hooee! Hooee! Hooee!*" he barked like a coyote. "We got fresh Gulf shrimps here!" He yanked the trip line in the bottom of the net and spilled the bag out onto the deck.

A casade of shrimp and fish spilled into the light. There were starfish and crabs, squids and baby octopuses, rock shrimp with their hard shells and scant but delicious meat, sponges, a bright orange filefish, redfish, small sharks, a brilliant red scorpion fish with needle spines which can give you nasty stinging wounds.

We got the trawl back overboard. The cable went out with its angry complaint.

Now we sat sparddle-legged on deck, sorting and heading the shrimp into wire baskets that hold sixty pounds of shrimp tails.

The head has to be separated fom the tail immediately or the shrimp will not keep. The head contains the heart, stomach, thorax—virtually all of the shrimp's internal organs. We grab a shrimp in each hand and flick the tails from the heads into the baskets. A good header can fill a sixty-pound basket in about half an hour.

We flushed each filled basket with the hose and lowered it into the hold, where we packed the shrimp in bins between layers of shaved ice.

Ezequiel salvaged whatever fish we would keep to eat from the trash left on deck, cleaned it, and put it on ice. There is always more good fish among the trash than we can ever eat.

The good fish go back into the sea by the shovelful along with the bright parrot fish, the striped sergeant majors, sea lice, thumb splitters, sea horses, angelfish, baby sharks, and sea toads like something out of of a drunk's delerium.

"The Gulf is the devil's slop jar!" Ezequiel exclaimed, shoveling one of the toads in a load of trash over the side. "There are all kinds of things in the sea."

We worked over that bed hard all night and brought up shrimp on every drag. It took about two hours to make each drag.

Around two in the morning three of the other boats had worked over and two were dragging inside of us while the other was working on the Gulf side. They were bigger, newer, company boats. I could see they were doing goddamned well, too. Well, there is nothing you can do about that. No one holds claim to a shrimp bed. As long as they did not crowd me, let them fish. We were getting all we could handle in any case.

One of the captains called me on the radio and told me, "Hey, Johnny! I think you've found the mother lode."

"Beginner's luck," I replied. "You can keep all we scare your way."

"Much obliged," he called back. "Hear ole Johnson took a hundred and fourteen bucks off you at five card stud. Said if the storm had lasted longer, he'd of gotten your rig, your boat, and your shoes."

"Well, that's all right. Where's he when the shrimpin is so easy?"

The other man laughed. "Stay out of card games, boy, and you might amount to somethin yet."

It was getting light when the captain working nearest to the shore saw the gunboat coming out and gave us a call.

I put the big seven-fifty glasses on the coast and saw it. It was steaming. The Mexicans had two gunboats down there. I knew and so did the others that we were inside the Mexican limit.

Shrimp might belong to God and whoever can catch the crazy sonsabitches, but the Mexicans insisted that everything that swam, crawled, side-wheeled, or squirted along inside twelve nautical miles of their coast was natural-born Mexican property. Our government said we were not legally obligated to recognize any but the international three-mile limit. But after the recent shrimp war we formed the Shrimp Association of the Americas with the Mexicans and signed we would abide by their coastal laws. But if the shrimp are running inside and they aren't running outside, we are going where the shrimp are. If the shrimp are running, we are going to follow them into the kitchen of the Seven Virgins Café and worry about getting out with them when we have them on ice.

Not many of us are what you would call good navigators anyway.

I can find north for you anywhere on earth without a compass, day or night, but I do not know one end of a sextant from the other, nor do I personally know any shrimper captain who does. We have charts, our fathometer, a compass, and use dead reckoning. We aren't out to steal anything from nobody. We just want to make a living without shaking someone else's jolt. Given a world that logical, dead reckoning ought to be good enough.

We had just dumped our bag. The net was up on the boom. The big company boats inshore were still on the drag. The boat outside us had completed its run and was dumping its bag.

"Get those doors on the side!" I yelled.

They had already seen the gunboat.

The radio crackled with conversation between the boats.

"Here we go again!" someone exclaimed.

"We still got our tommy guns by God!" another replied.

I got on the radio and told the others I was going to run for it as we had our rig up.

"You're having all the luck today, Johnny. Wish I'd lost a little something to that Johnson."

"Good luck."

I opened up the *Shea,* heading straight out into the Gulf, calculating to keep as much distance between me and the gunboat as I could.

When Eli came in, I asked him what was happening.

"They're going to get two of them. Us and the one outside us are goin to get away."

"Fuckin world is full of gunboats and horseshit laws."

"Yeah. . . . and football coaches," Eli said.

I left the radio open. I heard someone saying—I think it was Bluff Jorgensen—"Jesus Christ, Henry, they're shooting at us again!"

I gave Eli the wheel and went out with the glasses to see.

The gunboat was firing its three-inch bow gun. They did not seem serious about hitting anybody. They were better gunners than that. They just did not like the fact that some of us were making a run for it. But they hadn't shot at us in a long time.

I ran back to the pilothouse and called the other boats.

"Listen, maybe they're shooting because we are running. I'll stop if the other one will."

Eli looked at me as if I were crazy.

"Listen, Johnny, this is Henry Watkins, you just keep goin. They ain't about to hurt us. Just report we been fired on again to the Coast Guard. If this shit's startin again, we're goin to get us some bazookas and torpedoes and take on the fuckin Mexican navy once and for all. Don't feel bad, boy, if we hadn't been on the drag, we'd of run too."

"OK, Captain."

"OK, Johnny. See yuh. Shrimpin's getting rough again, boys!"

At least they had a big company behind them. Watkins owned two boats and his son owned one and had an interest in another. They both drove air-conditioned Cadillacs and had sprawling new houses in a good part of Brownsville on a *resaca.* He was going to be all right. His son was captain of the other boat that was making a run for it.

I wondered if the gunboat made us through their glasses. If

they had, they would be watching for us. They would be looking to catch us any way they could and get us into a Mexican court. I could lose my catch and probably my boat.

When we were far out in the Gulf, I turned toward home.

CHAPTER FIVE

The next day we were where the water is deep blue and cold if you have to go into it.

We made a few passes out very deep and came up with some Royal Reds, huge ruby-colored shrimp almost like lobsters first-class gourmet shrimp to top off our catch.

Ezequiel stripped naked and showered under the hose on deck, snorting and talking to himself when the cold water hit his skin.

On the hatch cover were all his possessions laid out neatly as if for inspection, divided into five groups of items to coincide with the pockets in his patched and repatched biballs.

He hauled in a line on which was tied his laundry. The wake of the boat had twisted his overalls and shirt tightly around the line, so he had to work to free them. He had tied them tight, for if he had lost them, he would have been naked. He never brought a change of clothes. He hung his laundry up to dry and sat down with his knife to pare his toenails. I went back into the pilothouse to leave the old man his privacy.

The windows were open, and the breeze out there was sweet. I took the wheel from Eli, and he went over on the seat along the side windows and rolled us a couple of joints. He reached me one.

A lot of captains would not permit smoking marijuana or drinking anything stronger than beer on their boats. But neither Eli or Ezequiel was a serious pothead or drunk. I did not see anything wrong with a little smoke and a shot of brandy after a good day's work.

I was feeling pretty good. We had between nine and ten thousand dollars' worth of shrimp in the hold as best I could figure, plus those Royal Reds. I felt bad about the others back there, but that did not make me feel less good generally.

I didn't have anything against the big company boats. Hell, we were all "company" boats in a way. The whole fucking country worked for the "company" one way or another. The rest was just a big a con. Soon it would all be big company operations or all one big company. Already they had refrigerator mother ships out there which could take your shrimp, freeze and package them at sea. A boat might stay out forever except for repairs. It was soon going to be like when the big canning companies moved into the Midwest, bought up all the little farms in a place, tore down the fences, and farmed with armies of equipment. All those farm houses were left sitting out there derelict. Where had the farmers gone? What happened to them? Moved to California, to places like Hayward and Fremont, bought anonymous little houses of plywood and became anonymous. Soon we would all be anonymous. And what a true tomato or peach tasted like was already but a memory.

There was no sense in kidding myself, the dream Shea and I had was never really going to come true. I could maybe have a boat or two—one boat pays for the other, was the shrimper's adage—but it would be like the truckers who own their own rigs, there was nothing all that independent about it. The companies and the people who rigged markets would always have us by the balls.

Still, it was a pretty good way to go. The money was good when everything went smooth and nothing broke down. Even when things went wrong, short of winding up on the rocks or lost at sea, it beat almost everything else.

His clothes dry enough to wear, Ezequiel came in carrying the rocket we had hauled up near the Navy's Matagorda ranges. I had forgotten about it, figured he had gotten rid of it long ago. It made me angry to think it had been aboard all that time. It especially made me mad for I had been feeling so good.

"God damn it, Ezequiel!" I yelled. "We got nine, ten thousand dollars' worth of shrimp on here! Get rid of that fucking thing—*now!*"

"Hey! *Poco a poco.* There is no danger. He is a dud."

"How the hell do you know?"

"Because he don't go off." He thought that was very funny.

He had been smoking, too. The stuff he smoked was so clean and strong, the merest little sliver of a joint was just right. A regular-sized one was too much. He had let me roll myself a normal-sized joint the first time he offered it to me and I thought a lot of things were very funny too, until I had to go lie down.

He was grinning. There were about a dozen teeth left in his mouth, each the color of rotting bronze pegs stuck haphazardly in his infected gums. I had seen him pull out a rotten tooth while working, curse it and throw it away, and wash out his mouth with sea water.

Eli was smiling. When the old man came near enough, Eli goosed him. Ezequiel let out a whoop, straightened up very straight, and began bobbling that rocket between his claw and his right hand which was occupied with a cold can of beer.

I swore at Eli and let go of the wheel to make a grab for the rocket, but the old man got it back under control and still held onto his beer.

"He is pretty tall when he is straightened up good," Eli observed.

"I want you to take that fucking thing out of here and throw it way out over the fantail—*now!*"

"OK. But I think it make a nice lamp for my house. A present for my wife."

"By the same token so would a live rattlesnake. Get rid of it. That's an order."

"Whoo! Hey, *compadre*, you hear him, he gives me an order!" He nudged Eli. "Hey, *Capitán*, you never give me no order before. Maybe I do it, maybe I tell you to stick your order up your ass."

"Do it!"

"OK. Maybe. But you owe my wife a lamp for your pleasure."

He left me shaking my head at the Gulf, feeling suddenly a long way from anything anyone would think of as home. I realized I had become a strange man. My ties to the hopes and dreams of my kind had become too thin ever to trace back to a bungalowed way to go, grass to mow, talk of sports, movies, last night's TV show, watching a pretty good woman wasting a little more each day, wasting myself, or both of us just growing goddamned silly. Out there on the Gulf it was easy to imagine all the rest of the world had died. It was easy to consider that somewhere, when I was too young to know what happened, I had died too in a way; that nothing logically followed as it ought: that there were those on earth who were so able to cheat and steal and lie that nothing followed logically and never would again. Living had been turned into a game, a killing game, with television and sports and sex as reward for the winners. Only hardly anyone wanted to kill for himself. They wanted to send somebody to do it for them and get the results by telephone. Fuck it! There was nothing left in the bungalowed world that fell close enough to my heart to matter.

This moment, with the hull of the trawler balanced on the surface of the Gulf, out of sight of land, with all the remarkable and mysterious and awful living things teeming in the long soup of the sea, I felt alive, so alive I did not need a name. The sunset was on one side, moonrise on the other. It was good. Like in a movie, my mind lifted and rose, soaring slowly backward and upward until I could see the boat on the great belly of the Gulf, a toy boat with a toy wake. Ezequiel, Eli, and myself mere specks. A little farther back, and we disappeared to the naked eye.

Ezequiel returned with an arm load of beer, which he sat on the shelf that runs across the front of the pilothouse.

"Where's the opener?" Eli asked. "You have a church key, Señor Cavazos?"

"Of course, stupid. I am well equipped," the old man answered in Spanish, clutching a gob of his bagging overalls at the crotch and offering it to number forty-four.

Eli scoffed, "Nothin in them *pantalones*, old man, but shrimp heads and poverty."

"You are so dumb, you queer, you cannot find your asshole for yourself," Ezequiel instructed him in Spanish. Switching to English, he wondered: "Maybe it is not so much your knees you lose playing *futbol* as your *cojones*. You are married now one year and your wife has nothing in the oven. Maybe she don't give you nothing yet. Maybe you don't give her nothing."

"That's all you know, old man. We are modern. Not like you. When we want a baby, we will have one. Fuck you and the Pope too. You old farts always braggin about your balls. How many of those kids you think is yours anyway? No one as ugly as you could have made a daughter as beautiful as María-Antoinette. That is someone else's work."

"You keep your mouth off her name. That one is my salvation. We can only dream of such things as that one is blessed with," he added in Spanish. "One day she will marry a gentleman with much money who will do the right thing by me.

"I will wear good clothes, "He flipped his faded suspender straps like fine lapels. "I will smoke good cigars. I have told her since she was a little girl that she must not waste her gifts. She can love a gentleman with money as easily as a nobody. She can have the life of her dreams."

"*Your* fucked-up dreams," Eli corrected.

"Ah...you know nothing. You are full of shit. One such as her comes maybe once in many lifetimes. When this happens, the things you think is so changed is so much bullshit. This modern talk is a trick to sell you cheap, my friend. For those touched with enchantment," he continued in Spanish, "there are rules older than human gods. This girl of whom we speak was sent for something. She is not a witch, but she is enchanted, truly."

From a pocket he produced a beer opener tied with a string to a button somewhere. Holding each can tightly in the vise of his two-fingered claw, he popped neat wedges in the tops of the cans.

The cold beer was good on top of the pot taste on my tongue.

Eli must have been feeling the same way because he was smiling when we looked at each other. We raised our cans in an unspoken toast to good feelings and to making some money. The old man lifted his can too and laughed.

"Maybe I will buy a little TV just for me and my wife to put at the end of our bed. The kids fuck with all the knobs on the old one and you can't get shit on it no more."

"Why don't you put a toilet in your house instead?" Eli suggested.

"Why? Something like that costs more than a little TV. There are no pipes for a toilet, and you must have a tank. Besides, the toilet is useful to me as it is."

"How many kids you got now, Ezequiel?" I could never remember.

He thoughtfully counted on his fingers. "Seven." He held up all the fingers he owned. "If I have more, I have to start on my toes."

Eli tapped Ezequiel's deformed thumb on his claw hand with its nail growing out the side. "That one is an ugly brute, Uncle. You could have lost him with no regret."

"He serves, shithead. But this, this is my María." He held up his other thumb as if measuring it for clothes, examining it from all angles. It did seem to glow a bit, but that could have been the stuff we were smoking.

"She is my salvation," he said, kissing his thumb with fatherly primness, closing his eyes as he did so.

I was suddenly very hungry. Each of the crew kicks in for his share of the groceries and can provide himself with anything special he might want to eat during the trip.

Now I can eat fish tree times a day for a long time. I can eat it fried for breakfast, hot or cold for lunch, and any damned way for supper. I really like fish. But there comes a day when I

cannot *think* fish without my throat closing against it entirely.
That is when I want meat. A steak if I can get one, black as
something that has been napalmed on the outside and sort of
pinkish at its center. Unlike some captains, I cannot sit down
and enjoy a steak in front of others if they do not have one. In
the freezer there were three big T-bones which I had been
saving until I felt the urge or that the time was right to eat
them.

I said, "Ezequiel, why don't you cook us those steaks tonight?"

He laughed "I was just waitin for you to tell me. You want
to give me another order? I told you this one was goin to give
us steak tonight."

Eli nodded.

Then Ezequiel pinched me with his claw, and I yelled. He
scooted off, laughing.

The crooked nail on that thumb went right into you.

"Goddamn, I hate that!" I told Eli.

"Me too. He can make your heart stop."

He could also head shrimp faster and cleaner with one
hand and a claw than ninety percent of the others could with
two good hands and a helper.

Although everyone called Ezequiel "old," I doubt if he was
much over forty-five. He could have worked on a better boat,
a bigger boat, except for the fact he was often quarrelsome
and could not resist pinching the shit out of you with that
damned claw. No one liked it, and most would not stand for
it.

Eli spelled me at the wheel. I took his seat against the side
of the pilothouse.

"Hey, Johnny, when you goin to get married and quit living
like a sea turtle on this boat?" Eli wondered.

"Sometime, maybe."

"Yeah? My wife has this girlfriend. You would like her. Real
good-looking, big fuckin tits like your head man. When we get
in, you come to supper some night, my wife will invite her."

"Sure."

Mexicans are Indians, not Spaniards. They are landsmen. The earth and sweet water and the things of the earth feed their souls more than it does mine. Though I was born and raised in a landlocked county, I know somewhere the sea rolled my ancestor's bones. I was no less wary or scared of the Gulf than Eli or Ezequiel; it was just I felt no more secure on dry land. I thought that was probably why there would always be sailors, men who damned the work of trying to make a living from the sea, but who would always come back to it after a spell ashore. If the sea has ever rolled your bones, a part of you will be hooked to it forever.

"If I had finished college, I wouldn't be on no stinkin shrimp boat," Eli said. "I'd be makin good money and be at home with my wife at night."

"What was it you wanted to be . . . an engineer?"

"Civil engineer."

"What do they do?"

"Design water plants, sewers, streets and stuff. Lay it all out, make it work."

"Why the hell you want to do that?"

"You get good money for that stuff, man. Some of those guys make twenty thousand a year. I was pretty good at mechanical drawing and math. I had a talent. Man, I couldn't read that Shakespeare and such shit, all that *old* history. I always liked to make things."

"Well, why didn't you keep on studying nights or something after you lost your scholarship at TU?"

"Hell, I never got close to studyin what I wanted to. I was up there to play football. They tell you what to study and how much. All that required shit first. Before I got hurt, they had brainy guys to help me make my grades. Then, when I got hurt, the coaches didn't want to *know* me, man. All they wanted was my scholarship back, so they could give it to another chump." He drew deeply on his cigarette. "I tried, man. Shit drills twice a day. There was this big tackle, a real good friend of mine. He'd broke his leg completely in two, and it wasn't ever goin to be right. We had to go head to head against each other, doin train wrecks—*Bang! Whup!* We almost killed each other. I *wanted* to kill him! He wanted to kill me too, I know. Both of us were crying like babies, man, tryin to kill each other. For what? Nothin! I couldn't do it after a while. I hurt and he hurt and we wanted to kill each other's ass. Fuck that. I quit. I didn't check out. I just left, man. Sneaked away that night. Left my clothes and everything. Let them have that fuckin scholarship. They wanted it. Let them have it. I just cut out."

I had known he'd had a football scholarship to Texas. He had been one of the best fullbacks in high school anyone had ever seen in the valley. He had told me how he had torn up one knee in his freshman year and then the other the next year and had lost his scholarship, but he had never spoken of it as he did now.

"I quit, man," he said softly to the Gulf. "You know they say Mexicans can't really cut it in football when it gets big time. That's why you don't see so many Mexicans at Texas or SMU or any big school. All the coaches think like that. I knew that, and I was goin to show them. But I quit. I couldn't cut it when I got hurt. There was nothin lower than a quitter up there. Coach used to yell at us, 'You quit here, you quit now, and you'll quit in a game, you'll always quit!' I'm not a coward. I never run from nothing since I was little. I coulda broke Coach in two. I mean, I know my guts are great as his, but man, I quit. I got hurt and I quit. And I know that coach and his assistants think, the Mexican quits."

"Aw, fuck, that doesn't matter, Eli," I told him, though I knew it did and was sorry I had said it. "I know how you feel. I've quit a couple of times myself."

"It matters! Don't give me that shit! You know that."

"Yow. It matters. It will always matter. I still have bad dreams about the times I quit when I was just a little kid. I expect when I'm an old man, I'll still dream those bad dreams and feel as punky and rotten and unforgiven as ever. You're right, Eli. I know how you feel. All you can do is try to even it up in the long run. But it matters. It'll always matter."

I clapped him on his broad back where the orange number forty-four was now faded and stained by hard work for which there was no glory under the sun.

I headed back toward where I smelled meat being burned.

Ezequiel was sort of dancing around in front of the cook-stove, more just sliding a little one way, then the other with the motion of the boat, his shaggy old head loose on its stem, nose open to the smell of meat. A cloud of smoke boiled from his skillet and tumbled out the open door on the lee side of the galley. I had shown him how I liked steak done: coated with crushed peppercorns, thrown for about seven minutes on each side in a big iron skillet which should be almost red hot. In another skillet he was frying potatoes in bacon grease. With the steak and potatoes we would have a big platter of sliced Bermuda onions and sliced tomatoes. We would drink beer. Afterward we would have ice cream and coffee and maybe a big shot of Fundador brandy with the second cup of coffee. We bought the brandy tax free by the case from the sailors off ships that put into the port of Brownsville. We would light up Havana cigars and sit around telling lies until it was time for two of us to sleep.

"It is a good life, *viejo*," I cheered him. "If you don't weaken."

"There are many things I will do with more pleasure if you have been sent to ask me." He had taken off his shirt to work over the hot stove. He was a powerfully muscled little man. Veins slid around beneath his taut dark skin like those you see in the legs of a horse.

I liked Ezequiel and knew he liked me and Eli. He liked the boat, he liked his twelve percent of the catch, but what he liked best of all was to be thought a man of talent, an inventor, engineer, scientist, seer, forecaster of hurricanes, and he claimed he had once fixed clocks for a living when he was young.

We all ate supper together in the pilothouse rather than the galley. It was cooler.

When the food was gone, Ezequiel started talking about

how the sky was Grandfather, the earth Grandmother, and
how the sun was Father and the moon Mother, and how all
four major directions of the compass were also relatives of our
spirit.

"What kind of religion is that, Ezequiel?" I asked.

"The one we had before the Spaniards come and sold us
that fuckin Virgin," as if I were responsible for *that*.

"Who told you that stuff?" Eli wanted to know.

"My own grandfather told me these facts. His grandfather
told him. In the old days it was hard for a man to grow old
without becoming a little wise."

"Now it's hard for them to grow old without becoming
damned fools," Eli baited the old man.

"Sadly, that is true. But because your grandfather's grandfather told him nothing, and he in turn has told you nothing,
you are a fool to begin with and will be one always unless
something magic touches your spirit. You will father children, if you have any balls, which has yet to be shown, and
tell them nothing but bullshit, and soon all wisdom will be
gone from all people, and then we will see terrible things happen. Even worse things than now."

"What sort of things?" I asked.

"Terrible things! We will be worse than the worst of beasts.
Worse than sharks. Yes. We will be like the sharks, but
worse."

Ezequiel hated sharks more than any living thing.

"We will use the atom bombs on each other when all wisdom is gone, worse things too. Those who are left will tear at
each other and eat each other like sharks in a killing frenzy. I
have seen all this."

"You mean you dreamed it?" I asked. "Or—"

"Yes. No, not a dream when you sleep. I seen this in that
other dreamin. What do you call it?"

"A vision."

"That's it. I seen this, and it was more real than a dream.
And absolutely true."

"When, Uncle?" Eli asked in Spanish.

"When wisdom is gone from this world."

"How long is that going to take?"

"Not long. It is goin fast. When things were different and people did not have to move so much the grandfathers and grandmothers could speak the wisdom to us. Now they die or we move away to get a job, or our grandfathers and grandmothers don't know shit no more. It is a very bad situation. My own father was too busy to listen to nobody. He just worked in a field, breakin his back; now he is dead, and he didn't learn nothing. I learned from my grandfather these many things when I was very young. My sister learns from our grandmother. I have not seen her in years, but I know she is no fool. I tell these things and more to my children because there is no one else to do it, but I don't know if it is the same. Children don't like to listen to their fathers. They don't believe their fathers. What we need is some good grandfathers and grandmothers."

We talked like that for a while. Then I took my plate back to the galley, scraped and rinsed it, and put it in the dish rack. I went outside for a smoke, walked back to the fantail, where I leaned to look up at the stars. When the cigarette was finished, I went inside to my bunk to sleep until it was my turn again to take the wheel.

I dreamed awhile of Ezequiel's daughter María-Antoinette, but nothing came of it. When I dreamed again, it was of Lupe Contreras. She would come to the boat as soon as she was able after we got in. She would take off her clothes, and her skin would eat up my touches, her soft body seem to try to wreck itself with my own. She would kiss me better than anyone had ever kissed me and roll my bones in a way that was fulfillment of the old sea's promise.

If I ever owned more than one boat and did not marry one of Ezequiel Cavazos' daughters, I might name the second the *Lupe Contreras*. She would like that. Someone sure as hell ought to name a boat for her.

The explosion blew me out of the bunk. I heard it, and then I was in midair and crashed onto the deck, looking into the pilothouse, where the wheel was spinning wildly and Eli was down, his back up against the bulkhead onto which I caught hold to keep from sliding down the steeply tilted cabin floor into the galley. We seemed to be standing on our tail. Stuff was thrown all around the boat. Through the windshield for a second or so I could see nothing but the starry black sky. Then the bow crashed down and plowed under, throwing a wave of water back over the pilothouse. The screw came out of the water and ran wildly. I was afraid we were going to the bottom. Eli skidded forward on the wet deck as I went head-long through the door and came up beside him in the pilot-house. The boat rocked and plunged like that for a while, twisting and turning. All sorts of stuff in the galley and cabin were crashing down.

I thought we had hit something, a whale, except boats don't hit whales and whales don't hit boats. I thought maybe we had hit a private yacht, ran up on and sank it, that Eli had dozed off at the wheel, or the other boat was out there without lights, maybe a bunch of Cuban revolutionaries or something. I remembered hearing the explosion. Then I knew what had happened.

As soon as I could, I got hold of the wheel and headed the boat into the sea and yelled for Eli to take it.

I ran out on the deck. There was nothing to see forward. Nothing in the water. We hadn't hit anything. I raced back to-ward the long fantail, yelling for Ezequiel. There was no an-swer. There was a big hole across the back of the boat. I went on back. I knew what had happened. Ezequiel had not thrown that rocket over as I had ordered him to do. He had been back there fucking with it, and it had gone off. I felt sick.

The hole was about four feet across, right down to the decking. The deck is heavy planks, which were splintered a bit but were not broken. They were discolored in a sort of star-pointed arc away from where Ezequil had been sitting on or against the rail when the rocket went off. I could smell the ex-plosive in the old wood. I leaned way out over the hole to see if we were damaged further. Everything looked OK.

I cut on the big floodlights and yelled for Eli to begin cir-

cling the area we had just covered, though I knew we were
not going to find Ezequiel. There were the fins of sharks he
hated so along our wake as we recrossed it.

"Goddamn sharks," I said aloud.

Water blurred my vision.

But you have to look.

There was nothing to find. Not meat or rag.

After checking everything topside once more, I took a bat-
tery lantern down to check everything below. Shrimp and ice
were thrown all over hell, but I could not see anything that
looked like a leak.

In the engine room I shoved some batteries back into the
brackets, but the engine seemed OK. Tools and stuff from the
workbench were all over the place. There was some oil
spilled.

We were going to have one hell of a cleanup.

I went back and cut off the boom lights and joined Eli in the
pilothouse.

I shut off the emergency bilge pumps to keep from burning
them out.

The floor was slick with water that had been thrown in the
open windows and doors. There was some broken window
glass. A couple of beer cans rolled around on the deck.

Our radio was none too good. Sometimes it worked, and
sometimes it didn't. I finally raised the Coast Guard and told
them what had happened. our location, that we were all right
and were coming in. I also raised the wife of a trawler captain
who had her own radio to keep in touch with her husband
and sons and told her the story and that we were coming into
port. We were probably picked up on the radios of other
shrimper wives, and the car dealers in Brownsville who had
radios to know who had made big catches so they could meet
the boat at the dock with the latest model to tempt the crew.

The freezer doors had been blown open. I picked up stuff
and threw it back into the reefer and closed the doors. Ezequiel's soup was all over the place. The coffeepot was on the
deck, coffee grounds mixed with the other crap floating in the

galley. I tried to clean up the mess, but my heart wasn't in it. I closed lockers and cupboards and just left the shit as it was. Do it later.

The bottle of Fundador rolled out from under the table. It was all right. I took it with me and went back to Eli, pulled the cork, and offered him a drink.

He was glad to see it.

"Ezequiel?" Eli asked.

"Gone."

"Gone?"

"Yow. Just gone. Blew a big chunk out of the rail, but I checked real good, we seem to be OK above and below."

"That thing went off!"

"Sure as shit did."

"An he's just gone?"

"Gone! Nothing back there, Eli. Not meat nor rag."

Eli shook his head and reached for the bottle. When he had drunk, I drank again. I rolled us a couple of joints and gave one to Eli. My hands shook.

"But we're all right? You're sure?"

"As far as I can see. Yow, we're OK."

We drank again.

After a little Eli exclaimed, *"Whooee-shit-man!"* He shook himself like a pup.

I looked at him and did the same thing—shook all over.

Then Eli laughed. It was just a bit of a laugh as if it had been jarred from him. He looked embarrassed about it.

Then we both laughed.

"Man-oh-man!" Eli howled. "That fuckin thing went *off!"*

"It *did!"*

"Can't you see Ezequiel's face, man? Oh, God, he'd of given his precious old balls to take back that surprise!"

"You know it!"

"He was a crazy old man."

"But a good one."

"Oh-yow. Whooeee---*GONE!"* Eli cried.

"Just gone!"

"Man, back there screwin on that fuckin thing. . . ."

"Eli, we oughtn't laugh," I howled back.

"I can't help it."

"Me neither."

"*Whoo!* I mean that motherfucker went *off!*"

"Oh, man, it went *BOOM!*"

We drank again and stopped laughing.

I went back to check the boat again. Hanging from a hook in the galley was Ezequiel's faded old chambray shirt. It seemed uniquely bent to his body so if you knew Ezequiel, you would know it was his shirt. It was the only thing of his left aboard. Everything else he needed he carried in his pockets.

CHAPTER
SIX

A boat came out to meet us. It was one of Wesley Slocum's boats, captained by a pal of mine, Pete Gatliff.

I stopped down for it to come alongside so Pete could jump over onto our boat and ride in with us.

"There's a dockful of folks waiting for you guys. There's TV and radio and newspaper reporters. It got all confused. First they thought you'd been shelled by a Mexican gunboat. The reports got all screwed up."

"Well, we were with Henry and the other boats when the gunboat came out, but we had our rig up, so we ran for it. You heard anything about them?"

"They're OK. Nobody got hurt. They got them tied up at the dock down in Tampico. Goin to be some fines over it. You bastards were right in there, you know that? That near boat wasn't even three miles offshore, the Mexicans say. Now what the hell happened to you?"

"Aw, Ezequiel blew himself up with a goddamned rocket we brought up off the Matagorda ranges. I told him to get rid of it, but he didn't do it. We're going to have to be hauled. I want the shaft and bearings checked out. Godamn the luck. We did good before that happened."

"Way it goes, *compadre*. Way it goes."

There were bigshots from the shrimp companies there on the dock, three kinds of police; the Navy had sent down a couple of officers. There were other shrimpers there, people from the port, Mexicans, rummies, dogs and cats. We came up the ship channel and tied up at the main dock.

Radio and TV people kept shoving microphones at Eli and me.

I told them what had happened, described the rocket for the Navy and the press, told them my location where we picked the thing up. I wanted to make sure they got the idea we were not in the restricted area. That was going to be important when it came to working out who was going to pay for fixing my boat. I showed everyone on our chart where we hauled up the rocket.

Everyone went to stand around the hole in the back of the boat. I had one of those feelings like you have seen something before, only I was seeing Ezequiel sitting there, screwing on that rocket just before it went off. He looked up and smiled at me. It raised the hair on my neck. I felt faint and had not heard someone's question.

"What? Oh, well, after we got the boat under control, we searched for him, but he was gone. There were a lot of sharks out there following us," I told them.

I kept looking for Lupe Contreras in the crowd, but I did not see her.

Deputies from the county sheriff's office cleared a way through the people on the dock for Ezequiel's rusted-out old gray Studebaker, which bucked and snorted and backfired along as much as rolled.

Farther back another sheriff's car was coming with its top lights flashing.

From the Stude climbed the driver, a slender crop-haired girl, who ran around to help her mother. The woman got out of the car carrying a baby wrapped in a *sarape* against her breast. From the backseat tumbled a younger girl and two skinny small boys and a ratty old red chicken that kept blinking and cocking its head at the doings on the dock. One of the boys saw the hen, chased and captured it among the feet of the spectators. He hung onto it with both arms wrapped tightly around its middle.

In the back of the crowd a man was selling ice-cream bars, cold drinks, and slices of *sandia*—watermelon—from a cart beneath a colorful umbrella. Ezequiel's boys eyed the cart longingly.

A way was made for the family to approach the boat.

Now what the fuck am I going to say? I wondered.

Ezequiel's widow and her children did not seem certain what this was all about. The TV crews and all the people frightened them. They were not sure Ezequiel had not done something very bad.

"Eli, get me his shirt," I said out of the corner of my mouth.

Ezequiel's wife was nursing the baby beneath the *sarape.*

"I am sorry, Señora Cavazos," I told the woman, who stared back at me stoically. Her eyes were black and questioning.

The woman nodded, yet seemed to be looking for her husband on the boat.

"She does not speak English good," the slender girl with short curly hair said, standing protectively at the woman's side.

"Please tell her I am sorry about what happened."

The girl spoke to the woman.

"She wants to know what has happened. We were told there was an accident on the boat. My father is dead?"

"Yes. We found this Navy rocket. He wanted to make a lamp out of it. I told him to get rid of it. But he didn't do it. Then last night he was evidently fooling with it, and it exploded."

The girl translated all that to the woman.

"Tell her Ezequiel was a fine man. This was all he left on the boat." I took the shirt from Eli and handed it to the woman, who draped it over the bundle in her arms.

She was a flat-footed woman in sandals. Her belly was broken down from childbirth so it pooched out as if she were always pregnant. She was settled low now between her hips.

From the other car came Ezequiel's favorite daughter, *la Encanta,* along with the daughter who was very pregnant and was accompanied by her husband, the would-be bullfighter, Small Billy Champion.

All eyes went to María-Antoinette, also called Toni, as well as Encanta. There was a collective intake of breath. The TV camera had swung around to pick her up as soon as the police car stopped. It was hard to figure. She *was* as beautiful as any young woman you will ever see, but it was more than that.

I think I saw it! In that moment there was something about Encanta so soft, perfect, flawless, it made you want to destroy her, mess her up, and consequently you ended up wanting to protect her, even from yourself.

She wore a tan and white dress with high-heeled shoes. She crossed the splintered old dock carefully, looking down so as not to catch one of her stiletto heels. The deputy, Bobby Joe Solar, a big, handsome fellow, steadied her by the elbow as if she were precious. Her pregnant sister with a cowlike, complaining face followed with her husband.

Small Billy wore a pigtail, though no real bullfighter had actually worn one in years. They clipped false ones onto the backs of their heads when they fought. Small Billy carried himself as if he were hearing applause, turning his peeny head slowly this way and that, moving as if he were on ball bearings or about to ask someone to tango.

Encanta came and kissed her mother, placing an arm around her shoulders.

Eli nudged me. He had Ezequiel's old wooden-handled pocketknife.

"I found this back stuck in the side of the galley bulkhead."

I took it and handed it to the girl whose hair was chopped like a black cauliflower. Our fingers touched, and I shuddered involuntarily. She stared at me as if she could see into my head. Her eyes were like Ezequiel's. He was wrong. Of all his children, that one was definitely his own.

To look into her beautiful sister's eyes was like staring into the Gulf. There was all sorts of things in them, but no man knew for sure what he might come up with if he dipped into them. As flesh she was so blessed she hardly seemed real, yet

more real and more fleshily so than any other. Her eyes
seemed to have been touched with stars as in a cartoon, her
words slipping between her beautiful red lips in oblong bal-
loons. Yet the sound of her voice was a weightless caress. To
think that any man might fuck her was a maddening notion.

The business on the dock lasted too long. The cameras and
reporters and officials stole the souls of us all, turned our his-
tories into a little bit of passing news, made us all oddities. I
hadn't known that was what it was going to be like. News as
opposed to history made men anonymous. It left me feeling
cranky and depressed.

It was late when we got unloaded, weighed out, and
cleaned up.

Eli's wife came for him in their new two-toned Edsel hardtop convertible.

I worked around until after seven cleaning up the cabin and
galley, expecting Lupe Contreras to be along any minute.

She should have been there, if she was coming. There were
reasons why she might not be able to get away, but I was angry nonetheless.

Fuck it, I told myself.

I put on clean khakis and a short-sleeved pullover shirt,
locked up, and headed for town in the truck.

CHAPTER SEVEN

The Cuba Libre is in an alley and you have to go down into it, so anyone coming in the door stands for a moment at the top of a short flight of open concrete steps where everyone in the place sober enough to focus can turn to see who comes in.

It had not been there long, but it had become popular with all those looking to buy or sell or arrange something outside conventional mercantile channels on the U.S. side of the border. It was where I arranged to buy a case of tax-free Spanish brandy or scotch from seamen off merchant ships. Watches, radios, and such things could also be bought from the seamen at bargain prices.

I ran into Pete Gatliff outside and invited him to have a drink.

The two young women who worked behind the bar said they were Cuban. They ran the place and hoped to give the impression they were the owners, though they were not. They also said they were sisters but looked and acted less like sisters than did Pete Gatliff and myself.

It was common knowledge that the place was owned by a very bad man from San Antonio who controlled everything illegal from the Alamo to the Rio Bravo. The place had become a den for all sorts of border jackelry, so naturally there was always an off-duty cop or two up front and a couple of queers farther back and all sorts of people with revolutionary ideas in and out all the time.

The shortest girl behind the bar with the biggest tits was named Teresa and might have been a budding Cuban movie star as she claimed, though my guess was she would photograph about as wide as she was tall. She also claimed to be a personal friend of Fidel Castro, a very personal friend. She had his picture framed behind the bar, draped with an armband of the 26th of July movement. There was also a photograph of President Eisenhower just to forestall debate.

We were on our way across the river but had stopped at the place on my claim of needing a drink to make it over the border, though I'd had several drinks and was really interested in seeing if Lupe Contreras was inside.

She was in the back room with the two young men she had brought to my boat. I saw her as soon as I was on the floor of the main barroom and one of the gay young men who made the back room their office scintillated out to deliver his order to one of the young women behind the bar.

At the table with Lupe and the two young men who wanted a boat that could go to Cuba without causing suspicion were two other men and two girls. One of the other men was tall, blond, wearing sunglasses though it was night, and was plainly just *with* a shorter, older dark type with some gut, who carried the jacket to his dull metallic summer suit because it was a hot night and he was sweating through his white shirt, and the place was not air-conditioned. One of the other girls I recognized as Lupe's girlfriend Berta Garza.

A beaded curtain hung in the arch divided the more private back room from the main bar. The back room was where wine and vegetables and such things had once been stored. The whole place had been the cellar of a merchant's business and his home.

If Lupe saw me, she made no sign.

Pete and I ordered a beer and a tequila on the rocks at the bar.

There were the usual types in cowboy hats and hand-tooled belts and boots in the place. The editor of the city's newspaper was at the bar in earnest converstion with the local FBI man and the American consul from Matamoros who wore a white *guayabera* Mexican shirt and smoked a long Cuban cigar. The consul was a decent sort who had spent ten years in Morocco before being transferred to Matamoros. He was much better at trying to get you to trial and out of jail across the border than had been the previous consul. The editor's name was Bill Roth, a Texas Jew who could pass for being half Mexican and who was nicknamed Gordo because he resembled the cartoon character by Gus Arriola. Bill was a hell of a nice guy who never wore cowboy boots or Stetson hats. The FBI man was named Parker. He was a tall Lyndon Johnson type, starting to grow a potbelly beneath his hand-tooled Western belt. He blended into the place in a tan Palm Beach suit, good boots that were handmade in Mexico, and a neutral shade of Stetson with a medium brim blocked in what they call stockman style. He was all right too, as far as that kind of guy can ever be OK. Both he and Roth bought their personal brandy and scotch there too.

In a booth a reporter from the *Herald*, a new guy I had only met once, with his pretty German wife, were chatting with Bill's tough and funny wife, Ruth.

"I don't know what the hell they let them fruits hang out in here for," Pete complained when another *maricón* came out to see what had delayed his friend.

The girls were busy behind the bar, and there were others more forceful about placing their orders.

"They got to drink somewhere," I allowed.

"Gives me the shivers to see how a man can get that way."

"That one is the son of a big quartermaster general. His old man gives him two hundred a month to keep his name changed and stay lost."

"How you know all that?"

"I had a drink with him and Bill Roth and Teresa one night. He's sort of interesting. Cops run his little ass off, use him as an informer. He's one scared little queer all the time. One side turns him one way, and the cops turn him the other. Both sides got a handle on him. Bill says someone threatens

to kill that kid about three times a week. Must be a hell of a
way to live. Takes something."

"I don't give a fuck. What you doin drinkin with queers?"

I grinned. "Got to drink with somebody. Least he was able
to stand his round, unlike some always broke shrimpers I
know."

"If you're meanin me, you can go across the river with your
queer friend if you'd druther."

"Tell me, Captain, how much you share out from the last
trip of fishing you claim you did?"

"I told you, " he grumbled.

"Yow, I know. I just like to hear it. It's a funny fuckin
figure, *compadre*."

"Fourteen dollars and seventy-nine cents."

Every time he said it I had to laugh. He had been out for
over two weeks, fished as hard as we had, was a good shrimper, and when the divees were cut up, Pete had fourteen dollars and change in his pocket, and *he* was the captain! That
was shrimping.

"Way it goes, *compadre*," I told him. "Way it goes."

Lupe heard me laugh, for when I looked back past Pete's
skinny back as he leaned on the bar, I saw her looking at me
through the beaded curtain. We looked at each other for several beats; then she looked away and did not look back.

Well, fuck it, you know. If that was the way it was, her and
that Raimundo, that was the way it was. And good luck to
her.

"Drink up *compadre*, let's go eat some goat."

"I'm ready! I could eat a whole one."

"How come you are always hungrier when I'm treating
than when you do?" I wondered.

"I'm not so anxious then, " he replied reasonably.

Before we could get out, Bill called us over to have a drink
with him and his wife and the reporter whose name turned
out be Crumbie or Crumpie and who was very afraid his
round-assed blue-eyed German bride, Erica, was going to be
lured away from him any moment, it looked like.

Bill always drank red wine. The reporter had scotch on the rocks; the women went with margaritas; Pete and I had another tequila on ice.

Bill wanted to know about the deal with the Mexican gunboat down below Twenty-four-ten.

"Well, we might have been a little inshore down there," I admitted.

He laughed. "I hear if you had been in any closer, you'd of been arrested for a traffic violation instead of illegal fishing."

"Well, you can hear a lot of things."

"True . . . Heard there are some people looking to move some stuff to Castro, offering tempting money, too."

"Well, if you run into some of them, you tell them to come see me or Pete here. We could use some tempting money. Pete here is about ready to start running wetbacks and Chinamen. Hey, Pete, tell Bill what you cleared this trip."

"Fourteen dollars and seventy-nine cents," Pete repeated gloomily.

Bill laughed, then so did the others. The German girl's boobs jumped and wobbled in the square-cut neck of her pretty pink and white checked dress. Made me swallow. Our eyes met, and she smiled. Her blond hair was short, her eyes blue like tiny transparent flowers, and her skin so milk-white where it was not tan it made me start thinking back to when I had known skin so white. Nipples would be pink as a baby's tongue. She sort of cocked her head slightly and widened her smile when I hung onto my thought while staring into those funny eyes. She had eyes and a curve of lip like that actress Maria Schell. Same thing. You knew if you ever put out your hand, something was to come of it—maybe not what you had in mind—there was danger in there not even she knew about. Her husband reached over and took her hand and squeezed it to remind her of something. She seemed to make me some sort of promise while at the same time expressing disappointment in her husband within the space of a second before looking away to say something in German to her husband.

Outside, Pete said, "Man you see the white titties on that

schotzie? Haven't seen anything so goddamn pretty and nice since I was weaned. Plumb spoils my evenin now lookin forward to them brown and yellow titties across the river."

"Did I say I was buying you titty, too? Well, let's start with goat and see what we feel like."

"That Mr. Crumbie is sure worried about his wife, ain't he?" Pete grinned.

"Seems to be. Wonder if he has good reason?"

"Man, I sure would like to find out. You know how long it's been since I pronged a full-bloodied white woman? More than three years, man! That's too long. I get all anxious and upset just thinkin about it now. Don't know what I would do with a bunch of white meat like that and nice yella hair an all."

He was looking way ahead dreamily.

"Settle down there, *compadre*," I cautioned him.

He shook himself and came back, spat on the sidewalk.

"She-it, sometimes I just wonder how Missus Gatliff's little boy ever got to here."

"Know how you feel, Pete."

Lupe's border guard husband waved us across the bridge on the US side. A Mexican with a Mauser rifle across his back waved us in on the Mexican end. You had to start watching for water-filled potholes in the street which could break an axle as soon as that.

We pulled into the Pemex station for a tank of gas. Mexican gas was a lot cheaper than US gas. It will run your car all right, if you invest a dollar in a little ceramic filter which you put in where your gas line joins your fuel pump to take care of the water, seeds, and small wildlife which are part of the bargain.

We cruised slowly around the main square in Matamoros, past the sentry at the maw of the constabulary armory, the cathedral with the huge wrought-iron studded wooden doors on which formal handwritten banns were still tacked.

On the far side of the square near the New Houston Café

we found a place to tuck in the truck in front of a tourist trap full of alligator bags. The bags were replete with head and feet of the now unnaturally colored and glazed little monsters.

Why a woman would ever want one of those fucking things is eternally beyond me. If it were another age, do you think those ladies with their blue hair and elastic stockings would have subdued their own little gator and tanned its hide? Like those fox stoles with heads and feet around some little old woman's turkey neck, it would ever puzzle me.

Whole store *full* of alligator purses.

I fished for shrimp for a living and had just cleared about eight hundred to a thousand dollars for three weeks' work, after deducting the boat's share of the catch, which was also mine in that I was owner of the boat. On the other hand, my buddy Pete had come out ahead fourteen dollars and seventy-nine cents—You have to laugh. Hell, anything is possible. Somewhere there is a factory with breeding pens full of those little gators for purses. You can sell anyone anything. Shrimp are just seagoing bugs. You can do anything to goddamned people. You could go straight to hell through a pair of smiling German-blue eyes. There is no end of craziness where people are involved.

"Want an alligator purse, Pete?"

"What? What the hell for?"

"I'd like to buy you an alligator purse."

"You're drunker than shit, man. Buy me something useful. I don't want no alligator purse."

"Come on, Pete, let me buy you one. I never bought anyone an alligator purse before. I always come over here to Mexico, and I can't ever buy a souvenir for nobody. One little alligator purse, Pete. It isn't so much to ask."

"I don't *want* no fucking purse. Now I don't want to hear no more about it."

There were two old tourists in crepe-soled shoes coming out of the New Houston full of stuffed green peppers and two other entrées. He wore a flowered Hawaiian shirt and broad-brimmed straw planter's hat. He was picking his teeth. His

wife had hair the color of a woman just dying to be offered an
alligator bag. Both she and her husband wore rimless bifocal
glasses. Her left ankle was wrapped in an Ace bandage beneath her stocking. She had a little blue sweater thrown over
her shoulders and sported a wooden necklace of fake tiger's
teeth and nigger toes.

"I'm going to buy that lady an alligator purse or know the
reason why," I vowed.

"You're drunker than shit, man," Pete observed, dropping
a step behind.

"Excuse me, missus . . . sir. Where you folks from?"

"Why, Findlay, Ohio!" the woman chirped brightly.

The husband took her elbow and eyed us warily.
"Edith. . . ."

"Now just hold on a second. I'll bet I can tell you, ma'am,
what you want to take back to Findlay from south of the border more than any other thing."

"Edith, come on." The man tried to nudge her around us.
"Now you fellas have had a little bit too much to drink, it
seems to me," the husband observed.

"Don't mean any harm. Just now, when I saw you and your
missus come out of the New Houston, I just knew what she
would like more than any other thing is a genuine alligator
purse with the little head and feet right on her. Hunh? Right?
Ma'am?"

"Listen now, you fellas, let us by." The man tried pushing
me a little.

"I want to buy Edith an alligator purse," I explained my
mission. "Just have to step up to the corner to that little shop.
It's full of alligator purses. Be *happy* to buy you one, ma'am.
All you got to do is pick one out." I hauled a wad of money
from my pocket and waved it under their noses.

"Just what the devil is this all about?" he wanted to know.
He was getting hot. His face was very red. He had a black
string tie clasped with a Western slide around his neck; otherwise he was wash and wear head to toe.

"Nothing sinister, sport. Just want to buy the little woman a nice alligator bag to take home to Ohio. Nice little genuine alligator bag with the head and feet on."

"I don't understand!" The woman blinked like a rabbit caught in a bright light.

"Nothing to understand." Pete said. "He's crazy. Just loves to buy women alligator purses."

"Now I am asking you, young man, to step out of our way," the man said, his jowls starting to shake.

"Don't get tough, sir. Just want to buy your wife a nice alligator purse. I know she would like one. Now wouldn't you, Edith?" I smiled.

"Well. . . ."

"Sure you would!"

"They're so *expensive*."

"But if they weren't, you'd like one, right?"

"Well, they are about half of what you'd have to pay back home." She glanced at her husband.

"Edith, for God's sake! Young man, get out of our way."

"Not until you let me buy your wife an alligator purse!"

"Well, by damn! I never—"

"What will it hurt? She *wants* one. It'll save you fifty bucks. Get a hell of an alligator bag here for fifty bucks."

"I just don't know what your game is."

"No game! I want to buy your wife an alligator purse. No strings attached. Just step with me to the store and pick one out. I swear, that's all there is to it. With my thanks."

"When he wants to buy someone a purse like this, it is dangerous to refuse him," Pete warned them. "He tried to buy me one, but I already got a closetful, if you see what I mean, so he would sure like to buy your missus one. I mean, I think it's crazy myself, but I sure wish you'd let him do it. We're on our way to supper, and I'm getting hungry."

"This is the nuttiest darn thing I ever heard of." The man was positive.

" Well, if *that's* all there is to it." The woman sized me up as if she was figuring what she would do if there *was* some catch.

I found myself between them, the three of us arm in arm,

as I hustled them along toward the leather shop on the corner. The man complaining but stepping right along. The
woman was sort of half huffing, half giggling, her cool, flaccid
bare arm clasped in mine, the back of my arm bouncing
against her huge corseted breast. The smell of the powder and
perfume beneath which she was decaying was too sweet. She
smelled like something rubber that had been powdered.

Right into the store and up to the counter where the startled and curious Mexican proprietor hoped we were serious
customers, though he plainly had his doubts.

"For the *señora* we would like to see a nice alligator purse
with the head and the feet on it so we know it isn't plastic."

"We do not sell plastic goods, *señor.*"

"That's good! That's why we came to you."

"What color of purse!" the shopkeeper wondered.

"Well, I don't know," Edith said, fussing with her necklace.
"I just hadn't thought too much about getting one. I liked
them, but they were so expensive for just a purse."

"Show her some colors."

He returned and spread half a dozen bags on the counter,
still dubious about ever making a sale under such circumstances.

After a goodly debate with herself, Edith decided on the
brown, then just as I asked, "How much?" she changed her
mind and went for the black.

"It will go better with my fur coat." she explained.

"You bet!"

That purse was fifty dollars.

"What do you take us for?" I asked the Mexican. I'll give
you twenty-five."

The man made as if to reclaim his property merely by placing his hands on it and looking at me wearily as if those days
were gone forever and he was bored with the memory of
them. "I give you twenty percent off."

Now I'm not too swift with percents when I've been drinking. "Give you thirty bucks."

"No thirty bucks!" He edged the purse farther back toward

him, though Edith still had the strap over her shoulder, a good grip on it, and a disappointed look on her face.

We got the purse for thirty-five US dollars.

Outside she said, "I always tell Harry to bargain, but he just can't bring himself to do it."

"Well, you enjoy that purse now. You can always tell it's real, got those little feet and the head right on her. "

"Yes. Well, I don't know what to say. This is the darndest thing that has ever happened to me."

Damned if she didn't look right at my cock. She sort of stopped talking. Then she looked up. "Uh, well, thanks, I guess." She giggled.

"Um, yow, uh, thanks," her husband grumped.

"Perfectly all right. Bye."

The woman turned and waved and called good-bye.

We did not go the New Houston. We went off the square down a side street to a place that just served charcoal-roasted *cabrito*. We each had a hindquarter of young kid, served with a deck of tortillas and a salad. We had a couple of good beers with the meat.

Eating sobered me up a lot. It was a good meal, but I was a bit depressed when we went back out into the street. A nice breeze had come up as it often does in the evenings, and it would probably rain before morning.

We did not discuss it. We just got in the truck, and I headed it out along the Washington Beach highway to see what the old-timers still sometimes called "the little painted girls."

CHAPTER EIGHT

The unpaved streets of Boystown were made mud by the cantina owners and sidewalk crib girls to lay the dust. The girls along the sidewalks who posed on their beds in the well-lighted cribs tossed the contents of their washbasins and their slops into the muddy street. On a busy night you had to step lively past the cribs.

If Western movies were true, I am sure the main streets of all those cowtowns would be mud, too, or no one would have been able to do business for the dust. Boystown surely resembled an electrified old cowtown less the bank, post office, and the houses of the righteous.

The large cantinas in which the prettier, more expensive *putas* performed are linked by rows of the jerry-built cribs in which less blessed women wait. Some of the crib girls are as large and better padded than the beds on which they sprawl as invitingly as nature permits. Some are consumptively thin, sick in the blood. A few are mere children. Between the grotesque and the sick and underaged are that majority of women too unexceptional to work in the cantinas.

From the cribs, with the fronts hinged like carnival booths swung open to show there was nothing but happiness inside, the crib girls beckoned with their eyes, a finger, their lips and tongues, while others merely waited, dully, hopelessly, bitterly, witlessly, mad or drugged, for whatever found its way into their cribs with some money in its hand.

Between the gross *putas,* as obscene as something scrawled on a shithouse wall, and the sad, little, still frightened Indians, every size, shape, and denomination of whore offered herself in the cribs and cantinas which blazed like an incandescent cruciform set with neon jewels out in the mesquite between Matamoros and Washington Beach.

Like strange birds, the girls in the sidewalk cribs preen nightly in their poor finery. In every crib is a calendar to count the days: a gift of a Brownsville department store.

How do some of those women ever get up the rent?

Had man's tastes ever swung so wide a loop?

But then, look at it from the girl's side of things.

For down the sidewalks strolled, shuffled, gawked, stumbled, reeled, straggled, and pitched headlong a variety of men as varied in configuration, needs, and desires as the girls who expected them—times ten thousand. Soldier and sailor, driller and roughneck, roustabouts by the carload, fishermen and those who never wet a line, hunters and the hunted, fantasts and straight shooters, geeks and gargoyles, common border jackals of all stripes, young and old, and the agelessly haunted, obsessed, or merely kinked, the idly curious and the curiously idled, those on vacation and those eternally displaced, the motherless lonely and wifeless lost, big spenders and cheapskates, those who can count their change blind and those born to be bilked—all passed before the clean, well-lit cribs. Nobody *sent* for them, yet they came like patrons of a Men Only sexual zoo, where while you were judging the inhabitants, by their own measure, they were judging you.

"I would take a whore's honest opinion of a man before I'd take a preacher's, if it really mattered," I put it to Gatliff.

"Wished I was a woman," Pete yearned, pursing the line of open-sided cribs. "Sure would beat workin."

"You would starve," was my guess.

"The hell! If that big fat sow can make her nut, I sure as shit could make mine—with one arm tied behind me."

"Four bits a crack, Pete, no matter what tricks you develop."

"That's crap! I could get a dollar over here just for bein so freckled."

At the top of the main steam, like a cocked diadem, slants

the Dos Equis, which with the Yellow Bar, is one of the best cantinas out there. It is a two-story hacienda topped by a one-story double cross of thousands of light bulbs outlined in red and green. The sign is a gift of the company that brews the beer of the same name. Visible from the highway, the sign lights the street outside the cantina, the open inner court-yard, and the dusty mesquite that brushes up against the walls.

We came through the barroom with its colorful tile floor, dark wood, and plaster walls like the bowls of old clay pipes. The place is cool and dim as a cave. There is the scent of roses and jasmine from the open double doors that lead to the courtyard from which there is the feminine mutter of a lazy fountain. The four-piece mariachi band was on its break when we came in, so we could hear the fountain over the voices of those in the bar. It was too early for the Dos Equis to be rowdy.

I think it is the influence of the fountain, but the Dos Equis is never as rowdy as the other places.

The women there too are generally quieter, better dressed, and better-looking than the women in the other cantinas.

We ordered beers and went back through the courtyard to the toilet.

On the left of the fountain there is a little chapel of the Virgin of Guadalupe where the *putas* can pray. A reddish glow of votive lights in red glass windshields tinted the otherwise dim and doorless room.

A pretty woman in a skintight sky blue dress came from the chapel, her breasts hoisted in her low bodice like offerings, her wealth of dark hair twisted and lacquered in an exotic hive as if she were going to a party. She smiled and asked with her fingers if we would care to accompany her to the rooms that ringed the balconied court—two eyeless tiers of numbered red doors.

Not now. Check with us later.

On the right side of the courtyard is the latrine. The door opens on a tiled urinal. To the right are four washbasins. It is about as clean as Mexican latrines go.

"*Hola.* You have a cigarette for me?" a woman called from behind us as we addressed the urinal.

We both looked over our shoulders to see a medium-little *puta* a bit past her prime on the stool in the first cubicle. She neither looked nor smelled good.

Pete did not know whether to laugh or explode.

"Goddamn . . ." he drawled.

Well, why the hell not? A coed crapper in a *puta casa* is a practical solution to the need.

"You don't look well, *mamacita*," I observed.

"I am sick," she agreed mournfully.

"Maybe someone you ate," Pete suggested.

Overcome by a terrible internal eruption, she bent over her bare yellow knees, holding her guts, her eyes closed in pain. When she looked up, her forehead popped beads of sweat.

Pete held his nose. "Jesus Christ!"

"Yes," she agreed. "It is terrible. Please, you give me one cigarette." She flushed the stench away.

Both of us dug for our packs.

I offered her a Camel. She preferred Pete's Lucky Strikes.

"And I take one for later, OK?" She helped herself to two cigarettes.

Her preference earned Pete her dubious offer: "You look for me another day when I am well. I am the best. I will feel well soon. You look for me."

We went out pretty fast, half wincing and half laughing.

"Don't let anyone tell you, you can't pull a sick whore off a piss pot, Pete," I encouraged him.

"That's a first for me, *compadre*. Man, that really kills it for me. My old pajonk has crawled up in my belly to hide." He shook himself. "Brrrr. . . . A white woman wouldn't do that, would she?" he wondered.

"I don't know. I sort of like the idea of women and men using the same facilities in a cathouse. Anything else seems pretty silly when you think about it. You feel better if a sick man taking a dump bums you for a cigarette?"

"Man, I don't *know!* I'm just not used to a woman doin that in the same place as me. It just spoils everything. Let's drink our beers and git on down the road. This place is always too quiet anyway."

We drank up and went.

"This is more like it!" Pete exclaimed as we stepped through the swinging saloon doors of the Yellow Bar like two cowboys.

The bar itself is fifty feet long and solid as a fort. It is not yellow at all. The room is noisy, open, garishly bright. Tobacco smoke on a busy night hangs over the half acre of tables like fog.

Chairs scraped, glasses clinked, men talked loud, women laughed or protested shrilly in a stream of border Mexican spat with the rapidity of machine-gun fire.

Along the wall, across the vast room from the bar, was a long bench the length of the room where the *putas* waited to be invited to drink. If you did not soon invite one or more to drink with you, one or more would soon come to your table as if they bore a warrant and want to know why.

At the far end of the room a little stage is provided for the relentless band honking away for your dancing pleasure. There is also a stage show later, nightclub and whorehouse, it was a real old-time cantina, so much more civilized than the furtive prostitution in the U.S., the call girls rated for big business types on expense accounts and so beyond the means of someone who works for a living.

"Forget what they tell you, Pete, you can judge the depth of democracy in a society by what it costs a man to fuck. Mexico isn't any more democratic for the Mexicans than the U.S. is for us, or Korea or Japan or Germany is for their people, but it is a whole level higher for us than we could afford at home. Every country is set up to force a man and woman to get married, and then they are so saddled with responsibility they have to think twice before throwing over their jobs or speaking out for themselves. All because a man who works for a living can't really afford the cost of sex in his own country anywhere. You ever think of that?"

"Just always thought I was bein stinted that way to some degree."

"Well, think about it. It's true. It's one of the major ways everyone is kept in his place . . . the cost of sex. As long as there is a price on it, what they call democracy is a lot of shit."

When a girl goes back with a trick, she stops at the far end of the bar and hands the young man at the ever-busy cash register the money paid in advance. He gives her a token, which she hangs on her own hook on a board affixed to the butt of the bar.

Two girls came over to see if we would buy them a drink.

"Is Lena working?" I asked the wide swaybacked whore straining the seams of her red brocade gown.

"You want her?" She made a face, looking me up and down as if I had crawled in on hands and knees.

"If she is here."

"She is busy now, I think. She will come. Buy me a drink, and I will make you forget that crazy one anyway."

They were both pulling out chairs.

You just smile and let them tell the waiter what they will drink, for the waiter is at hand before their asses kiss wood. You can tell them to go away if you can't afford to buy drinks and fuck too, or you can tell them to go away during the day or on a slow weeknight. But if it is a big Saturday night, you should not go into a cantina unless you expect to buy a few drinks for the girls.

"A brandy alexander," was their choice.

It is a true drink, not cold tea. You can taste it if you have any doubts.

The young one, a rather shy, unhappy-looking girl of common prettiness, began a conversation with Pete by asking his name and telling him her own. We could all be at a party. The plump older whore scooted her chair over until she and I were joined hip and thigh. She wrapped my right arm in both of her arms, slithering the cool, smooth, meaty flesh of her flabby arms against my skin. It was as if my arm were being loved by scaleless snakes. Her fingers wove and unwove my own. My arm was hugged against her big, deep bosom. She prattled and chatted, posed and pressed herself against me, the master of a million secret little touches and insinuating sounds. She nipped the hairs on the back of my hand with her garish red lips, ran her tongue between my fingers, dunked one of my fingers in her drink and popped it into her mouth, sucking it up to its last knuckle, closing her fluttering eyes while making greedy sounds in her throat.

Maybe she was forty. Maybe she was older. She was one of those ageless *putas* working to stay out of a sidewalk crib where her price could skid to fifty cents a trick and she would have to take up the slack working out back of the town where old women did the younger women's laundry. Her name was Aurora. Her left eyetooth and the molar next to it were capped with gold.

"I am better than Lena," she purred, sneaking a hand into my lap, "I promise. If I lie to you, you go free."

It was a tempting offer.

"¿*Que* No? You are crazy, *Capitan*. I make this offer only to you. How about it?"

"Maybe later. You like to dance?"

"Sure. OK." She got up and led me by the hand to the dance floor, giving the hand half a dozen different intimate squeezes en route.

She was some Aurora.

A short, plump woman, she danced with me better than anyone had ever danced with me before. It was amazing. I have never been known as much of a dancer. But that little plump whore molded herself to me and seemed to know what move I was about to make before I knew myself. How much work did it take for her to seem weightless and me so smooth? All the while, every turn, every beat was a small act of sex. She rolled her breasts almost imperceptibly against my chest, brought her wide belly up against my cock, touched me, it seemed, in a hundred small ways. Her lips nibbled my neck. In her throat she made tiny sounds like a woman fucking and liking it, but so softly it came to me as a shock when I realized she had been doing that since we began to dance. Were she a wife, her husband could have danced alongside and not known what she was up to. She purred and cooed and exuded a whorishly sweet perfume that made the cantina as dizzily cloying as a hothouse.

I became aroused against her belly.

"Come with me, *chico,* I take care of him for you. I give you a real good time. You will be my first today, hunh? OK?" She was all but tugging me off the dance floor toward the rooms beyond, all but digging in her spike heels and horsing me out of there with her bare hands.

I laughed. "Maybe later, *mamacita.*"

"You like me. I know. I do anything you like."

"Maybe later."

She shrugged and began automatically casting about for another possible trick, her face a bit high in color for having been rejected.

"You give me one dollar for the dance," she demanded, not half hoping she would get it, eyeing four tourists in sports shirts who came self-consciously through the swinging half doors.

"It was worth a dollar," I agreed to her surprise. "You dance with me better than anyone, *mamacita.*"

"I do everything as well, *estúpido!* You should trust me." She kissed the dollar and stuffed it deftly into her brassiere.

"Another time," I promised.

"OK. Sure."

Soon she was at the table with the tourists. Her young friend remained at our table, and it looked as if Pete would go back with her.

Two of the tourists had cameras and wanted to take pictures when drinks were brought to their table. Three other *putas* had joined Aurora.

The girls did not want their pictures taken. The waiter tried to tell the tourists they could not take pictures. There was a

row about it. Presently the bouncer came over to explain pictures could not be taken in Boystown. If you want pictures,
you can buy them from a licensed vendor on the street. They
are the same pictures your father brought home from Mexico. One monkey is not so much different from another, is an
old Mexican *puta casa* cry.

"He wants a bribe." One of the tourists had a brainstorm.

Another produced and handed the bouncer a dollar. He
took the money but placed his considerable mitt over the photographer's lens.

"No photographs!" he insisted. "It is forbidden."

"He says it's *verboten*," one tourist sought to translate.

"Give him another dollar," another suggested.

He did not turn down this dollar either, but neither did he
permit them to take a picture.

When the second cameraman set off *his* flash while the
bouncer was busy with the first, it became busier still. The
bouncer snatched the man's camera and damned near
yanked him in two as the leather strap was still around his
neck. Then the tourists started squealing and making threats,
and pimps came to help the bouncer, and it was not settled
until two members of the constabulary with carbines and pistols slung on them came on the run to straighten things out.

The constabulary levied fines on the spot for taking illegal
photographs that might embarrass the Mexican people. The
tourists paid the fines to keep the soldiers from confiscating
their cameras. Before they left, the constabulary officer
opened the cameras, exposed the film, and left the tourists
protesting indignantly about being cheated in Mexico.

They left vowing to damn the name of the place everywhere, as if they were actually a threat to continued business
success at the Yellow Bar.

The whores did not even bother to make naughty gestures
at the tourists upon their departure.

The men had not really been there to go back with a girl
anyway. They had come out to pretend to get drunk and flirt

and talk dirty, but none of them would have had the guts to make the first move to go back with a girl. Alone, each might have furtively gone back with a girl, but together they could creep back to town, to their wives in the hotel, feeling they had dared so much and been cheated by whores; for having cheated and been cheated in the normal course of their lives, they would not trust a real bargain now if it came up, crawled in their laps, and licked them on the face. Americans have been offered so many bullshit alternatives for so long they may be incapable of making a good decision for themselves if one ever does come along.

It is funny how the middle class never trusts the lower, taking their cues from the upper class. It is incredible how the lower class is ever bent to trust the one above them as they are educated to accept that their own failure to rise is due to a moral lack, when the contrary is more likely the case. So the fucking captains and lieutenants lead the lower ranks down trails to stupid deaths and ambushes generation after generation, having over them ultimately the power of life and death. And the rich form clubs more powerful than governments. And however you really look at it, everyone except the rich busts his guts for relative peanuts.

So there was not a *gringo* in the place who worked for a living who would have gone to the tourists' assistance if they had chosen to make a stand against the constabulary. The tourists were foreigners there as Pete and I were citizens by virtue of values that broke differently from arbitrary notions of boundaries.

She came around the bandstand beside the bar and said something to the man behind the cash register. She entered with an authority no other girl there possessed.

Lena—Cleopatra of the Yellow Bar—she dressed as professionally for her game as Yogi Berra did for his. In her especially high-heeled silver shoes, tottering on tiptoe higher than all the other whores, her spine arched radically against the prospect of pitching onto her face, she seemed something crippled for any purpose save sex. Her coarse Indian hair had been bleached pale as sisal and pressed straight, then cut into a peaked bang above her incredibly made-up eyes. Great sweeping wings of rose, gold, green and blue outlined in black swept away from her nose to a point over each temple. Glitter dust sparkled on her eyelids and brows, and specks of it caught the light in her unearthly taffy-colored hair, on her shoulders and back and breasts. She minced into the room in a silver satin sheath that dipped in a V below her navel and was scooped out in back to show her dimpled coccyx. It was widely latticed up both sides to demonstrate she wore nothing at all underneath.

Most of the other whores seemed to shrink and fade when she came into the room. They thought she was crazy. So did most of the customers, much to Lena's regret.

"Man, I do not *see* what you have to do with something like that for," Pete voiced his thought.

"I like her," I told him. "She is what a whore is all about."

"Hell! She ain't even natural."

"If you want a whore as natural as another woman, why cross the river?"

"OK. Just don't bust a gut. I don't give a fart if your taste in *putas* is off base. Everyone is titled to his little kinks if it don't get in the way of my good time," he teased.

Cleo was not the hit on the border she had been in Mexico City. She had re-created herself so on the side of Latin fantasy she missed all those conservative souls looking for surrogates for their daughters, secretaries, a face off a billboard or movie screen or out of a magazine. You had to be pretty sure of what you are and no bullshit about it to walk out of that room before God and everybody with your arm around that whore's middle even though she would never again be the hit she once had been or the hit she yet rated herself to be.

A whining lot of complaint had begun to work itself into her act, especially if she thought you were in the least sympathetic.

But she was still very young and rated top dollar at the Yellow Bar as well as a room with its own toilet and shower and a window air conditioner. She was a four-dollar *puta*, short-time, when the standard was two bucks, and far prettier and more considerate girls went for three.

Up close, stripped naked save for the gold crucifix around her neck and the little gold hearts on a chain around her ankle, she was not really pretty at all. There were half a dozen prettier girls at the Yellow Bar. She was short of leg once she got off those shoes, and rather knockkneed. Her breasts, which looked great cantilevered in her gown were unexceptional in repose.

But her pubes were neatly trimmed and shaped like a valentine. She also operated on a high big bed when most of the others had to turn their tricks on twin-sized beds. The bed was mounted before a big three-panel mirror triptych in which she and her trick could watch themselves. She liked watching herself. She was very dramatic and always feigned a violent, death-defying orgasm and may have in fact gotten off watching herself now and then. Her vanity was of an order seen in the giddiest, most determined movie starlets.

She would tell you in her room, "I am a good actress. This is my stage." She would pat and smooth her high soft bed, then lie back, cock a knee and make a mouth at you, checking herself in the mirror so she was mostly always looking a little past you at your reflections.

She also pulled for compliments.

"You like my body, yes?"

"Good body. *Es buena. Muy bella.*"

Yet, whatever you said, it would fall short of what she needed to hear.

She bleached her skin with chemicals to make it whiter, achieving the pallor of a Latino corpse or mock albino. But the light in the room casts a rose-colored tint, and as both you and she watch your bodies moving together in her clever mirrors, the aspects of fucking are multiplied and reangled in your mind until feeling and seeing are rebuilt and curious—

not better necessarily, just different. That muscular ass pumping up and into that accepting pale woman flesh is your own.

But if you are too sympathetic, you will not be able to go back with her for long.

"I am not appreciated here. Here is only *peónes*, Latinos and *gringos*. I am artist. In Mexico I have men give me one thousand pesos, *por nada*, for the tip. It is true! You do not believe me?"

I shrugged.

"It is true! You are *peón*, too. I thought you were my friend. You are no different from the others. You do not understand me."

Her cunt was smooth and grippy, and she worked it every minute of the ride like a well-oiled fuck machine, then "came" so dramatically, cutting glances at herself in the mirror, that it would have been embarrassing even if it were genuine.

I had become much too sympathetic ever to go back with her again. We were becoming buddies. She chewed my ear before we got on the bed about how unfairly she was being treated, processed me mechanically and fast so she could bend my ear with dreams of what she might achieve if she were but understood by an inferior world.

"Baby, do you ever reckon if there *were* justice where *I* might be?"

She had not. It was a silly question.

She kissed my cheek at the cash register and made an obscene gesture with her arm and fist at the men who were staring at us to let them know I was a good fuck.

"*Swee! Swee! Swee!*" she whistled, tucking her lower lip over her small white teeth and pumping her arm.

She sent me on my way with a blaze of her lipstick on my left cheek.

Seeing no customers among the civilians, Lena turned along the bar to stalk playfully with exaggerated strides and glower a young sailor being hustled by two *putas* at the bar.

The kid, who looked a lot like Alfalfa Switzer, saw her coming and swallowed so hard his Adam's apple dipped to his breastbone and rebounded as if he had swallowed an eel.

I would have paid another four bucks to watch Lena and that kid go.

The little square-assed *puta* smiled and gave away her place to the only headliner the Yellow Bar ever had.

Frank Smith saw me before I saw him so there was no way to avoid insulting him.

Frank was a rummy. He had been a big-time Chicago lawyer, held a license or whatever to plead cases before the U.S. Supreme Court. Now he could not be bothered to find laces for his scavenged shoes or socks for his feet. Someone had to carry him across the border, for no guard would let him pass on foot.

But he had wet and combed his hair and put on a reasonably clean shirt. He had shaved within the last three days.

"Johnny, I've been looking for you," he said before he got to me lest I turn away before he had stated his mission.

"Hey, Frank. How's it goin?"

"You know, Johnny. It's rough right now for me. I've been working on a coonass boat, but I can't keep doing that, Johnny. They aren't decent men like you and me. They're like animals, Johnny. They treat me like something lower than low. I can't take much more of it, Johnny. I—"

"Yow. Want a drink, Frank?"

"Well, that isn't why I stopped you. Maybe a beer. I'm really trying to kick it, Johnny. I'm really trying. I'm going to make it this time. I know it. I can handle it. I can't live like this, Johnny."

"Well, that's good, Frank."

We sat down with Pete, who looked a bit rumpled and slumped over his drink as if guarding it with the fortress of his arms. His little *puta* was right there.

"You going to take that poor girl back or what?" I wondered.

"Already been and come," he slurred.

The little *puta* hung onto his arm with both hands and nuzzled his ear in hopes of inspiring him to go again.

"You need some more money?" I asked.

"Fuck no!"

Every time, after Pete had his ashes hauled, he got morosely drunk and sometimes mean.

"Fourteen fuckin dollars and seventy-nine cents!" he bellowed and banged his fist on the table. "This damned little cunt made more'n at tonight layin back on her butt an openin her legs."

"What you say?" she asked.

"Said what you do for a livin beats the shit out of shrimpin."

"*¿Que?*"

"Never mind."

"Listen, Johnny." Frank scooted his chair a bit closer and would have put his shaky hand on my arm, but I saw the intention in his mournful face and let him know with my eyes I did not want him to touch me.

Frank was OK. But he was hopeless. A Jonah. A man you could pity for having fallen so far, yet despised for ever having so far to fall in the first place, then *doing* it. He was a man who could recall having shirts made just for him . . . bespoke shirts. If I were an alcoholic and had fallen upward as fast as Frank came down, how helpful would he have been to me? On the level where we met, Frank was tolerated, accepted even for what he was—a rummy—and even employed from time to time in hope something inside him would go against all odds and outward sign to let him again become a person. Working on a Cajun's boat was not the way for anyone who had ever worn bespoke shirts to go. They would make him as near a donkey as they were able. If they became displeased with his work in the extreme, they could throw him alive to the sharks trailing the boat and circle around to watch the fun.

"They aren't like you and me, Johnny. If I don't get off that boat, they'll kill me or I'll kill myself. I mean it. Johnny, I know you need a third man. I'd like you to give me a chance,

Johnny. One trip. If I don't cut the mustard, you don't have to pay me. How about it, Johnny? I'll get off the booze. I can do it."

"You aren't going to get off the booze, Frank. You just conning yourself. You don't even believe it."

"I'll handle it."

"Aw, shit, Frank. You know how I hate for you to put me in a spot like this. You're no damn good on a boat, Frank. You get sick. You're a rummy. You can't cook for shit. All you got to offer anyone is a goddamned crying need. You make it so someone who would like to see you get yourself straightened out has to say such things to you. That's a hell of a presumption, man!"

"I know that, Johnny. I don't want to put you on a spot. I just—"

"Then don't, Frank." I shoved back my chair. "Hey, Pete, come on, let's cop a mope."

"Hunh? Sure. So long, Conchita *mía*." He leaned over and kissed the little *puta*. She was about fifteen or sixteen years old. "You work on him." He indicated Frank. "He is *muy hombre*."

She knew better.

"Johnny, listen, I'll do you a *job!* I can be a hand. For God sake, Johnny, give me a chance!"

I turned away and started to walk out of there.

Hell . . . I turned back.

"Come down to the boat tomorrow afternoon."

I got away. I did not want to hear him say thanks.

Outside a small barefoot boy tried to sell us Chiclets or condoms from an open cigar box. An old man wearing a hand-whittled wooden pegleg and sporting long wispy chin whiskers sold peanuts, candy, soft drinks, and dirty postcards from a tin and glass casket on bicycle wheels.

Down the street a young airman without trousers drilled with a piece of broom in the ankle-deep mud, giving himself commands.

The constabulary patrol was busy farther along with a big white air-conditioned Cadillac which they had hailed over to the curbing. Two Anglo couples, obviously tourists, were in an argument with the police.

The police were trying to make the tourists understand the women in the car could not remain in Boystown.

"If you wish to see what goes on here, you must see a doctor and have an examination. Then you can get a permit from the police," he explained to one of the irate women in the car.

"You mean we can't even drive down a public street!" The woman's high nasal voice cut through the soft, humid *puta casa* night.

"No. No. This is not a public street," the Mexican insisted. "No. You must turn around and go away."

"Shit, give him a couple of dollars, Bob," the woman turned to the man at the wheel.

He pulled out his wallet and handed a two-dollar bill to the woman, who turned it over to the young constabularyman.

"*Gracias.* But the women cannot be here without a permit to prostitute." He made as if to offer the woman two dollars, indicating between himself and her, with thumb and little finger that they could be together.

"What the hell is this, Bob?" the woman wanted to know.

Pete shouted across the walk, "They're tellin you the only women out here are whores, and if them women want to stay, they better be ready to perform."

"Well, I never in all my life!" The woman chose to be insulted. She was a redhead with her hair twisted and lacquered in a hive, big tits depending in a halter over a roll of suet above her waistband. Her skirt was hiked high, and her knees spread to catch the benefit of the car's air conditioning.

"Oh, sure you have, honey!" Pete informed her. "I'll take a couple of dollars' worth myself."

"Let's get out of here," the man in the backseat insisted.

"You mean you sonsabitches are goin to let a Mexican and a godknowswhat proposition me like that and get away with it!"

The man spun that Caddy around in the slops, hitting the electric window switch, all but decapitating his wife as she leaned out, cursing Mexico, Mexicans, American scum, and men in general with such a richness of profanity that I would have hired her to work on the boat if she had cared to apply.

We heard a pig. It was very near. We looked all around for it but could not see it.

"That's a pig," Pete assured me.

"Yow. I can hear it."

Definitely a pig making piggy sounds.

We were near where I left the car between the Yellow Bar and the Dos Equis. There was only a high adobe wall along the sidewalk. The pig sounded as if it were on our side of the wall.

Then I saw it. Just its snout, wet and deckled with rooted earth. It had rooted beneath the wall far enough to get his snout just outside in a little declivity at sidewalk level.

Pete and I laughed.

"Poor fuck."

"It isn't any better out here than it is in there, pig," I told the snout.

It grunted as if it heard, but it remained clearly determined.

Pete suddenly took out his cock and began to piss on the pig's snout.

The snout made snuffling, unhappy sounds and withdrew from the hole until Pete had finished. We continued to watch, and soon the snout was back.

The sight of the snout wrinkling and snuffling under the wall made me shiver.

I went ahead and got into the car.

Pete came along, got in, and we drove back to the highway without speaking, then through Matamoros, and headed toward the bridge.

"I'll be damned!"

"What?" Pete stirred himself.

"Coming out of that motel."

Ezequiel Cavazos' most beautiful daughter called Encanta was coming out of the place arm in arm with Sheriff's Deputy Bobby Joe Solar.

"What about it?" Pete wondered.

"I just never thought she'd do something like that."

"Why? She squats to pee like any other woman."

"Yow. But he's married."

"I don't give a fuck." Pete turned away. He was morose and touchy.

I felt the same way after seeing María-Antoinette Cavazos coming out of the motel at three in the morning with that sheriff's deputy as I felt finding the pig's snout snorting hopefully beneath a *puta casa* wall—a mix of fear, anger, disgust and pity, now with the added misfortune of envy.

I had seen her at the boat when the deputy brought her out to learn of her father's death. Now here she was, the same night, coming out of a motel with the handsome bastard. Was she so easy after all? I felt bad for the old man who had dreamed she would be his salvation.

There is no salvation.

Fuck it. You know. If that was how things were, that was how they were.

I woke Pete up in front of the place where he kept a room. He mumbled something, got out, and went away as if we need never see each other again. That was it, too. If Pete and I never saw each other again, neither of us would ever wonder why. It did not matter. We were buddies, not friends. You can feel that way about most of the people you know. The farther along you go, the more all right that becomes.

CHAPTER NINE

Parking the truck in the lot at the head of the dock, I looked for a moment out over the masts of the fleet. I was part of it. A fisherman, captain of my own boat, twenty-five years old. To state such things to myself at that moment was like having a pocketful of nice, heavy silver dollars.

The breeze had died. It was hot, muggy; mosquitoes zinged past my ears. There had been lightning but no rain. It was going to be very hot on the boat to try to sleep, even with the fan. On deck I would be eaten by mosquitoes. I could take an air mattress and go down on the beach and sleep in the truck. But with the heat now moving off the land, the mosquitoes there would be bad as well. There would also be thousands of little dead sharks on the shore stranded by the tide. The smell would be rotten until the tide and the scavengers cleaned the sand.

Going over the two-by-twelve plank from the dock onto the boat, I felt suddenly apprehensive. I tried to shake off the feeling. There was no reason for it. Yet, rather than go directly to the entrance of the main cabin, I went up the dock side of the deck to the bow; then, turning aft, I knew someone was aboard. There was someone slumped down beside the pilothouse.

I heard myself let go a startled challenge and leaped for the figure, ready to destroy whoever it was. My reaction was instinctive.

"Johnny!"

"Damn! You scared me!"

She was in my arms, crying softly, frightened, digging her fingers into my back and shoulders, seeking my mouth, her lips wet with salty tears.

"Lupe, Lupe, what's the matter? What happened?"

"Nothing. Nothing happened. It is just me. I am a crazy girl, Johnny. I warned you. You forgive me?"

"Sure. Nothing to forgive. Just glad I didn't hurt you."

"I'm sorry. You do not deserve to know such a crazy one. I am afraid I will die, Johnny. I feel my death trying to take me over. I am sick. Johnny, I'm afraid.

"Don't be afraid, Lupe."

"Yes, I'm afraid.

"Let's go inside. I'll heat up some coffee. Have a little brandy, hunh?"

"I don't want no brandy. I don't want your coffee tonight. It is too strong, too sweet. I can't keep nothing on my stomach."

"You see a doctor?"

"I don't need no doctor. It is not physical. I have a sickness of my spirit. When your spirit is sick, your death can come into you. Mine is trying to take me over. I feel so weak, Johnny. I feel I can hardly resist. Sometimes it feels like it would be nice to let my death have me. But I am afraid. I don't want to die, Johnny. But I can't think of no good reason to live either."

"Well, if you don't want to die more than you think you want to, that is reason enough. So you won't die. I won't let you."

"Oh, Johnny, I love you. I really do. I am a crazy girl. I'm sorry. You are good to me, Johnny. You are the only one I have except myself."

"That's funny. Because, I guess, Lupe, you are the only one I have too, except for myself."

"It is so hot. It is hot everywhere. In town I can't breathe, so I came to your boat. But I can't breathe so good here either. There is no air anywhere."

"We will go out into the Gulf."

"Yes?"

I led her to the pilothouse, unlocked it, got the engine started and checked the gauges. I just had on the low red night
lights inside, so we both were a shade of red, her lips, nails
and rouge neutralized so she was a monochromatic pale red. I
went outside to cast loose the lines, hopped back aboard,
rushed to the pilothouse and eased the boat out into the
channel. Lupe hauled our lines aboard.

As soon as we were moving, it seemed there was a breeze.

Lupe stood just outside the open door of the pilothouse in
the low red glow from within. She ran both hands back
through her thick hair. When we cleared the light at the end
of the jetty which ran along the top of enormous chunks and
blocks of broken concrete, she began to take off her clothes.
She stripped naked, tossing her clothes back into the pilothouse.

"You are a beautiful woman, Lupe."

"The wind feels good on my body."

She stood with her legs spread against the motion of the
boat as we cleared the pass and opened her arms to embrace
the wind. With her hands, she laved herself with the night
breezes.

She came inside and began tugging at my shirt.

"You too. We go naked."

"OK. But I have to steer through here. Four boats out of
Port Isabel were lost here not long ago. Good boats with good
captains. No one knows why. There was no trace. It was as if
the Gulf or something had swallowed them up."

"Don't make me afraid again. I am starting to feel better.
Get naked."

She unbuckled my belt and hauled down my trousers.

"Step out. Step out."

Maybe a waterspout had taken the four boats. One guess
was as good as another.

Of course you can be killed crossing the street, but think of being picked up and whirled in the cone of a waterspout, tornado, hurricane; dying acquires a horrible, inhuman majesty beyond our ability to alter or explain. Indeed, all explanation in the face of such phenomena seems sadly presumptuous. President, king, bum, there is no protocol going up or coming down in a funnel or spout.

Lupe pressed her naked body against my bare back. I felt the soft squash of her breasts against my lower ribs, the tickle of her pretty bush below my buttocks. Her arms wrapped tight around me as if she would weld us together.

"I love you Johnny Hand," she said, with her soft lips against my shoulder.

Then, she slid around between me and the wheel.

"Is this OK? You can see to drive OK?"

"Um."

She nuzzled the juncture of my neck and shoulder.

"Oh! Phew! You stink like a *puta!*"

She disengaged herself, stepped back to examine me.

The sparkles from Lena the Cleopatra of the Yellow Bar were like some sort of devil dust in the red light of the cabin on my shoulders and chest.

"What is that shit?" she demanded, picking at the specks.

"Glitter dust, I think they call it."

She punched me hard on the chest, mumbled something and went outside again.

"Lupe!"

"No! Not now."

She went forward to stand on the bow like a beautiful, living figurehead. Her hair blew behind her. The moonlight off her naked skin made her look as if she were silvered.

Soon we were far enough outside the pass to anchor. The land was but a faint glow behind us. I anchored and let the boat swing on the tide. I went aft and just threw out a sea anchor to keep us from swinging on the anchor.

I went forward and took Lupe in my arms.

"Wash yourself so you don't smell like a *puta*. It makes me sick."

"OK."

I went back amidships, threw over a Jacob's ladder, and dived into the dark sea. The surface still retained a little warmth, but a few feet below, it was very cool. I dived into the darkness, tumbled about, and was quickly disoriented as to up and down. I relaxed, and the way my head ultimately pointed was up. I could just make out the dark shadow of the boat.

I broke the surface and swam strongly against the sea until I felt the end of the burst of energy that had sponsored the effort, floated a bit on my back, then rolled over and swam back to the boat. I could see Lupe leaning anxiously over the side watching me.

"Come back!" she called. "I am afraid if you leave me on this boat alone."

I swam easily. I felt good. My head had cleared, my nose opened. I felt nicely taut and tired.

I climbed back aboard.

Lupe was there and hugged me tight, drinking the cool water from my lips and off my skin. In the heat of my body chill standing there, her mouth opened upon mine, drew me inside her kiss until I shivered from the warmth.

"Bring the bed out. Let's sleep beneath the sky," she urged.

"Yes." It did not smell so good inside the boat.

I lay the mattresses and blankets on the deck so we could look up at the sky full of stars.

"Are the stars Mexican or American?" I wondered aloud.

"They are nobody's," Lupe said.

"It's crazy when you think we live on something like one of those out there. That from out there we would look just the same as one of those."

"It is not true."

"It is! Out there on one of those stars there could be a world like this one, or a world very different, but just as real. There could be a planet like this one, with a gulf on it and a man and a woman on a boat who looked just like us. Maybe there could be a whole chain of us to the end of time."

"Hey! You make me afraid again. I will believe many

things. There are many things that are mysterious, but there can only be one place as ugly as this one. It would be too cruel if our troubles traveled out into the stars. No. You are wrong. It is not possible."

The sky seemed too full of stars to support them all. While we watched, by ones and twos, stars fell and streaked briefly across the sky.

We fucked and lay close to count the falling stars until we fell asleep.

In sleep I saw stars continue to fall and fell myself, falling forever through space. It was a feeling I associate with extreme contentment—a sensation of falling backward, headlong through eternity without fear of crashing or death. I hope death is like that. If I were God, I would be sure that death felt like that forever for everyone.

I awoke at first light. I was not certain where I was, yet aware of the slow rise and fall of the boat, the smell of the sea. I heard a large fish jump and splash.

The sea had become glassy. The boat rose and fell on long, lazy swells.

I tucked the head of my cock between the sweaty deep globes of Lupe's fantastic ass. She stirred, muttered something, and bent double to afford me passive access to her cunt.

She was tight and made a quick, pained sound when I popped into her, but she bent and snuggled backward to afford a better angle and deeper way.

I whipped it to her, uncovered now beneath the lowering sky, selfishly, almost cruelly, yet loving her nonetheless, holding her fleshy cunt from the front between her legs with my right hand, trumming her clit, gripping her left tit tightly with my left hand. Then she carried my hand from her tit to her lips and slipped my middle fingers into her mouth to suck them as I came in her hard, crying out loudly in the gray Gulf dawn—all at sea—no one to hear but the sea, the fish, Lupe, and God. I yelled loudly.

She purred then and motored her ass back nicely to run out my orgasm.

Then she asked, "Let me be on top, *querido*. I want to come, too."

I rolled quickly over, and she got astride me and inserted my still mostly erect cock into herself. Soon she closed her legs and humped me close, tight, grinding her pelvic arch against my own, working hard, talking, grunting, breathing rhythmically.

"Yes! Oh, yes! Um. Feels good to me, Johnny. Um, yes."

She seemed to want to be between my legs. I opened my legs as if I were a woman and she went wild, fucking me hard, short, like a man, yet not like a man, tossing wildly back and forth, her hair whipping my face.

"Suck my tit!"

I fastened on her left breast.

"Yes! Um. Fuck me!"

I gripped her big, soft ass with both hands, spread it wide, felt my cock between the slick lips of her cunt with my fingers, started to run a finger in her asshole.

She shook her head she didn't want that and reached back and carried my right hand to her other breast.

"Yes! Oh, Johnny, fuck me! *FUCK ME!*" she screamed where there was no one to hear but me and fishes and God.

"Hold me!" she cried.

I had become excited again; she had never been quite so passionate, never taken over the fuck. I felt myself about to come again.

"Yes!" she cried. "Hold me, Johnny! *HOLD ME!*"

She came, shivered violently, screamed, collapsed, seemed to come again with another body-racking shudder. She was a comer, but she had never been like this.

"I feel dizzy," she said weakly.

"Me, too."

"I love you, Johnny. I want you." Then, she said, "I'm sorry."

"Why? What?"

"Nothing. I don't want to hurt you."

"You don't hurt me. What are you talking about?"

She rolled off and curled with her back to me and began to cry.

"What's wrong? What did I do? Wasn't it OK?"

She turned quickly, her face like a little girl's.

"Oh, yes! It was wonderful, too wonderful. I want things like any woman, and I know I must not."

"Why?"

"There is something wrong with me. I am not like other women. I am a monster."

"Bullshit, Lupe. What happened to you can happen to anyone. How do you know it was not your old man's fault the baby was not all right? Why blame yourself?"

"Because I know what is inside me. And he made two good children before he met me."

"That doesn't really prove anything, Lupe. Have you talked to a doctor?"

"Doctors do not know what is inside you unless they can see it with their eyes or an X ray or under a microscope. Blood doctors don't know nothing about feelings. They are not geniuses. They are mechanics. And they are rich. I do not trust rich people."

"Maybe you just have some bad blues."

"You can call it that. But it is something worse. I can die, Johnny. I know this. I don't want to die, yet I feel drawn to do it. I don't want to."

She hugged me tight.

"Hold me, Johnny. Don't let me go."

"I won't, Lupe, I won't."

"Hold me."

After a while, I said, "Lupe, if we don't eat something, we will both fade away. I'm hungry."

"Swim with me first. I want to wash me."

"Sure."

I got up and picked her up in my arms and carried her to the rail above the Jacob's ladder.

"Don't throw me," she begged, hanging tight on to my neck. "You go first."

I got up and set her down and dived from the rail into the glassy water. She climbed naked over the rail and down the Jacob's ladder and dipped cautiously into the water, then settled in up to her neck.

I swam over to paddle around her. Our limbs and bodies brushed slickly against one another in the foggy, glassy sea. We kissed long, lovingly, holding each other gently in the water.

Then a big fish bumped us, brushed across the back of Lupe's legs. Her nails dug painfully into my shoulders. Her eyes flew open with fright. She screamed. I could see the gold fillings and the little doodad at the back of her throat. I thought of a cartoon scream. But she was terrified long after the big fish had gone.

I told her to stop screaming. It hurt my ears, reverberating off the water like a spray of needles straight into my brain. I could understand how a prowler so surprising a frightened woman might destroy her, how a parent faced with a hysterical child might beat it to death.

I shook her, then slapped her. She shut up.

I carried her up the ladder and set her feet on the deck.

She stood staring at the puddle forming on the deck around her feet.

"Sorry, Lupe. It was just a big ling probably. They like to hang around the boat. It wasn't a shark."

She put her arms around me again and lay her head on my chest.

"I don't know what to do about me, Johnny. I'm sick."

"I'm going to get you to a doctor, Lupe. If you feel so bad, you got to do something about it."

"No. I am not sick that way. You don't understand."

She turned away and went into the cabin.

"I'll fix some breakfast. That'll make you feel better."

"I am not hungry," she said and went back out to bring in the mattresses and blankets.

Well, if she felt good enough to do something, she could not be too sick, I reasoned.

I made breakfast—bacon and scrambled eggs—while Lupe made up the bunks in the main cabin. The galley was a mess, but I had to use it.

"Hey, Lupe . . . I like this going without clothes," I called to her.

"Yes, it's nice.

"You read lots of books," she called from the cabin.

I had a small library of books in the cabin, mostly paperbacks. But I have always been a reader.

"You read Shakespeare!" She laughed.

"Sure. In the original English, too."

I was suddenly very aware of her accent for some reason.

"I nayver look ah ch-yore books bayfore."

Instant tenderness and pity for her melted and expanded to unspecific concern and pity for myself, then for us both.

I went to the two steps up into the main cabin and stood silently watching her, bending to look at the books in the seagoing bookrack I had made beside my desk.

"You are beautiful," I told her.

She jumped and smiled and was embarrassed slightly upon realizing I had been standing there watching her. She smiled and looked more beautiful still. She glanced from my face to my shoulders, my cock, legs, and back to my face. On her knees before the bookcase, she opened her arms toward me, with a look of giving on her face that made me want to give her something better than I owned, was, or would ever be. She made me happy to know her, to see her. I wanted to make her happy, too.

She stood on the first step, so we were about the same height, her arms across my shoulders.

"I feel better about you than any man I have ever known," she said softly to me.

"You make me want a house," I told her.

She laughed inside herself happily. It left her little motor running. I could feel the tremor in her belly against me. It was in her lips when we kissed.

We made love standing on the stairs, she rising until her head was higher than mine, her breasts close enough to kiss. Crazily, we came together and fell about on the steps and into the galley on rubbery legs. There was almost a cramp in both of my calves. We tried to catch our breaths and laughed and felt weak.

The eggs were cold and hard. Lupe nibbled on toast and jam. I ate the bacon and some toast. I drank about a quart of cold milk. Lupe thought milk was disgusting to drink. Then we had mugs of my heart-kicking strong coffee in the pilot-house as we headed back into port.

We stood arm in arm at the wheel, naked as the day we were born.

"This is the life, hunh?" I asked, squeezing her pretty pointed tit.

"*¡Ai, hombre!* That is a tender thing, not a bell to ring. *Suave.*"

"Boy, Lupe, if you could head shrimp and we could just run this boat with you and me, this would be a perfect life."

"I can head shrimp."

"Then what we have to find is a deaf and blind third man about ninety years old who can still do a day's work."

She laughed. Her left arm was around my waist. With her left hand she traced the muscles of my belly, played with the hair on my chest, tickled my paps until she raised goose pimples on me.

"You know what I would like? I would like for you to read to me from your books some time. The thought makes me feel warm and safe."

"I'll do that some time, Lupe."

"But on the sea or during a storm in our bed."

"Lupe, if I got a place, would you come and live with me?"

"Oh, Johnny . . . you mean that?"

"Yow. I just feel so good and grown up all of a sudden with you, like a lot of cheap shit is all behind me. I mean, when I say 'woman' now, I mean you more than anyone. It has a special meaning when I think of you in the same breath. You know?"

She shook her head vigorously.

"I don't know. But you make me happy. You don't know what it is inside me. You don't know my dark self. I am no good, Johnny."

"That's bullshit, Lupe. You are good. One of the best people I know or have known. I'm no fucking fool, Lupe. I like you. I really like you."

"I love you, Johnny!" She squeezed me hard.

"I love you, too, Lupe. But liking you seems more important now than loving you. I mean I have loved a lot of people I did not really like. You can even sort of love everyone on earth in a general way like the Bible says, but there isn't two percent of them you would like to know, be around a lot."

"Yes, that's how *I* feel! Oh, Johnny, you know my heart. But now I feel I do not know your heart. Now I feel scared. I have known too many men. They have all been like little boys. You make me feel afraid."

"You make me feel afraid too," I confessed.

We smiled at each other. She was so pretty, even without the makeup which made her look like a Mexican movie star, looking at her made me feel silly.

"If I got a place?"

"No. I do not want a place, Johnny. I am sick of a place. A little house. I would live on this boat with you if I could. I would go fish with you."

"You would break those fingernails."

"Yes. I would cut them. I would work like a real person, cook for you, be a woman."

"You are a woman."

"I am a big ass, *chi-chis,* a cunt, something to put on a bed."

"I like you when you are all dolled up. I like to see you walk, wear women's things."

"I like me as I am now."

"Oh, yow! I like you better this way than any other. But I like you all dolled up, too. I mean, if I never saw you like that, it wouldn't matter much, would it? But I have and I like it too. I'm spoiled."

"OK. Sometimes I spoil you to keep you off the *putas*," she joked.

Only then I knew she was not serious, that I was uncertain whether I was serious or not.

Were we just playacting?

It did not matter, I guess.

I felt empty, sort of back to where I began, only older, a bit of me used up.

You can spend some of your life and know you have spent it surviving some danger or bad hurt or by experiencing such joy that everything this side of danger and hurt that isn't joy seems a waste of time.

"Better get some clothes on, Lupe, we are coming in."

"OK."

She was sad then, too. Very sad. She seemed sadder than she had been when I found her on the boat.

She had taken a taxi out to the port, but she would not let me drive her back to town in the truck.

"I love you, Johnny. I will remember this time always."

"Me, too, Lupe."

I had a feeling we had said good-bye when she walked away up the dock, that I might never see her again.

If that was so, there was nothing to be done about it.

There were things now I had to do.

Up the dock I heard someone whistle and cry out a profane compliment as Lupe passed.

I had to smile, though I knew she was in no mood for such play.

It must be terrible to be beautiful, sexy to men, when you are feeling so ugly and frightened inside.

The only thing worse than being a pretty girl in this fucking world was to be an ugly one.

Somewhere there is a tight little society of multimillionaires where it is all so different . . . isn't it?

But then it was time to get to work.

CHAPTER TEN

We hauled the boat just before noon. Out of the water, on the cradle, it looked a considerable thing to own. It was big as a house.

I went up to the Good Eats Café at the head of the dock. It was a sagging white painted shack like most of the buildings of the port. Three sides of the place swung upward from waist-high sills like the cribs over in Boystown, like the sides of a stand. Green-painted screening, many of the little holes clogged with paint, was meant to keep out the clouds of flies which rose from the heaps of oystershell, trash from the canneries, and rotting fish and shrimps parts which littered the port. Yet inside the Good Eats half a dozen curls of tacky tan flypaper were dark and nubby with dead flies.

A large propeller fan mounted in a round hole cut through the back wall over the griddle drew some of the hot, greasy air outside. You can look through the spinning prop out over the port as if the hole were a whirring, round window.

Mother Cayce, called K-C, was behind the counter at the griddle. Her daughter Babe was the waitress. A Mexican woman washed dishes, peeled potatoes and such things. The menu was on a chalk board over the griddle and steam table.

The place was always full at lunchtime with shrimpers and office personnel from the shrimp companies who brought pretty secretaries with them. Most of the girls were Latinos, young, and let the men pay for their lunches. Only a couple of the men were Latinos.

The workers from the processing plants ate from mobile

canteens or brought their lunches. They spilled out onto the docks to sit in the shade, play cards, shoot craps, pitch coins, catch a quick nap next to the side of the building where ice is stored. Several of the young women brought transistor radios and were occasionally moved to get up and dance with each other. As a general rule, the workers segregated themselves sexually during lunch. They would shout back and forth at each other, teasing, but they rarely invaded the other group's lunchtime territory.

I sat on a wobbly stool next to Charles Principal that was still warm from the tail of J. R. Boone. On the other side of Charles was Hobie Glass.

Hobie weighed over three hundred pounds. He weighed himself on the commercial scales on the dock. You did not want to sit next to Hobie. He sweat puddles around him even if it was cool. He also breathed as if his next breath would be his last. You could hear the air being sucked into him and down into the wet tissue of his lungs; then out it would come again. When he held a fork, it disappeared into his hand except for the tines. He ran one of the big steel trawlers, hauled two nets. Over in Boystown most of the girls hid when they saw Hobie coming along the *calle,* but there was always some larky whore who considered Hobie a challenge. He more resembled a huge wild boar than a pig. He wasn't sloppy. His lower incisors were even canted so they resembled tusks. Sometimes he playfully made a face so those teeth protruded over his upper lip to frighten taunting children or scare the little painted girls across the river. I have seen bears to whom I felt more a brother than I did to Hobie.

"Whatchyall havin, Johnny?" Babe Cayce asked, shifting gum from one side of her country mouth to the other. From each of her plump earlobes hung tiny plastic tomatoes on gold-colored chains. She was a pretty girl, sixteen, with a broken tooth in front that was kind of cute. She had seen an Ann-Margret movie and changed her hairstyle, piling it over on one side of her head where it gleamed like a dull brass breaker running to a foam of curls. Some Babe. Some to-matoes.

"The chicken-fried steak's good today," she said, her stub of a pencil poised to record my desire.

"I'll have it then."

"You want the green beans or the corn?"

"Ah . . . green beans." Just because they would look bet-ter next to mashed potatoes and gravy than would corn. I didn't like green beans as well as I liked corn. Sometimes you have to make those kinds of decisions.

"Coffee, iced tea, or lemonade?"

"Your ma make the lemonade?"

"I did it! It ain't out of no can if that's what you mean."

"Lemonade."

When she went to get my lunch, Hobie observed, "That child is sure proud of herself. I'd like to get her little ass down and see what she thinks she's got to be so proud of."

The vision of that made my stomach tighten as if expecting a blow just to consider. Charles Principal went quite pink next to me.

Charles Principal was a quiet freckled man, growing prema-turely bald, a shy man who did not put himself forward. Though utterly reliable, sober, and saving, he was never long considered by an owner to become a captain, nor would he ever likely get a boat of his own, though it was rumored he had money enough in a bank to make a down payment on a good boat any time he wanted.

"Mother Cayce is sure anxious for that Babe to find a hus-band," Hobie went on. "Way past time. Don't want her run-nin around sinnin an all. I'd consider it if I hadn't been mar-ried once and didn't like it at all. Like tryin to live with two brains. One of them that don't like you for shit. How about you, Johnny? You'd be a pretty pair. I'd pay five dollars just to see you two go."

"Scares me, Hobie."

It was plain to me that it was Charles Principal who wanted

Babe. The talk across his lunch had made his rather elfin ears
dark red. Though he was a dozen years older than the girl,
that would not be a barrier to his desire if he had ambition
and drive enough to get a boat and amount to something.
Mother Cayce married Pop Cayce when she was fourteen and
he was near forty. All their children except Babe had married
almost as young as had their mother, including their only
son, Robin, who was lost when the four boats disappeared just
outside the pass a year back.

Mother Cayce was a very religious woman. A fundamental-
ist. The Holy Bible was the only book she had ever read and
the only book she thought anyone need read. She even disap-
proved of newspapers for their lack of divine inspiration. So
she lived uncorrupted by the news beyond the name of the
President of the country, "General Eisenhower." In that part
of Texas, the President's military rank was always recalled.
Mother Cayce and Pop came over from Tampa years ago.
There was no Pentecostal church nearby, so Mother Cayce
started one. A couple of times a year they got a real evangelist
to come and preach and heal. The rest of the time Mother
Cayce did the preaching and healing herself. Babe played the
piano. It was a going little church.

"Why don't we ever see you at church, Johnny Hand?"
Babe asked, as if reading my thoughts, setting down a plate
that all but needed sideboards. Mother Cayce fed her customers as well as she fed her family.

"Well, I like to go now and then," I told her. I did like to
hear a good preacher get after sin now and then. I liked the
music, too.

"Why don't you come with us Sunday then?"

Mother Cayce left the café with the Mexican woman on
Sundays.

I was very aware of Charles Principal keeping his eyes on
his plate as he waited for my answer.

"Well, I got my boat up on a cradle in the yard and want to
get it back into the water as soon as I can. I'll be workin on her
day and night."

"Like you was workin last night?" she asked archly.

What the hell did she know about last night? No one had any secrets there.

"We saw you goin out with that Mexican woman who used to work out here. That one who swings her butt all over the place." Babe swung her own in a grotesque imitation of Lupe Contreras' famous walk. Cute, but not the same thing at all.

"She can't help the way she walks," I insisted. "Has knees like Marilyn Monroe," I explained. "That's why it moves like that."

"*Knees!*" Babe hooted, and the little plastic tomatoes hanging from her ears danced happily.

"Yow! It's all in the knees."

"You can believe that if you want to. Anyway if anyone around here needs some savin, it's you. I mean there are some who need it more, but they are beyond hope, and you may not be yet. I'm goin to look for you at church."

She turned and went away with a bit more flip to her bottom than usual.

She looked more like June Carter than she did Ann-Margret. And that was entirely as fine a way to look.

"There you go, Johnny," Hobie Glass grunted. "The first step right down the old chute. You'll be that girl's husband before Christmas."

Babe heard him and called back, "You can kiss my foot!"

"Honey, I'll kiss it right up to from where it growed and you don't even have to wash it," Hobie offered.

Mother Cayce gave Hobie a stern look over the top of her rimless spectacles, but you could see the flickering tail of a smile she had swallowed.

Babe blushed and looked angrily at Hobie.

Pop Cayce came in just as Babe was setting a wedge of her mother's homemade banana cream pie in front of me next to a mug of strong black coffee.

"How's it goin, Pop?" Charles, I, and Hobie asked at the same time.

The old man peered at us to see who the hell we were. He

ought to wear glasses but never would. An old dead reckoner, he only carried a radio on his boat so his wife could keep track of him and know that he was all right. She had a set in the house. Most wives of shrimpers had radios and tried to speak to their husbands every day.

"Goin to wreck and ruin," the old man advised us. "There ain't nothin in it."

Everyone liked to rile the old man.

"What do you mean, Pop? Lots are gettin rich. Like Johnny here," Hobie said. "Be a rich man before he's forty."

"Where's the fun of it? The good of it? All these fancy damn boats with ten thousand dollars of instruments on em, goin off to Mexico or China next maybe. You make a lot of money. But it ain't no good livin."

He searched around under the counter and found an empty Coke bottle to spit in. He always had a big cud of tobacco in his cheek. Those who worked for him had to stay to windward of the old man when they were out in the Gulf. His teeth were the color of old piano keys.

"Old days you'd go out a couple of miles and catch your shrimp and be back home for supper. You'd shrimp like that for six months, oyster three, and the other three months you'd go bootleggin. Them was what I call good times."

Hobie jabbed Charles Principal with his elbow and winked.

"You never ran in no wetbacks or Chinamen, though, between all that shrimpin, oysterin, and bootleggin, did you, Pop?" Hobie teased.

"Oh . . . I mighta given a couple of fellas a lift."

Everyone laughed. For Pop was rumored to have been one of the primary independent carriers of live cargo to Florida. It was said that knowledge became so common that Pop decided to move to Texas.

"Never carried anyone who was a Commie or not a Christian. They all had to swear to that," the old man vowed with a wryness so fine you had to know him to know he was not a fool.

And you could see if you were sitting as close as I was then that in his eyes there was a hardness and trueness of stunning certainty. He was capable of surviving any folly to which he might be bent.

He spat again into the bottle. He was a man destined to die gracefully in his own bed no matter who else sank, of that I felt certain.

Suddenly he fixed Charles Principal with a look and asked, "Young man, you ever goin to get yourself a boat and amount to somethin or are you goin to shrimp for some other son of a bitch all your life?"

"Well. . . ."

Charles was caught with his mouth full of pie. He swallowed hard.

"You come to talk to me pretty soon," the old man told him.

"Yes, sir, I will. . . ." He swallowed.

That settled, the old man looked at me and Hobie. "I hear there's folks goin around lookin to have something carried to Cuba."

"You can hear all sorts of things, Pop, you know that."

Pop knew all the sorts of things a man can hear. He silently dismissed Hobie from the face of the earth and switched his inquiry to me.

"Yow, Pop. There's some people around looking for a charter. Price I heard was six thousand. I don't know if it is serious or not."

"That's what I heard," the old man said thoughtfully.

"You interested in something like that, Pop?"

"Always interested in easy money, son. I don't know, this revolution reminds me of oh nine and seventeen in Mexico. The kind of fight a man can understand and maybe get something out of. Had a brother—Jessie—went and rode with Pancho Villa. Son of a bitch had his hands on most of a hundred thousand in gold and silver once and let it get away. That would be worth most a million nowadays. You could buy a good damn boat then for ten thousand. A *good* boat. All the son of a bitch got back across the border was two Mauser bullets clear through him, a cough that eventually killed him, and a dose of clap that wouldn't quit."

We all silently contemplated the fate of Pop's brother.

"Anyway this revolution might be a little fun. If I was young as you boys, I think I'd go have a look-see. Specially if there is a little money in it. Might go anyway."

"Daddy," Mother Cayce called him from the griddle, "will you go get us a gallon milk real quick. I don't think they left us enough this morning. We're about plumb out."

The old man looked at the woman. He spit again into the bottle. The world had gotten beyond his control and would never come to terms again. He turned away and went to get the milk.

Outside, picking the stringy bits of steak from my teeth, I thought about Charles Principal and Babe. I thought I wouldn't mind screwing that Babe one time or so before she decided to settle for Charles. She and Charles would be all right. She would run him, and he needed running. She would tell him where to put his chair. I grinned. "There you go, right down the ole chute." Charles would be that girl's husband before Christmas, and I would be in her pants before we slipped the boat back into the water . . . or so was my thought at the time. . . .

I hoped Lupe would come out again that night. But I also wanted a change from Lupe—it suddenly occurred to me that women probably felt the same way sometimes. The thought shook me somewhat. Of course, they would feel like that. I loved Lupe. Part by part, and by all that made her a person, she was far and away more what I had in mind than Babe. I mean, Lupe got inside me to some crazy uncontrollable place where I was as vulnerable as a nameless child. Yet I wanted to join meat and breath and spit with someone like Babe. And women were walking around feeling the same way. The thought made me feel a bit lonely. It was OK. It made sense. I could live with that. But it made me feel as vulnerable as I felt when being with Lupe made time stop. Maybe people were not made to live together two by two. Maybe it is unnatural.

Romantic. What would the world be like without romance? It was a puzzle. It was a puzzle that could sponsor a lonely dream. It was a puzzle that made me feel glad I felt strong and had good work to do.

My boat up there on the cradle—large and traditionally homely against the blue Gulf sky in which new white clouds were boiling up—was something by which I could define myself, gain some measure of myself against unknown meanings, unpredictable possibilities.

"Captain Johnny Hand," I said silently, then grinned, for the strange fear had passed.

But maybe I knew nothing about women after all. They did suddenly seem a large part of—maybe the whole of—an essential puzzle.

It was a good thing to have work to do.

You know—damn!

Frank Smith was waiting for me. He looked so hungry and anxious I felt guilty about having just eaten my fill. He was standing looking expectantly toward me rather than toward my boat up on the cradle.

Staring up at the boat from under the bow was a slender, shaggy-haired Mexican kid in Levi's and a sweat shirt. It was Ezequiel's daughter, Chelo. I did not think about or wonder why she was there.

"Hi, Frank," I told the rummy. "I'll give you a buck and a half an hour to scrape and help me get this cleaned up and a new coat of bottom paint on her."

He was shaking a bit.

"You eat today?" I asked him.

"No. But I'm all right, Johnny."

"The hell you are. You look hollow." I pulled a couple of bucks from my pocket and handed them to him. "Go up and get yourself something to eat. You can pay me back this evening."

"Thanks, Johnny, I'll hurry back."

His eyes looked like a goddamned dog's.

My dad had been a rummy: even if they join AA and get

dried out and never touch a drop again, there is still the worm in them they tried to kill with alcohol, and you live knowing it is there every minute of their lives. It is an imposition they impose on the rest of us, a self-mutilation you have to resent, no matter how sympathetic you may be.

I could see Frank's whipped form shuffle up toward the café without turning to look.

The girl had moved along the boat and was touching the thick crust of barnacles on the hull. She turned when Frank left and watched me walk toward her. I felt she was studying me. Her large eyes were narrowed and her lips tight.

"I am Chelo, Ezequiel's daughter."

"Yes, I remember you from yesterday."

I was wary of what she might want or of what she would say. There was the same intensity in her that was in the old man. The same pride, not yet bent to be accommodating and so employable.

"I want my father's job," she said.

"I'm sorry?"

"I said, I want my father's job. I want his job on this boat."

I had to smile.

"I am serious," she insisted.

"It's hard work," I replied. I didn't want to insult her.

"I'm not afraid of work. I am strong."

I smiled again.

Her eyes quickly fined down to bright points. I remembered Ezequiel saying, "I am a little afraid of her." I stopped smiling and forced myself to regard her seriously.

"It is not a job for a girl," I tried. "I mean, being out on a boat with two men for weeks. That boat looks big up there, but when you have been on it for a while, it seems pretty small."

"I have lived in a little house—two rooms—with my brothers and my father and sisters. You think I am bothered by men?"

"Well, no. I mean . . . I really don't think you would like shrimping."

"I have heard my father talk of it. I would like it better than picking cotton or fruits and vegetables. I would like it better than working in someone's house. I would like it better than being in an office all day. Besides, I have no skills or patience for such things. I can cook like my father, but not for people I do not know.

"Besides, my father makes good money shrimping. More than I could make doing anything else. Now we need money. He is dead."

She was tall and very slender. She noticed me sizing her up and said, "I am one hundred and twenty pounds. I am much stronger than I look."

I felt I *owed* her a goddamned job. She was a fifteen-year-old girl, and she made me more uncomfortable than any man I had ever met. Every phony bullshit thing about me felt as if it were breaking out all over me in a rash.

Some fifteen-year-old.

"Well, I don't know . . . I could use some help cleaning up—painting."

"Sure. I am ready to work now. How much?"

I could get a grown Latino man for a buck an hour. I told her a dollar an hour.

"I heard you tell that other one you pay him a dollar and a half. I am worth more than him. You will see."

Son of a bitch . . . I grinned. She smiled a little, very little.

"OK—a buck and a half."

"OK. But if you see I am truly worth more, you will be honest enough to pay me more?"

"Well . . . yow. But that's pretty good money."

"The day you pay me what I am worth to you, we will both know it and be honest and feel well about it."

"You are some tiger, aren't you?"

"No, I am gentle."

She looked steadily into my eyes as she had the first time I saw her with her mother when they came down to the boat. There was no place to hide in yourself from her desire to see.

"But you can kill me and I will not be a dog or *puta* for no-body. . . ." Then she smiled truly for the first time and tossed back her hair that was like black feathers. "I am not so bad. You will see. Where do you want me to work?"

"Uh . . . start inside. It is a hell of a mess in there. Eze-quiel had a pot of his famous soup on the fire when that rock-et went off. . . ." I stopped myself, sorry I had mentioned it. Her look did not change.

"You will find cleaning stuff in the lockers under the sink. There is a swab and buckets and rags in the tall locker outside the galley on deck."

She was already mounting the ladder up against the side of the boat.

"If you need anything else, let me know, and we will get it."

"OK," she called down, already on her own.

I watched the way she moved up the ladder. There was more than just a little bump for her to sit on. Her father had very old-fashioned standards. She had a high waist and long legs and between the bottom of her sweat shirt and the belt-less top of her faded Levi's there were two large, shallow dim-ples, in creamy, pale skin. Neither she nor her sister, *la En-canta*, was as dark as their parents, nor as dark as Lupe, I thought suddenly. Then I put such thoughts out of my mind.

The carpenters came from lunch, picking their teeth, and went up to go to work.

Eli arrived full of a lunch that was too big and he would have rather gone and had a nap than go down in the hot en-gine room with me.

"Who's that?" he asked when we passed the galley and he saw a girl inside up on the table to clean the overhead. She was going to clean that place from the top right on down. That was the way to do it. I would not have been so clever.

"Chelo. Ezequiel's daughter. The one he is a little afraid of." I grinned. "She wants his job on the boat."

"What!"

"Well, she can clean up that shit in there. I wouldn't even know where to begin without thinking about it awhile."

"She's kinda skinny."

"Don't fuck with her. She'll hand you your head quicker than the old man.

"How's the wife?" I wanted to change the subject.

"She's mad as hell about you letting the little shark bite me, man. She says I am mutilated on my ass. Before, she says, it was pretty and smooth. She is really pissed off. She *liked* my ass the way it was. I didn't even know she notices it. She tells me, yes, women look at men's asses. I didn't know that, did you? That gets me all worked up, an we fuck our brains out. She is sure she gets pregnant this time. I am, too. You know, Johnny, there was the first time we did it last night, I know everything goes right into her and sticks there. You know, you can just feel it. She says she felt it too. . . ."

"Yow?"

"Um. . . ." He shook himself. "She says when she has the baby, she wants me to find a job in town and not be gone like I am. I think I will look, Johnny. There is a job in the recreation department soon. Her brother told me. He is with child welfare for the county, and maybe he can put in a word for me. They want somebody with a degree, but maybe they would let me study at night or something like that. I don't know if I can get it or not. Probably not. But I think I will look into it, hunh?"

"Hunh? Hell, yes! I mean, sure, if I had a wife I loved like you do yours, I'd find it pretty rough being away so much. I always told you that. And anytime you want out I'll settle up with you."

"Oh, don't worry about that." He waved that away. "It's just when my wife heard about the trouble down there with the gunboat and then thinks we are blown up, she is afraid I am dead or something. She says I will make her an old woman before her time from such shit."

"Me too."

He laughed. "Me too, man. I never forget how that fuckin bomb went *off!* And old Ezequeil *gone,* man. Whoo. . . . I would like to work in recreation. It is easy. I would live long and get fat like my wife's brother . . . and important." He laughed again. "I don't think I have a chance. But I will look for something if she is pregnant."

I just knew the propeller shaft was out of true, maybe the screw, too. I would have to have them pulled and micrometered to be sure. But coming in, I could feel something wrong—out of balance down there. That was going to cost a lot.

CHAPTER
ELEVEN

If the rummy was worth a dollar and a half the girl was worth twice as much. She was a marvel. She did not have to ask a lot of questions. She did not make mistakes. If I complimented her on what she had done, she looked at me as if I were a fool, as if she were somehow insulted, until I got the idea she *expected* to do a good job of whatever she undertook.

She stripped the cabin bare, scrubbed it cleaner than it had ever been, then came and asked me what color I wanted it painted—not *if* I wanted it painted. I gave her some money and the keys to the truck.

She painted the cabin and galley white with a soft gray trim, which beat the hell out of the grimy pale yellow and boarding-house green it had been.

A couple of days later she arrived with a large parcel and carried it up the ladder though it seemed half as large as herself. If she needed help, she would ask for it. She rarely asked.

On the way down to the engine room I looked into the cabin and saw she had hung very snappy blue curtains on the windows, held back with neat ties. She was putting up curtain rods and matching curtains on the berths.

I went inside.

"It will give more privacy," she explained. "And darkness. My father says you sleep in the daytime."

"I thought about doing that," I told her.

"Well, now it is done."

"It really looks nice, Chelo. The whole thing." I swept my hand around at her work.

She stopped what she was doing to study the full effect of what she had done.

"Yes. It is pretty good." She smiled quickly to herself; then, as if embarrassed at her satisfaction, she returned to the job at hand. "I made the curtains. I have a receipt. You can pay me."

She was standing on the railing of the lower bunk. I patted her leg above the knee. She did not feel so skinny beneath the cool faded denim.

"Thanks, Chelo. The fu— She looks like a real ship."

She did not reply. I was beginning to see what I had taken as a kind of sullenness was simply a dislike of a lot of unnecessary words.

I went out and down into the engine room, where Eli was stripped to the waist, greasy and cursing in Spanish and English.

The propeller shaft was bent and magnaflux showed it was flawed structurally. We were putting in a new one, rebuilding the bedding while we were at it. The screw too would have to be rebuilt. You can trade a salvageable propeller in on a new one, but anything for a boat costs like hell. The repair of the boat was going to run between five and seven thousand dollars. We were already in the yard longer than I had hoped. I told myself in the long run it would pay. In the short run it was going to tap me out. Payments on her had to be made if she was fishing or not.

"You see the insurance man?" Eli asked me.

"Don't talk to me about fucking insurance," I told him.

I had insurance. I had to have insurance with a mortgage on the boat. It cost like hell. Marine insurance for any kind of boat is expensive. For a working boat it is so expensive a lot of shrimpers let their policies drop as soon as they paid off their boats.

"What fucking good is five thousand deductible?" I asked my minority partner.

He shrugged. It was not his worry.

I was pissed off. It was *my* worry.

"You have to goddamn sink to get anything. Insurance is a damned racket. You ever been able to understand a fucking word any insurance man ever said?"

"My brother-in-law sells a little insurance," Eli said.

"Your brother-in-law is an asshole."

"I will never fight nobody about that."

"Insurance men are born weird or have to study like hell to be like they are." I was sure. "I mean, you can eventually understand a doctor or a scientist, pin them down, but not the most tedious and chintzy mind can make any sense of what an insurance man says. It has to be a racket or they would make it understandable in short paragraphs even an old dead reckoner could understand. Hell, I watched my grandma sock away quarters and four-bit pieces forever to assure she and the old man would have a spot to be buried and funeral expenses. She must have put in enough to have buried their whole little house. Then, when she got sick, she ran out of quarters and four-bit pieces. No one knew. The old man didn't know. And she lost all she had put in."

"I buy insurance from my brother-in-law. He is an asshole. But if he fucks me, he fucks his sister too. He would do that maybe. But I would bust his ass."

"Your brother-in-law doesn't handle marine insurance?"

Eli laughed. "Man, he sells insurance from places you never heard of. And it is not so cheap either, *compadre*. Poorass Mexicans can't put themselves in the hands of Allstate. So my brother-in-law fills a need, I guess. You seen them insurance companies with the Rock of Gibraltar, with a big fuckin deer, a studhorse Minuteman? Well, the insurance my brother-in-law sells me got a picture of the Alamo on it. . . . But what can you do?"

"Man, it's hot, Eli!" I wiped sweat from my face with the back of my arm.

"You goin to the big fiesta tonight?" Eli asked.

"I don't know."

"You come. I will introduce you to my wife's friend with the big *chi-chis. Big,* man! And pretty, too, all over elsewhere."

"Maybe."

I hadn't seen Lupe since the night I found her on the boat. I had called her house once and got her old man. Woke him in the middle of the afternoon. He works nights at the bridge. He was not too happy to be awakened. I hadn't gone across the river to see the girls either. All work.

"Maybe I'll come eat some barbecue."

"You see my wife's friend you will want to eat somethin. That's for goddamn sure."

"She's that good, hunh?"

"Mmmm!" Eli smacked his lips wetly. "When she stays with my wife and I am there, my wife makes love to me four, five times a day, man, just so I don't get no ideas. I saw her naked in the bathroom. Man, if I wasn't married. . . . She is prettier than that Italian movie star."

"Sophia Loren?"

"That other one."

"Gina Lollabrigida?"

"Yeah, like that. Only better tits, man. Lots better tits. It's true."

I almost believed him.

"Maybe I will go to that dance."

"Yeah. You will like her. She will like you."

"How do you know that?"

"She always likes you sorry *gringo* types. That is her only flaw."

It was too damned hot to go up to the Good Eats for lunch. The rummy went up there. Eli's wife came for him in their new Edsel hardtop convertible and drove him off someplace for lunch.

That was a funny car. But Eli would not take any shit about it. You could bum-rap his wife before you could knock that goofy car. It looked like a goosed guppy to me. Eli kept finding some wonder in it each day to inspire his loyalty.

An enterprising car dealer with a good radio receiver un-loaded a lot of those Edsels on shrimpers after a particularly good catch earlier in the year. I mean people drive a lot of crazy things that year. But *Edsel?* Why not an Elmer?

Well, it was Eli's money.

"Why are you smiling like that?" Chelo asked me.

She was eating a cold *burrito* and washing it down with a tepid Coke she had brought from home.

"Eli's car," I explained.

"It looks like a fish in front," she observed.

"My thinking exactly!" I laughed. "A guppy that has been goosed."

She smiled.

"If you aren't ready to get your Cadillac, you just get a Ford or Chevy, whichever will give you the best deal," I philoso-phized. "Forget Plymouths or anything else. I never met a man who really knew anything who drove a fucking Ply-mouth. The odd Pontiac, Olds, or Buick can be all right. . . . But why pay all that extra? You are still miles from a Cadillac."

She nodded her head as if she agreed.

"That looks good," I said of her lunch.

"You want some? I bring another. It is too much for me."

"Yow. Thanks."

She handed me her other *burrito*, wrapped in a bit of waxed bread wrapper.

I saw the man with the cold drinks and beer and ice-cream cart and yelled at him to bring us *dos cervezas.* He came and climbed up the ladder with them.

The cans were wet and ice cold from his cart. The beer sharp with the cold. It was beautiful with the *burrito.*

"You make these?"

"My mother."

"They're good."

"I make them as good as this." She sipped her beer. The cold beer made her eyes water a little. She smiled. "I like this. So cold."

I liked her. We had never sat down and talked. I really liked her.

It was good to like her without a whole big sexual commotion up in front of it. She looked *good!* You looked at her, and she wasn't so damned skinny. She had nice little tits in there under her sweat shirt. High, round butt. But it wasn't that she had tits or didn't. She had a real face. There was a real nose on it. Her eyes did not play games with you. I understood what Lupe meant about being *good*-looking that time she tried to explain it to me.

Indian. I thought of Indians. I felt a crazy, dreamy sense of sitting in front of some place a thousand years ago with this Indian girl. Then that passed, but it left me feeling strange, as if I had seen something in a dream that was important but that I could not recall awake.

I liked the hell out of her.

I didn't want to *do* anything about it. It made me feel good to *know* it.

"Why are you looking like that at me?"

"I don't know."

"You think I look funny?"

"No!"

"Then why are you smiling?"

"I don't know. I just feel . . . friendly . . . looking at you."

She looked at me, raising her eyebrows and studying me head-on. Then she smiled slightly, as if deciding to trust me a little.

"Don't feel too friendly," she warned. But she was smiling.

"You are very pretty," I said.

She stopped smiling. I didn't think she liked to be told that.

She put her back against the pilothouse and leaned her head back and closed her eyes.

"That is not important," she finally said.

I was wrong. She was not pretty at all. She was beautiful. Not pretty-sexy like Lupe Contreras; not too beautiful to touch like her sister Encanta—beautiful like the Indian princess in Diego Rivera's murals in Mexico, the princess in the white beaded dress, so beautiful, carrying a human leg with her for lunch.

Mysterious. Pre-Christian. No man will ever look at her face and feel safe in his own bullshit. She might cook *your* leg for supper. She might. She could. All the mysteries of Creation, Art, Belief, and the Unknown were in that drowzing woman-child's face.

I liked her. But as her father said of her: "I am a little afraid of her."

I saw her belly rise and fall gently; below, the divided V of her tight faded jeans dipped between her slender thighs.

There has never been a woman I could not somehow *think* of fucking, if I was attracted to her. There was no way this side of rape I could even begin to think of how to fuck this one. And the mere thought of something like rape in her case made me feel very bad about myself.

I got up and went down the ladder to the yard to see how the rummy was coming along on the bottom.

We should be in the water again by Tuesday or Wednesday at the latest was my optimistic guess.

I went to the dance. There was good barbecue. Lupe Contreras was not there. The thing was in a local park. There were Japanese paper lanterns hung on wires above the concrete dance floor. A local band sweated a lot for a little money, a few drinks and barbecue. There were no plates. It was mainly a Mexican party. You took a big tortilla, and the boys cutting the meat laid a generous hunk of it in your tortilla. There was beer and pop and almost everyone had a bottle, not far away, of something that would make you drunk. Some of the local cops and politicians were there showing their constituents what regular guys they were.

Eli's wife's girlfriend was not Gina Lollabrigida, but she was

not dog meat either. Mostly she was silly. But as we danced, I
could see the sweat trickle down between her big boobs and
feel her hips flare beneath the long boned brassiere she wore
to cantilever her tits out so aggressively. When it was estab-
lished that I did not have a steady girlfriend, she began to fall
in love. She took possession of one or the other of my arms.
The biceps were actually beginning to get irritated from being
rubbed by her armored chest. It was nice for a while, but ir-
ritating in its insistence.

I was thinking about this and about going out of there and
trying to find Lupe Contreras, when Chelo's sister Encanta
suddenly marched from the crowd out onto the middle of the
dance floor. I hadn't noticed her before. She was dressed
nicely in a dance skirt, high-heeled shoes and stockings, and a
Mexican blouse off one creamy shoulder. There were three
white flowers in her hair. She was reaching into a white purse
made of plastic disks.

Just beyond the middle of the dance floor, heading straight
for Bobby Joe Solar, she took out a little nickeled automatic
and began pointing it at him. Some of the dancers nearby
stopped when they saw her. A girl shrieked. People fell back
from her.

Bobby Joe's wife saw Encanta and yelled, "She's got a gun!"

Bobby Joe just sat there stunned. As an off-duty deputy he
was surely carrying a gun himself.

"*My God!*" Bobby Joe's wife screamed.

Encanta pointed the little gun at Bobby Joe with her arm
extended. I could see her face. She was mad, scared, and determined. She was going to shoot him, no joke.

She pulled the trigger. Nothing happened. She pulled the
trigger repeatedly, but the gun did not fire. She looked even
angrier, looked at the gun, screamed something in Spanish
that ended with the threat to kill Bobby Joe if it was the last
day she lived, then broke and ran through the crowd.

An off-duty policeman made a halfhearted attempt to stop
her, but a boy I do not know sort of got in his way, and En-

canta was gone while everyone asked each other what happened.

I remembered seeing her coming from the motel across the river that night with Bobby Joe Solar, but I did not say anything about that.

I was fucking Eli's wife's girlfriend in their spare room which Eli's wife had already begun to make into a nursery for the baby they were expecting, when I heard the shots. There were seven shots as fast as someone can pull the trigger. I stopped what I was doing, and the sweating girl in love beneath me stopped telling me about it and making soft sounds of ecstasy, though she kept moving a bit as I lay on her and listened.

Hell! Bobby Joe Solar lived half a block from there.

"Where you go?" the girl demanded as I pulled out of her. "What's the matter? What is it?"

"Shooting."

"No! Maybe it is some car. Why are you going? Stay, my darling. You don't finish. I want. Stay with me. I love you—"

I was already hopping out of the room, buckling up my trousers. Eli stuck his head out of his bedroom and wanted to know what the hell was going on.

"Some shooting. Down the street."

"What business is that of yours?" he wanted to know.

"I don't know!"

I ran out of the house and up the block. There was already some people in the yard of Bobby Joe's house. I heard the first siren.

Most of the people were Latinos. They were not talking loudly, nor were they very excited.

Standing in the middle of the yard was Encanta. She was dressed as she had been at the dance. Now the flowers in her hair were wilted. On the little front porch across the three steps of the house were Bobby Joe Solar in his underwear and undershirt, face down, and his wife in her nightgown. His

wife was still alive, crying and screaming at the girl standing in
the yard.

*"She did it! Fucking Mexican bitch! She killed him! She
killed him!"*

The police arrived from both directions. The sheriff's cars
arrived. The street was full of police cars, and an ambulance
could not get through without coming up over the curbing
and across the grass, scattering the people who had come
from their houses.

"She did it!" Bobby's Joe's wife kept screaming as they got
her into the ambulance.

Encanta was not denying that.

She stood in the yard staring at the dead man on the steps,
his arms stretched down feebly toward her. She looked up
when one of the police came near. She remembered the gun
in her hand and handed it to him. They put handcuffs on her
and led her to a police car.

I went away before the police got through with Bobby.
There was a picture of a white outline on the steps where he
had fallen in the paper the next morning.

I did not go back to Eli's house. I got in the truck and went
back to the boat. I still slept on the boat. I pissed on the
ground and shit and showered up at the marina dock facilities.

The next morning I was reading the paper in the Good
Eats. Everyone was shocked by the news.

Everyone also somehow seemed to be greatly relieved that
something bad had happened to so beautiful a young woman.
I can't explain it. I don't understand it. In some perverse way,
I felt a nonspecific relief.

There was a picture of her in a bathing suit for some beauty
contest she had been in a couple of years back. There was a
picture of her being led into the jail in handcuffs. I thought I
would like to be her jailer. Those kinds of thoughts kept popping into my mind. I was eating hotcakes and bacon, drinking
coffee.

There were some letters from Bobby Joe in her purse.

"She wrote the son of a bitch that the first day I see you again is the last day you live," someone read aloud. "She sure wasn't shittin."

"Damned old gun didn't fire when she tried to shoot him at the dance. Said she got it at Sam's Army-Navy Store and it didn't work. Took it back and made Sam fix it!"

"Sam said," another took it up, "wasn't nothin wrong with that gun. She just had the safety on. He showed her how to take it off."

There was laughter.

"Took the fuckin thing *back* to get it fixed!"

"That little girl wanted to shoot his ass *bad!* No two ways about it."

"Found her in the front yard with the gun still in her hand. She didn't try to run."

"That's some fine-lookin little girl, I'll tell you. I'd risk gettin shot for a little of that."

"Wouldn't risk it but once. That's one *dee*-termined little girl."

"Be the second woman they string up in Texas history," an authority vows. "Shooting a deputy sheriff, putting a couple into his wife. Got them out of bed to do it, too."

"Says he had his forty-five hanging just inside the front door, but when he saw who it was, he went out onto the porch. His wife heard the shootin start and came running out and got into it."

"I bet ten dollars she hangs," the authority offered.

"Shit! Anyone hang a pretty little thing like that is just wasteful . . . and that's worse than mean where *I* come from."

"Who's her defense?"

"Ole Judge Cracher."

"She'll hang."

"Ten years suspended," I guessed.

Everyone looked at me.

"Well, there's been ten killings this year in this county," I argued. "The worst anyone got was ten years suspended."

"But shit, boy, she killed a deputy sheriff. You don't kill no deputy in Texas, even if he *is* half Mexican."

"I don't know. But she says she is pregnant by him. Says he took her with him when he went to Washington to the FBI Academy for eight weeks last spring. Says he promised her he would leave his wife and marry her. Says there's a letter to prove that. Says when she told him she was pregnant, he gave her five hundred dollars and told her to go stay with someone he knew out in Idaho and have the kid gotten rid of. She says she has most of the money and spent the rest to buy the gun."

"I don't care, you don't kill no deputy in Texas."

"I don't know. I just know from what *I've* seen, I would rather be tried for murder in Texas than I would for stealing someone's cow. There is just no excuse for stealing a cow. But Texas law does take into account there are some sonsabitches who *deserve* killing!"

I was willing to bet anything that was how it would turn out.

I just felt bad about Chelo's beautiful sister being in jail, being handled by all those people, looked up the cunt and rectum . . . though I was willing to apply for the job if it *had* to be done.

Damn!

Something like this happens and it just screws you up all kinds of ways. Nothing seems real. Nothing seems stable. Pancakes tasted like shit.

I was still chewing when I ran into Chelo on the way down to the boat. I still had the paper under my arm.

She fell in beside me.

"I heard about your sister," I said.

The girl looked as if she had been up all night. She said nothing.

"Is it going to be all right?" I asked.

"It is all right."

"Listen." I stopped and took her near arm at the wrist. "You don't want to work today. We're about through anyway."

"If I didn't want to work, I would have stayed home."

"I just thought. . . ."

We walked on.

"She did what she wanted to do," the girl said. "Now it is important for me to work more than ever."

"OK."

I didn't know what I was going to do when the boat was back in the water. She was going to want her father's job. I couldn't see any way in hell I could take her on. Oh, I had no doubt she could do the job. She had shown me she could do damned near anything she set out to do. But you can't go out shrimping for three, four, sometimes six weeks, with a young girl aboard.

As if reading my mind, she stopped me again at the boat.

"I want you to tell me, do I go with you or not?"

"Christ, Chelo. It's rough out there. It's no place for a woman. It's *hard.* I really don't think you'd like it. I couldn't run you in in the middle of a trip."

She just stared at me. Her lips were thin. I saw her chest moving beneath her sweat shirt, her long fingers with the short nails on her hips.

"OK," I breathed.

I was sorry I had said it as soon as the word was out of my mouth.

She nodded her head once, short and sharp as if tacking down the agreement and turned and climbed the ladder ahead of me.

I looked up at her slim, yet womanly bottom and shook my head.

Now what the hell had I done?

God damn Ezequiel and *his whole crazy family!* I thought.

Man, the others were going to carry my ass high. "Meet my new header, boys." Oh, yow.

Oh, yow. . . .

CHAPTER TWELVE

Back in the water, the boat looked so clean, bright, new, Eli went and got a camera and we took pictures. She would not look that fine again for a long time.

We drank some cold beer, snapped the pictures, and had a nice time.

Chelo was reluctant to loosen up, enjoy herself. Then I gave her one of the flat-top, old-fashioned workingman's caps we all wore—like the golf caps Ben Hogan used to wear. She broke into a smile so wide and white it threatened the sun. She posed on the bow. She waved from the pilothouse door.

She was one of us.

The other captains kidded us a little, but finally, all I had to do was remind them she was Ezequiel Cavazos' daughter and they would sort of understand.

I did not think she would want the job after the first trip. Yet she had worked as well and honestly as any man I had ever known. With her sister in jail for murder, her family needed the money.

The first night out it began to blow some. There was some rain. Chelo got seasick. She fought it, then gave way and had to be put in a bunk and given some Dramamine.

We teased her a bit.

By the third day she was all right: rocky, wan, but OK.

She came into the pilothouse looking skinnier than ever. There were dark circles around her black eyes.

"I am sorry. You do not have to pay me for those days," she said. "I am well now. I will be OK."

"Everyone gets sick sometime. I still get a little upset once in a while," I told her.

"I am ashamed."

"Forget it."

"Listen, Chelo," Eli said, "your old man always brought some good weed with him to smoke. Grew it himself. You don't happen to have any of that with you?"

"*Ai,* no. . . . But if you want some, next time I can bring it."

"That would be a beautiful thing for you to do," he assured her. "Wonderful for seasickness."

"*¿Sí?*"

"Ah, very much *sí!*" he said.

"OK. If you want some."

"We should have thought about that before," Eli charged me.

He rolled a joint of what he had on hand and passed it to us. Chelo did not smoke.

"I think I would like to take a bath," she said.

"There's a shower in the head, or you can use the hose on the fantail," I told her.

"The hose is better," Eli said. "We use the hose."

"Then I will make lunch," she said.

When she had gone, Eli said, "She is a nice girl."

"Yow, I like her."

"You think she will be all right?"

"Sure. I think so. I would attend a war with her, if I had to go," I had decided.

"Ah, you are so *romántico,* Johnny."

We heard the hose going on the fantail. We looked at each other. The idea of a slender naked young woman taking a shower back there was a funny feeling.

Did fish pop up out of the sea for a peek? Were we trailing a fishy parade of voyeurs?

Eli and I looked at each other. He grinned and waggled his

eyebrows as if to ask which of us was going to wander back
there. I grinned back. Neither of us moved. He passed me the
joint. I took a smoke and passed it back. We grinned some
more. Neither of us was going back there.

"Son of a bitch," he said, grinning.

"Yow."

"We're some kind of a shrimp boat."

"Some kind of crazy."

Soon there was singing in the galley and the smell of food
being prepared.

"You sing almost as good as your father!" I called back to
her.

She laughed, for she knew her father sang like a sick cat
with a sinus condition.

When I went back to the galley, the table was set with red
paper napkins by the plates and some yellow flowers in a bowl
in the center.

"Where the hell did you get flowers?"

"I brought some. I put them in the refrigerator. Is that
OK?"

"Hell, yes."

We put on the automatic pilot so we could all eat together.
We laughed and joked. The sun streamed in the windows.
The food was good.

"If you head shrimp like you cook, *chica,* we are going to
have a good trip," Eli told her, rubbing his belly which was
beginning to make him look more like an ex-lineman than a
fullback.

"When they hear about this, there is going to be girls on all
the boats," Eli vowed.

There were women on other boats. Nearly everyone took
his wife and kids with him now and then. A lot of shrimpers
started out on their father's boats when they were ten or so.
One guy worked his boat with his wife and two daughters.
The girls never went to school. They seemed none the worse
for that.

If I had a good, intelligent woman and we had a kid, I could see going like that. We could teach him-her as much as, or more than, some half-assed school. I had books. I had seen some of the world. Most of what you learned in school was calculated to please the pushers of some immediate concept, was designed to train you how to work for some other son of a bitch all your life. I didn't think I wanted a kid of mine to do that. Better they should be around people like Chelo's late father, Ezequiel, awhile—crazy? I don't know. I don't think so. The old man was full of wisdom and a way of seeing behind such modern complexities as an insurance policy to essential mysteries that made your damned bones itch, while at the same time imparting a kind of peace, a sense that beyond the bullshit we were alone, or as a species, yet all right. All right.

I did not envy the doctors and scholars, scientists and politicians. Shit, with all their education they couldn't run the world any better than if they had left it alone; they could not run their own lives any better for all they said they understood than Chelo's sister Encanta who had killed her married-deputy lover because he said he would leave his wife and marry her, then, when she got pregnant, gave her five bills or something and told her to go get rid of the kid. I liked her way *better.* It was clean and passionate. I will never forget, the most beautiful young woman I have ever seen standing in her lover's front yard, the pistol in her hand, waiting for the cops to come take her away. No tears in *her* eyes.

What about the wife she widowed?

What about her? She will survive or she won't. She will. She will marry someone else. She will live. How does all the popular psychology make us better? I read. The people who are so hooked on psychology as a way to live better aren't any happier than anyone else. They just have a new, more boring way of talking about things. They take all the surprise and wonder out of things. They always think it terrible that an individual will take a gun and blast the life from some bastard that has done that person a mighty wrong, really crapped on their love, but they will rationalize or ignore that their society makes war for the wrong reasons against the wrong people most of the time. They are willing to profit from businesses that are as crooked as a dog's hind leg and support a government that goes along with it.

Maybe psychology is the intellectual's insurance policy, I thought.

Some things just can't be negotiated, fixed up.

Schools seem to have lost sight of what education is about—lost the wonder of delving into mysteries in the race to get answers. Almost all school was about, as far as I could see, was how to get into a position to skin some other chump for a living, get ahead of someone else. So the kids bored themselves silly or cheated if they cared about passing. What the hell is the point of living like that?

"You look troubled, Captain," Chelo said.

She had come into the pilothouse and had been sitting behind me over against the windows.

"Oh . . . I didn't know you were there. I was just thinking about things."

"What things?"

I told her my theories on education.

"I like your ideas," she said.

After a while she said, "I was afraid of you. I did not know what kind of man you are. My father tells me you have a good character and good spirit. He likes you. But I was a little afraid."

"Yow? Well, he told me the same thing about you. *He* said he was a little afraid of *you*."

"Are you afraid also?"

"A little."

She smiled.

"Good. We are even."

I looked back at her. You could see her father's bones in her face. She would look strong and beautiful when she was an old woman, or she would look like a witch.

"Come here. I will show you how to steer."

She got between me and the wheel. She smelled nice, of a clean fragrant soap, sunshine, the sea. I showed her what the gauges were about, the throttle, tachometer, explained about the torque curve of an engine. Then, I showed her how to hold a course.

I left her on the wheel and went to sit against the windows to smoke.

I studied her. We did not talk. I thought of her back on the fantail taking a shower, washing herself with soap, the suds running off her lithe body under the hose. I thought of Lupe Contreras. I shook the thoughts away and went outside.

Eli and I began to rig for fishing that night.

"The boat is better than new now," he observed.

"She's good. With her bottom all clean and fresh we have picked up a couple of knots. We'll save some fuel."

"There ought to be a way to keep her bottom clean. Someone ought to invent something," he said.

"Maybe they have. Some copper company has built some copper-bottomed trawlers that don't have to be hauled out but once every three years or something like that. I read about it. Very modern boats. Trying them out in the Indian Ocean, I think."

"That's good!"

"Yow. But then you think: when they make such improvements, it makes the boat cost so much no one man can own one. Soon it will be all big companies and everyone will be hired just like in a factory. Will that make our lives any better? Or shrimp cost less to eat?"

"Don't ask me, man."

"Well, maybe a man can still make enough to live OK for a while."

"You ever think what you are going to do when you quit shrimpin?"

"Not really. I don't know. I expect to keep at it until I'm pretty old. Then it doesn't matter much. Get some little place where I can grow most of what I need to eat, watch the sun come up and go down, drive into town to see some good ole boy or another. Just be like everyone else, I guess. I never wanted a lot."

"You have no ambition."

"What the fuck is wrong with *that* ambition?"

"You like your life!" Eli seemed surprised.

I thought about it for a second. "Yow. . . . I like my life." It was the first time I had thought about it like that. I liked it—my life.

The try net looked promising. We put over the big trawls to go on the drag.

The sea around the boat was obsidian. I had read that in a book and liked the word. It was like cruising over the surface of an enormous glass sculpture. If you did not know it was water, you would think you might walk on it. Long, low, glassy black swells slid along in a nearly moonless night. The kind of night for good shrimping.

I went into the pilothouse.

I put my arm around Chelo's shoulders and asked, "How do you like it so far?"

"I like it."

Then she turned to look up at me. Her face was close. I shivered involuntarily and let go of her.

"Someone just walked on your grave," she said gently.

"I wonder where it is."

The bag felt very heavy coming up. It looked as if we had found shrimp. A lot of shrimp.

A moonless night is better to fish by. A full moon will sometimes keep the shrimp from coming out of the mud. I wondered at this, for they were so far down, how could moonlight filter through to their beds? But it was a fact.

Chelo was excited as the cable came up streaming water from the weight it held, then the chain to which the doors were fastened. The winch whined. The bag broke the surface.

I was mostly full of an eight- or ten-foot shark twisted in the net, and angry, its big maw full of jagged white teeth slashing at a big hole it had sawed in the cord, its goddamned evil head hanging out of the hole. Shrimp and fish flew in all directions.

"*¡Chinga tu madre! ¡Mira! ¡Mira!*" Eli yelled.

I had already *mira-ed* and was going for my shark gun.

It was an Army surplus twelve-gauge Winchester pump riot gun, loaded with slugs.

The shark was held in the net only by its hind half's being twisted in it. It was thrashing wildly, swinging the net back and forth across the deck. You could see way the hell down its throat. You could see yourself going *in* there a twenty-pound chunk of you at a time.

I shoved Chelo back against the pilothouse. She stood transfixed and frightened by the monster held aloft by bits of cord which it was fast snapping into string.

I got up close to where it hung just above the deck, took aim on its skull. They allegedly have a brain in there. I pumped two slugs into the shark. The first made it lurch almost free of the net. I put in a third, and it hung limp in the great hole it had torn in our net. That was a nearly new net, too. I was mad then. Before I had been scared. I also did not think the shark was dead. I put in another shot up close, and its right eye popped out.

I reloaded the gun.

"Stay back!" I warned.

"OK."

I yanked the cord, spilling the bag onto the deck.

The fucker twitched and swiveled on its belly and made a snapping lunge at nothing. I did not like seeing its empty eye socket. It lunged back with a swipe of its head and bit into wood of the boat's rail. I pumped two more slugs into it. Chelo was holding her ears at the noise of the gun.

I got a gaff and poked at the shark until I was sure it was re-

ally dead. Even then we were careful. They can come alive after goddamn hours sometimes.

"I want to see what is in its belly," Eli cried, coming up with
the knife he wore on his belt.

"What are you going to do?" the girl demanded.

"Open it up," Eli said.

He plunged his knife into the white underbelly and sliced
the beast open.

"Whew! He stinks," the girl observed.

"It is a girl," Eli explained in Spanish. "See, she has two
sexual organs."

"¿ Por qué dos?" she wondered.

"Double her pleasure," he said in English. "Who knows?
God is unfair." He continued in Spanish: "You would not like
to see sharks make love. It is very cruel. The male will get a
female by the neck in his teeth and leave her missing a big bite
of herself when he is finished."

"The male, he has two organs as well?" she asked in Spanish.

"Sure. I think so. You think he just carries a spare?"

"They are horrible, but they are not ugly."

"You are crazy."

"Look!" He spilled out the contents of the shark's stomach.
"Sometimes you can find valuable things inside."

There were some fish in there, a yellow sou' wester fisherman's hat, a piece of a cork life ring, and a 1954 North Caroli-
na license tag.

"Maybe she ate the whole car except for this," Eli told the
girl solemnly.

"No?"

"¡Si! But maybe just a Volkswagen. She is not so huge a
shark. She is not so small either. This is a pretty good hat.
You want it?"

"It stinks."

"We will keep the hat. We can wash it."

"You want the liver?" Eli asked me.

"No. Let's get rid of the thing."

It was a sand tiger shark. The Mexicans called them "ragged-tooth," for their teeth were long and less even than other sharks. In Australia, they call this shark gray nurse. They say it is not a man-eater, that it prefers fish. But it is this shark whose young are cannibals in the womb. It births live young, one from each of its wombs. The two it births have eaten all their siblings before they have seen the light of day.

Eli slit open a womb. The shark was pregnant, and one of its intended young bit his hand before he knew what was happening. He shook the tiny prematurely born shark off onto the deck where it leaped around, snapping at anything. Very mad little shark.

Eli showed us the tiny crescent of where the baby had got him in the hand.

Tell *him* the sand tiger is not a man-eater. They may prefer fish, but that does not mean they are religious about it.

He sucked the blood off his wound and stomped the baby to death with his heel.

Chelo cried, *"No!"*

"There are enough sharks in the world," I told her.

We had to haul the mother shark's carcass over the side with the winch.

We watched as other sharks following the boat darted through the darkness and struck their sister in a frenzy that was soon gone from our sight below the surface of the water.

The girl watched passively, interested, noncommittal. I again thought of Rivera's young Indian princess carrying a human leg in a basket as from the market.

We rigged another net and put it over before cleaning up the deck. There were only a few shrimp to head and pack away, some fish for the pot. We hosed down the deck.

There were a couple of shark's teeth in the wood where it had bit the boat. I pried them loose and gave them to Chelo.

"They are beautiful," she said. "I will make a little hole and put one on my chain."

She was a lot like her father.

I examined the torn net. There was one hole over six feet around and another almost as large. It was going to take a lot of mending. A new net cost about four hundred dollars. That was our best net.

The shrimp had disappeared. There wasn't enough in the next two hauls to warrant separating them from the trash. Shrimp are like that. Maybe there was going to be a storm, though no weather report spoke of a storm. Maybe something down there was bothering them, though I could see nothing on the fish finder.

"They have just gone, *compadre*," Eli said.

"They burrow into the mud sometimes," I explained to Chelo. "Often it means there is going to be a storm."

I checked the weather frequencies again, both U.S. and Mexican. There were no storm warnings of any kind.

"Still, I think we will run in and lay out the rest of the night in the Boca Jesús María," I told Eli.

"OK."

"How do the shrimp know?" the girl wondered.

"I don't know. Your father says they are very old things. Maybe they feel something in the mud. It is a mystery. I know times when I haven't gone in and gotten pretty wet outnumber the times I have gone in and laid out some rough weather. Before a hurricane they turn apoplectic, get all red and bugeyed. True."

I showed her the island on the chart of the Mexican coast where we were headed and how to find the course to get us there. She was sleepy but interested.

"It isn't much fun. I warned you," I told her when she could no longer keep from yawning.

"I am sorry. My clock has not gotten used to being up all night and sleeping in the daytime. I will be all right."

"Go back and sleep."

"No. I will work on the torn net."

*   *   *

A freak local storm broke the next morning as we lay snug behind the island in the Boca Jesús María. Winds were up to sixty, seventy miles an hour. We listened on the radio all day to other boats in trouble. Someone went onto the rocks not far from where we were. We heard his May Day for a while, then nothing. It was the boat of a man Eli and I knew. He had a small boat. He shrimped with his twelve-year-old son and another man. Eli crossed himself and prayed for their lives.

We were snug. We had two anchors out and lay sheltered by the steep side of the long, narrow island. There was a pot of Chelo's good *caldo largo* on the stove. It was good to be in there safe with the wind howling over the top of the island, the rain coming almost vertically against our glass. We rocked a bit, but nothing to worry about.

We sat in the cabin mending the torn net, drinking strong black coffee, smoking, talking very little, listening to the rain.

Late in the afternoon a long white schooner made it into us, both masts broken, lines and sails lashed every damned way on her sleek teak decks.

We all went out and took lines so she could anchor and tie up alongside us.

Chelo wore the hat we had taken from the belly of the shark now. Eli had soaked and scrubbed it. She had turned up the cuffs of her foul-weather jacket a couple of times and looked lost inside it, and her father's boots were too big, but she handled the lines pretty damned well for having had no experience. She never stood back. She always pitched right in to try to do her share.

They were rich people, but they were pretty good with that big boat. The skipper was a man in his forties, handsome, tan, with a short black beard. He spoke with a New England accent. We invited him and his party aboard.

He said his name was Matthew. There were two other men and three pretty women and a hired crewman, a blond college boy.

"It's a girl!" one of the women said with surprise when Chelo doffed her slicker and hat and shook out her short black hair.

Chelo gave them soup and some bread.

The skipper sent the blond over, and he came back with some good brandy—the best I had ever tasted.

He told us of their difficulties.

"It just came up so quick. We were carrying a lot of sail. Suddenly the wind went up to about seventy, and there was a wave behind us about fifty feet high."

"I thought we were goners," one of the other men said.

"It broke over us and snapped both sticks."

"You should have heard it down below!" one of the women said. "I thought it was the end of the world."

She was a pretty, studiously thin woman, the kind you see in magazines, or as close to that as she could come. She didn't have an ass at all, like a board, like a man. But her hands were very long and thin with Dragon Lady nails and four diamond rings on her brown fingers.

Matthew's wife was also pretty, but quiet and strong. She looked at you the way he did, as if measuring you inside. She went to help Chelo right away and spoke to her as you would speak to anyone.

The other woman was younger, had dark-red hair; she sat back and looked at you in a different, half-amused, measuring way. She put her tongue in her glass, just touching the brandy with the tip of it and caught me watching her over the rim. She stopped and held her tongue there for a second, then circled the rim of the little glass with it slowly, looking right into my eyes.

I looked at her husband. I looked back, and she opened her eyes wide and cocked her head slightly as if asking a question.

She wore white slacks that fit her as snugly as pants can fit. Looking over her glass she sat with her legs up so I could see the big bulge of her twat framed by the soft bulges of her thighs and bottom. It lay in there like a peach.

I looked at her husband again. He was the handsomest man

I have ever seen in person. Tall, over six feet, with a great nose on a strong face, solid chin, wavy dark hair, gray at the temples.

His wife had to be just fooling around. A prickteaser.

His business was tax shelters. What I understood about it amounted to you paying him like five thousand dollars to save yourself fifteen thousand in taxes. Or something like that. It all sounded unreal to me. You paid money, good money, to take a loss.

All the time his wife was looking over the glass and fooling with it with her tongue.

The other man, short and heavy, married to the tall woman, was an attorney. Matthew was also an attorney.

He said they were going down to Yucatán, then on to the Caribbean.

The tall woman was interested in archaeology, had a degree in it, but she did not work at it except as a hobby.

"How's the fishing?" Matthew asked.

I told him about the shark.

The sexy one, whose name was Lee, got interested.

"I think they are gorgeous things!" she said. "They don't take any shit from anybody. So powerful and sleek. They are like jet planes."

"Well, this one ate up most of my best net," I went on. "A pregnant female."

"How can you tell?"

I explained about the peculiarities of the sand tiger shark.

"Two cocks!" she exclaimed.

"Yow."

"Wow! Are they big? You said it was how big a shark?"

"About eight feet or so, I guess. It was a real shark."

"Two? They must be *hung*. I would like to see a couple of big sharks screw," she said.

No one seemed to think what she said was strange.

"Lee is interested in seeing anything screw," the tall woman said.

"There is nothing more basic in the world, more beautiful . . . don't *you* agree?"

The other woman said nothing.

"Don't you agree, Captain?" she asked me.

"Well, the way sharks I have seen do it, it is pretty basic, but not so beautiful."

I told them about how the male gets his teeth into the female during mating.

"Fucking shark wouldn't be into it five minutes with Lee, right, honey?" the tall woman's husband teased. "If there was anyone losing some skin, it would be the poor shark."

"So I'm a little noisy and like to fuck a lot . . . I'd bite *you* that's for sure, just to see if you were alive."

I looked at Chelo where she sat in corner, sipping her brandy, working at something in her hand with the awl end of her father's old knife.

"This your boat?" Matthew asked.

"More or less. The bank owns the major piece. Eli has a bit, but the papers are in my name."

"You're pretty young, aren't you?"

"There are younger running their own boats."

Lee had gotten up and slipped around the cabin, examined things. She noticed my books in the rack I had made for them.

"Hey! You read these?'' she asked.

"Yes."

"Christ, there's a Shakespeare here, Plato's *Republic, Lives!* You go to college?"

"No. Never did. I like to read."

"Hell! I just thought you were a pretty face." She sounded disappointed.

"You are blushing, *compadre*," Eli said.

"Moreover, my dear," the tall woman said, laying her warm, beautiful fingers on my arm lightly, "you have probably just lost the chance for the lay of your long life. Lee is on a noble savage kick at the moment."

"Hey! My people were noble savages," Eli offered.

"Were they?" the tall woman arched.

"I can open a beer bottle with my teeth." He hung in there.

"Really? Is there a lot of call for that?"

"No. It is something I perfected at Texas University."
He showed her his teeth.

"Such nice even teeth too. You must have very strong mandibles."

"Those, too. But I am like the iguana, when I take a bite of you, I don't let go until the sun goes down."

"You hear this, Lee. Maybe this one is the one for you. He bites, too."

She looked Eli over. He sat up straight and threw out his chest and smiled.

"I don't like his number," Lee said, referring to his faded white and orange football jersey. "I never liked football players. I went with one once. He turned out to be queer. He just didn't know it."

"But you convinced him, right, darling?"

"He is probably happier."

Lee's husband kept crossing and recrossing his legs, looking as if he would say something, but then did not.

"What inspired you to read?" the tall woman's husband asked.

"I just always did. You know, you learn to read. Then, I would read a book and it would talk about something I didn't know or mention another book, and I would try to find out what they were talking about or pick up the other book when I ran across it. I live on the boat. I've never had a TV. I don't like TV much. Maybe when they get some good cheap color sets, it will be OK. But I read in color, I can see things better in a book than I can in what there is on TV. There are pictures in the words in books you can't *get* on TV or in the movies. I just read."

"I think it is wonderful," Matthew's wife said.

I didn't see it as wonderful. I began to feel a bit annoyed

that they were making so much over the fact that a man who happened to run a shrimp boat read a couple of books.

Their bottle was gone, and we had all started on our Fundador.

"Well, I envy you," the tall woman's husband said. "I don't have time to read as much as I would like. Too busy making money to keep my kids in their damned schools, paying off a castle of a house we don't need, paying for club memberships to keep us in shape, when a good day's work would do us a lot better. I envy you, Captain." He lifted his glass to me.

"Well, I don't know. I have always wondered what it would be like to be able to just go anywhere you wanted on a great sailing boat like that. I think I could take it for a while," I said.

"A yacht is a hole in the ocean into which you pour money," Lee's husband assured me.

"I know a bit about *that*," I promised him.

"Come over for breakfast in the morning and I'll show you around, if you like," Matthew offered.

"Thanks. I would enjoy seeing what a boat like that is like below."

"You have never been on such a boat?" Lee asked.

"No." I thought. "No, I've never been on anything you would call a yacht."

She had moved close. She laid her hand along my cheek. The palm felt fleshy and warm, moist.

"Come over now and I will give you the grand tour."

"Well, it looks as if it is time for me and my loving wife to call it an evening," her husband said, getting to his feet, finishing his drink. He was not angry, just weary. "Thank you for your hospitality, Captain. That soup is marvelous!" he turned to Chelo.

"Yes!" Matthew's wife exclaimed. "Will you give me the recipe, dear?" she asked Chelo.

"There is no recipe," she said.

"Really? But could you tell me what you put into it?"

"If you like."

"Come on, it's time for all of us to go," Matthew said.

"Perhaps you will tell me tomorrow."

"OK," Chelo said.

"Come on, Lee," her husband said, already at the door.

She bent down and kissed me fully on the lips, opening her mouth a bit, enough to quickly slip me the tip of her tongue. There was an electrical shock through me, then she was gone, waving cheerfully to all.

"Good night! Good night all."

But for a moment she caught my eyes and searched them of their surprise and wonder.

"Don't take it seriously," the tall woman whispered as she brushed past me, again touching my arm reassuringly. "A few days ago it was a country-western singer in a horrible little place in Galveston who had the most atrocious nasal twang." She imitated a snatch of the song the fellow had sung. "Next week it will be a Mexican beach boy or *something*. She likes to flirt a lot."

"Good night," I told her.

When they had gone, Chelo asked, "Why does that woman act like a whore?"

"I don't know," I said.

"Maybe she thinks she is being free, like a man," Chelo said. "She wants to be a whore or a man. That is not being a woman. She has a beautiful husband, much money, she does not have to work or anything. It is stupid."

"Maybe her husband is no good for her for sex," Eli pondered.

"I don't think so. He looks OK to me," Chelo said. "She is screwed up."

We cleaned up the things.

Eli went to sleep in the pilothouse. Chelo climbed into her upper bunk and drew the curtain. I lay down in the lower bunk in my clothes.

The sound of the rain was good to hear on the boat. It came in gusts, rattling against the boat; then it would slacken and

gust again. It should have made me sleepy, but I could not
sleep.

I could hear the voices of the people on the yacht tied up to
us. I heard the tall woman laugh. I heard a murmur in the
cabin close to where I lay. I was certain it was Lee and her
husband. I heard her laugh briefly, more a short burst, a snort
of laughter. Then it was still. I knew they were fucking. I
don't know how, I just knew. She cried out once. I was sure of
it.

I got up and put on my slicker, turned the collar up, and
went out on deck to smoke.

The rain had slackened. You could see the moon breaking
through the clouds, which were racing away north. The
schooner had a beautiful shape, sweeping back to the low teak
doghouse. I looked back up to the bow. When I looked back
to the stern of the yacht, someone had come out onto deck. I
could see the glow of a cigarette.

I walked back. Our sides were much higher than the
yacht's. I was looking down onto the deck. I thought it might
be Matthew.

"Rain's stopping," I said. "Be a nice day tomorrow."

"Hi."

It was Lee, barefoot, in a yellow foul-weather jacket much
too large for her.

"It's become warm." She put her open palm up to the rain.
"Soft."

"Can't sleep?"

"Hunh-unh."

She threw the coat back off her shoulders and arched her
body up to the soft rain. She was naked under the coat. She
threw back her face and washed her belly and breasts with the
rain. She was a very beautiful woman, more so naked than
she had been clothed. Rounded and sleek and tan.

I found I had put my hand on my cock, was holding it tight.

She came to the rail and stretched up both her arms. I
reached down and felt her bare arms snake up and grip my bi-

ceps. I lifted her up and onto my boat. She folded herself into my arms and her wet, open mouth made the rain seem chill again by comparison.

She placed one of my hands on her full, soft breast, and as soon as I touched the nipple, she jerked and ground her pelvis against me and moaned. Her small soft hand clawed at my fly, belt, got my pants open and searched for my cock. When she found it, she said, "Umm. Oh. *I want you.*"

I thought where to lay her down.

She dropped on her knees on the deck and got my jeans down and over my feet. Giving a small cry, she took my cock and popped it into her mouth, sucking and stroking me back to my asshole. It felt as if she were trying to bring my come forth into her mouth. I pried her loose before that and got between her legs on the deck.

She kissed me as if she would tear my tongue out.

"Fuck me! Fuck me! Oh, fuck me!" she breathed into my mouth. "Oh, yes! Fuck me hard! Fuck me hard!"

Her back and ass were banging against the deck. I banged her as if I were trying to hurt her and she asked for more, harder. I was breathing like a long-distance runner when she began to come. She tossed her head back and forth, started to scream the way I had heard her scream earlier. I clamped my right hand over her mouth, fucked her harder yet, let up a bit, then came, too. She bit my palm. Her eyes looked wild as I came and came in her.

Then I collapsed on her. She felt so warm and soft and small beneath me. Her cunt continued to squeeze me until finally it had all but squeezed me from her.

"Kiss me," she asked.

I kissed her.

"That was good," she told me. "You are very good."

"You too."

"I know."

We snuggled up against the pilothouse. It had all but stopped raining. We smoked. She played with my cock. When

it began to show sign of life again, she bent her face in my lap
and began to suck it once more. When it was erect, she scooted me down onto the deck and got astride me.

"This time, you bust your ass," she said.

She rode my cock for a long time. I felt I could stay hard
and not come for a week. She came three times before she decided: "That's enough. God!"

Her thighs and hairs and our bellies were slick with the
juices from our fucking. As soon as she was off me, I wanted
her again. I rolled her over and got between her legs.

"God, baby, I'm getting sore,"

"Now I want to come," I told her.

"Let me suck you off then."

But I wanted to fuck her cunt. I pounded her hard again,
not as hard as before, but hard. She whimpered and bit her
lower lip, but she fucked back dutifully, and when I came, she
gave a little cry and ran the coming out nicely for me though
she did not come again.

I still wasn't very soft when I rolled off her. I saw her looking at me. I was a bit curious, too.

She took me in her hand.

"Didn't you come?"

"Yes."

"Christ. You young guys can fuck all night."

"Not all the time. Only when I am inspired."

"Do I inspire you?"

"You must," I said, smiling at my cock.

"What are we going to do with you?" she wondered.

I looked in her eyes, kissed her swollen pale lips, then put
my hand flat against the back of her head and applied a bit of
pressure until she slowly lowered her face again over my lap
and took my cock in her mouth. She sucked lovingly and furi-
ously, cutting looks at my face with her large sexy eyes, jack-
ing the shaft of my cock finally until I came again a tiny bit in
her mouth. She sucked and licked me all around after I came.

"You do that better than anyone," I told her.

"Oh, I was famous for it when I was in school. Everyone says I suck cock better than anyone they have ever had. It was how I saved my virginity for my first husband."

"What happened to him?"

"He said I was a nymphomaniac."

"Are you?"

"*No!* Shit, no! I really just like to fuck a lot. I don't *have* to. I just *like* to."

"That's the difference, I guess."

"Damn right."

We smoked, sharing my cigarette.

"What if your old man wakes up and comes looking for you?"

"Scared?"

I thought a moment, grinned. "No."

"What would you do? He carries an automatic."

"I don't know. Maybe get shot. But I'm not scared. Maybe I don't care. I'd just like to fuck my brains out with you." I started to pull her down and kiss her.

She resisted.

"Listen, I'm sore. I came hard four times—five, counting once before I came out. I'm wiped out, baby." She gave me a long, friendly kiss, held my cock and balls in her hand, squeezing. It felt about half erect again. "How long has it been for chrissake since you had a fuck?"

"Over a week," I guessed.

"What about the little girl with you?"

"Chelo? She is just one of us. She doesn't."

"Never?"

"I don't know. I never asked her."

"Why don't you go crawl in with her and give her what's left of this. I'm really tired now . . . OK?"

I was squeezing her tit. I worked my hands between her legs where she was all sticky and warmly liquid inside the swollen lips of her cunt.

"Don't!" she asked and tried to twist away. She wrested her-

self up with her back against the pilothouse. I guided my cock
between her legs which were clamped tight, but as she rose on
tiptoe, the head of it slipped into her.

I humped her there while she protested, only about half of
me inside. Soon she quit protesting and began to come on.
She became wild. She clawed my back with her nails, arched
herself to get more of my cock into her, wrapped both legs
around my hips and began bucking like mad.

"Fuck me! Fuck me!" she again began to urge into my ear.

I came, but she had not.

"Let me be on top," she insisted.

I lay down on the deck, and she got on top and fed my now
half-limp cock into her sopping cunt and ground herself and
groaned against me, her cunt grinding against my pelvis until
she came again. She fell over me and shuddered in spasms as
if she were having some kind of fit.

"Are you all right?" I asked.

She shook her head that she was. But she shuddered several times more before she stopped.

"I've got to get back," she said.

It was about an hour or so before dawn.

I was aware that my knees and elbows were scraped raw in
places. She looked bedraggled, her hair stringy and wet. Her
eyes looked strange, as if they did not quite focus.

I helped her up. She leaned heavily against me. She came
about to my shoulder. I kissed the top of her head.

"I would like to keep going for a week," I told her. "I really
like how you are."

"I like you, too," she said softly.

"I wish I could see you again."

"Maybe you will."

"I'd travel a long way to see you again." I thought of all the
things we might yet do.

"You like me so much?"

"Hell, yes."

She kissed me long and gently. I held her soft, nice, deep
ass in both hands, pressing her against me tightly.

"I think I could go again," I told her.

"No, you can't!" She wrested herself loose.

"Maybe we could meet somewhere soon," I suggested.

"OK. Sure."

We were at the rail of the boat.

"How can I find you?"

"I don't know," she said.

"Tell me where you will be staying. I could get away from the boat for a few days maybe. Could you?"

"I don't know. Why don't you give me your address? I'll get in touch with you when I can." She sounded tired.

"OK. I will write it out and give it to you tomorrow."

"That's fine. Well . . . good night." She put her face up to be kissed.

I lowered her back down onto the yacht. I watched her go the hatch that led below. She stopped halfway down the hatch and waved and blew me a kiss. I blew her a kiss back.

"Very *romántico,*" Eli growled from the doorway of the pi-lothouse.

"You awake?" I said, embarrassed.

"What you think? Think I can sleep when you are fucking yourself silly against my wall? Now you make me so horny I will be miserable the whole trip."

"Sorry, *compadre.*"

"That don't make me feel better. You better go to bed. You look bad, man. She will kill a man like you in a week."

"Don't care if I do die, do die, do die," I sang to him.

"That good, hunh?"

"Good!"

"Goddamn!" He went back to bed.

I felt fucked out, almost happy. The scrapes on my elbows and knees burned. Man, I wanted her some more. I wanted her until I could not walk, could not twitch.

I went to sleep wondering if all rich women fucked so much better than anyone else, put so much of themselves into it. I'd sure as hell like to make a survey.

* * *

I was awakened by the sounds of the boat next to us untying, getting under way.

I dressed quickly and went out onto deck. Matthew waved to me. The day was clear and bright, already quite hot. I could see steam coming faintly from the yacht's teak decks.

"We are going to run on back to Brownsville. I called a yard there, and they can take us. We can just make it by dark on the engine."

"Good luck," was all I could think to say.

Everyone was out on deck except Lee and the tall woman. Lee came up on deck. She wore a short T-shirt with an anchor on it and very short white shorts that exposed the sweet bulges of her tan cheeks. She had a multicolored silk scarf wound around her hair. She waved, and I waved back.

The yacht was pulling away.

She shrugged her shoulders exaggeratedly, her palms turned helplessly outward at her sides. She made a sad face above her smiling mouth.

I smiled back. She smiled and threw me a big kiss at the full fling of her arm.

Her husband stopped working on deck and looked at her and at me with his hands on his hips.

She turned and went to him, linked her arm in his, and waved to us. He said something, and she reached up on tiptoe and kissed his jaw.

I watched the boat motor out to the inlet and disappear around the headland.

"Maybe you will see her again," Chelo said sneeringly near to me along the rail.

I had the note in my hand I was going to give Lee. It had a few words and my address on it. I felt stupid and crumpled it in my hand and let it fall over the side. It floated on the glassy water where the yacht had been.

"Those people don't care about you," Chelo said. "You should know that. Life is just for them . . . kicks." It sounded like "keeks."

I pinched her little butt. She cursed me in Spanish and gave me a wild shot that I caught on the arm.

She hardly spoke to me *or* Eli for the next few days.

"She is in love with you," Eli insisted.

"*Chelo?* Don't be stupid." That really pissed me off for some reason.

We worked, but we were not a happy boat for a while.

Nor were we catching any goddamned shrimp.

"The storm has made everything around here no good," Eli said.

"Then we'll run on down to Yucatán if we have to. We need a good catch. I have no money left from paying the bills on the boat. I'd have to borrow to get ice and fuel for the next trip if we don't make some money."

Chelo looked at me as if my fooling around with that rich woman had somehow jinxed us.

CHAPTER THIRTEEN

"Where are all the shrimp?" Chelo asked me. Her tone of voice sounded tinged with suspicion of my ability to fish.

I was beginning to wonder what was wrong myself. All sorts of superstitious nonsense flitted through my concern.

Maybe losing Chelo's father, Ezequiel, had forever lost our luck. Perhaps it *was* unlucky to have a woman aboard a boat.

"Who knows where shrimp go?" I said. "They are crazy. No one really knows what goes on with the things in the sea. There will be shrimp someplace for years, crabs, lobsters, oysters; then one day they will be gone and sometimes never return. They move. Maybe they realize they are about to be fished out and go someplace else to survive. Maybe they just get tired of someplace. Who knows why? All you get are theories. One is as good as another. Why do eels bust their slinky asses to get back to the Sargasso Sea to spawn? That is some trip. They will go overland on a light dew to get there if they have to. What are whales about? They say there are two great peaks among the species—man and the whale. And if some mutually applicable intelligence test could be devised, the whale would likely come out ahead, so they say. There are monsters out in the great oceans we have never seen, I am sure. Great sharks the size of whales maybe, giant squid longer than a ship, rays bigger than a bomber—throwbacks, survivors of prehistory who have dived deep and lurk yet. Things move beneath the surface in ways we cannot fathom. You have seen all the things we have hauled up in our nets. A madman in high delirium or an artist ultimately inspired could not dredge up the horrible, beautiful intricacy of a single catch."

"Yes," she said.

"Take whales now. A whale has feelings, is capable of love and vengeance, anger and compassion. A whale won't attack a boat unless it comes between it and its young. A shark will attack anything on instinct, yet it is incapable of intelligent anger or vengeance—love—forget it! It has the compassion of a storm of locusts. Whales support their wounded and dying to keep them afloat, give them comfort until all hope is gone. They may even have burial grounds like elephants. Sharks will turn on one of their wounded and eat him. There were a couple of big yachts, both over fifty feet, destroyed by a single whale in the space of a week in one area recently in the Caribbean. Then they found a young calf on the shore nearby with its back broken. Some ship had hit it and killed it. The mother hung about so bereaved she attacked any boat that passed that way. Porpoises are small whales. A porpoise can take a shark in a fair fight usually because it is more intelligent. There is wisdom and humor in the eye of a whale or porpoise. There is ignorance and blankness in the eye of a shark. Emotionally, I think man has become more like the shark than the whale who ought to be his brother. I think if there is a god, he must be more in the image of a great whale than a man."

"Yes?" she said.

"I don't know where shrimp go. Maybe they just burrow in the mud and let the world go hang now and then. I'd like to just do that myself sometime."

"You get very philosophical, like my father. Maybe you are around him too long."

"Maybe. Bad luck always makes someone who fishes for a living philosophical. Maybe rainy days make a house carpenter philosophical too. I wonder."

"I like you, Captain. . . ." She patted my arm where I leaned on the rail. "Even if you don't make me no money."

"I like you, too."

"Yes. I know. You know something? I feel like you are my brother."

I thought about that. I looked at her.

She smiled. "Don't feel bad, it is *good!* It does not mean I could not love you as a man too . . . maybe . . . sometime . . . Who knows what things move beneath the surface we cannot fathom?" she mocked me kindly.

I laughed.

"You are a little smartass, you know that?" I lifted my hand to give her a swat on the can.

She caught my wrist deftly and turned it to shake hands. She shook hands as Mexicans do—man or woman—her hand very soft and still in mine. Then she gave me a formal *abrazo,* holding her little belly well clear of me.

"*Hermano,*" she said, "I will go make supper. Maybe tonight we will wake up and find the shrimp."

We fished past Ciudad del Carmén and on past Campeche toward the islands off the Yucatan Peninsula. We were not even making expenses. Every other day or three one of those local Gulf storms would blow up, sending us for protection of land or leaving us fighting through heavy seas in high winds. In truth, we were young enough that the first few hours of the storms were thrilling. It was good to feel the power of the sea and wind pitted against the design of our boat, our skill.

I am sure if you could walk to work on water, ride a bike or take a streetcar on it, no one would go to sea except out of the same necessity they went to a factory. Boats *float* on the sea. Like the creatures that fishermen hunt, the boats are but specks, mere chips on a vast, deep, powerful element, controlled by no less than the amazing pull of the moon; literally a boat is caught between the planetary forces of earth and its moon. So is a pedestrian, but he is not going to sink into the earth if he makes a miscalculation. We were our own tiny three-person world busting through the tops of the large swells and liking it for a while. Our world was constructed of three-inch pitch pine planks on oak frames.

It was snug aboard. We smoked and drank hot coffee and ate sandwiches.

Bound together by the circumstances, by our concern, we were all a little in love with one another. We became very considerate and polite to each other.

"People are always nicer when there is some danger," Chelo observed after she did some small thing and got thanks from Eli and myself. "Maybe that is why people who are never in no real danger are often so mean to each other."

"Yow. You read a lot of books about how people in dangerous, castaway situations act badly to one another. I think most of the time they are just acting out the author's political notions and own fears—the strong preying on the weak, the rich on the poor. Maybe it is so. I don't think so. But you hardly ever read a book about how good people can be to one another when their asses are against the wall. Makes me wonder if politics and what we call society aren't against the better part of us. Maybe we don't know what our true best interests are."

"My father said, 'Live close to the mysteries of everything. Everything has its spirit. Those spirits are closer to you than someone of your own blood.'"

"The spirit in that bomb he was screwing on was a bit too damned close for comfort," Eli observed.

"He did not say the spirits were not dangerous," she said softly in Spanish.

We all stood aware that her father's remains had been blown into the waters on which we moved, into the waters we fished. His flesh would have fed fish, crabs, eels. Might we one day haul up in our nets a bone—the skull of Ezequiel? The thought made me sad, grim. I looked at Chelo. She looked back as if our thoughts had touched. I wanted to hug her to me, kiss her face, hair, mouth, take her into my bunk and enter her slender body, come in her womb. I don't know why. It felt as if the devil or the ghost of Ezequiel grown a thousand feet high were standing over my shoulder, casting a cold eternal shade.

"Go to bed," I told the girl. "If the storm stops, I will call you."

Eli spoke now often of how unhappy his wife was going to be when we got in. He spoke of having to go borrow money from his brother-in-law to make his car payment.

We had fished for nearly four weeks and had not earned our expenses. Now, we would have to go in, resupply the boat, buy fuel and ice, and work another month before we saw dollar one.

"How do you like it so far?" I asked Chelo.

"Maybe I bring you bad luck," she suggested.

"No. Don't think that." I looked at her. It seemed the most natural thing she should be there. If she brought us bad luck, then we were meant to have it. "There have been other times when it has been like this. It is like this for everyone sometimes. If it was so easy, there would be no chance for people like us to do it. I expect you will start smelling shrimp for me one day like your old man used to do."

I was sorry she had not made any money for her work.

We had to go in. I turned the boat toward Texas.

When I tried to give Chelo a hundred as she was leaving the boat to go home, she refused it.

"Please don't insult me. I will take my chances just like you and everyone. We will live somehow, just as you must. I know you like me and trust me. That is what we earn this time. I will be ready when you leave again.

She walked up the dock to the road with her meager bag of personal items over one shoulder, her cap upon her head, to catch a ride to the slum where her family lived.

Eli's wife came out to get him in their new Edsel.

She was visibly and vocally angry when he showed her his empty palms and flung a few snappers, shrimp, and redfish he had wrapped for their freezer in the backseat.

"You are going to speak seriously now to my brother about a good job that pays money—tonight!" she advised him in

Spanish. "The baby that is coming cannot live on a hatful of fish!"

I wanted to see Lupe Contreras. I wanted to see if those two jokers who wanted something moved to Cuba were still around. I wanted to see Lupe. I needed some quick money. I needed her.

Two boats had been lost during the time we had been out. One we had heard on the rocks during the first storm, the other boat had been from Los Fresnos.

Everyone was talking about how the shrimping out of Florida was great right now, especially around the Dry Tortugas. People were talking about maybe going over to Florida for a while.

"It's them fuckin Russians with their Sputnik!" Pop Cayce claimed up in the Good Eats Café. "Whoever got one of them things up first was going to rule the world, and they did it," he insisted. "And the Lord ain't goin to stand for it."

"You reckon shrimps know they got that thing up there?" someone wondered.

"Fuckin shrimp know everything," Pop said.

"The world is going to end in fire and destruction," Mother Cayce said, frying hamburgers, taking a long view. "And the time ain't so far away. The time feels right nigh."

Pete Gatliff and one of the Slocum boys got into a knife fight in the middle of the afternoon over a game of mumblety-peg for ten dollars.

They cut each other pretty good. Pete's left ear hung from just a string. Slocum's left cheek was open to the white bone, and he was missing a little bit off the end of his nose. They were gentlemen; neither had stabbed.

Charles Principal and I took them to the hospital in Brownsville in the back of my old pickup. They held towels and cloths to their wounds and passed a bottle of Early Times between them. I never did learn who paid for the bottle, and neither of them professed to remember.

It was while we were in the corridor outside the emergency room for the boys to get stitched up that I saw Lupe Contreras.

Her husband, dressed in his border guard's uniform to go to work, was holding her by one arm as they argued with a doctor.

"I'm dying! I'm not crazy!" Lupe insisted for all the world to hear, trying to wrench herself loose from her old husband's grip. She kicked at his shins. He swore.

She was a wildcat, that Lupe.

"She's goddamned crazy!" her husband yelled at the doctor. "She's barking the skin off me! She won't eat—do *anything*! Just lies in the bed and says all kinds of crazy shit."

"I'm not crazy, you bastard! I'm dying! You don't know the difference, you turd," she added in Spanish. "I know I am dying. That is what is wrong with me."

"That is what is wrong with us all!" the doctor, who was young, explained in exasperation. "There is nothing physically wrong with you." He turned again to husband. "There is nothing wrong with her. Nothing. She is very healthy. You are very strong and healthy." He turned to Lupe as if speaking to one who did not understand the language.

"You can't see nothing because you are blind to everything but the blood and bones and meat. *I* am dying!" She beat her breast. "*Me!* My body will follow. Shithead."

"If there isn't anything wrong with her, she's got to be crazy," husband argued.

"We can do nothing about that," the doctor said. "You will have to see a judge."

"She don't do nothing but lie in bed. The house is a shithole. She won't get off her ass for nothing."

"He wants to put me away to die where he don't have to see," she said. "He drags me here. He won't let me see the *curandera*."

"She wants me to take her to see some kind of witch across the border," husband offered as proof of her insanity. "I can't live with her like this."

"He locks me in the house when he leaves. Ties me to the bed."

"She'll burn down the goddamn house or something. She's off her rocker. I want someone to do something about her before she hurts herself or someone."

"You will have to see a judge. Get an order. I gave her some pills to calm her down."

"She won't take the damn things. Can't you give her a shot or something?"

"*No!* I don't want no needles stuck in me!" she screamed. "Let me go!" she screamed in Spanish. "Let me go!" She began kicking and trying her damnedest to get free.

"Godamn you!" husband yelled and let go of her with his big right hand long enough to slap her face.

"Let me go!"

"Won't you do something?" he implored the doctor. "Put her here somewhere for tonight. I got to go to work. I can see a judge tomorrow. Just for tonight. You can see how she is."

Her hair was wild. She tried to kick her husband in the groin.

"*No!* Don't touch me!" she screamed as the doctor started to help her husband.

I had been standing along the wall beside Charles Principal, smoking. I began to move before I thought what I was doing.

"Stop that!" I heard myself say.

People sitting along the corridor, who had been watching what had been going on impassively as people do in such places, noted my moving toward the trouble in the same noncommittal way.

I don't think her husband or the doctor knew what I was about until I was right there.

"Let her go," I told her husband, taking his hand to pull it away from her.

"Who the hell are you?" he demanded.

I could see the fear and wonder in Lupe's eyes. She could not believe I was there, how I had arrived.

"I'm not crazy," she promised me.

"Let her go."

"You get the hell out of here, boy. This is none of your business. Who the fuck you think you—"

I hit him in the belly right up under the ribs with all my might. I could hear the air go out of him as he doubled over my arm. I knew he could not see or breathe. I shoved him into the doctor and caught up with Lupe, who was already running out of there.

I could see out of the corner of my eye her old husband gasping for breath, mouth working, unable to speak yet, blindly fumbling for his pistol on his belt.

I grabbed Lupe as I passed her and hauled her along as fast as she could run. She had on high-heeled shoes, and I kept thinking she is going to break a heel off her shoe or stumble. I kept expecting to get shot in the back any second until we broke through the big double doors to the outside.

The heavy wet heat of a Gulf night was like running into a wall of cotton batting after the air-conditioned corridor of the hospital. It took my breath away, made my head ache, was like a hand grabbing my heart. Sweat suddenly poured off me. My shirt felt soaking wet.

"The truck!" I managed, hauling Lupe toward where I had parked the pickup.

I yanked open the door on my side and shoved her headlong into the cab, stuffing her fantastic ass after her, piled in, got the thing started, and was moving before I closed my door.

"Stay on the floor," I told her, gunning the old truck out of the lot.

In the rearview mirror her husband, the doctor, and an intern were out of the door. Husband raised his pistol and let go a couple of shots as we bounded over the speed arrester just inside the drive and screeched out onto the highway.

I cut on my lights only after I was on the highway and driving faster than the law allowed.

"You OK, Johnny?"

"Yow. Come on up."

She got on the seat. She seemed happy. Maybe she was crazy. Maybe we were all crazy. She was no crazier than anyone else.

"I was so glad to see you, Johnny. You cannot know how I felt when I see you there. It is a miracle. He wants to put me away in a crazy house. He doesn't know nothing. He is so stupid. I was crazy when I married him. Now I am not crazy. Where did you come from?"

"I was there with some boys who got in a knife fight."

"If you were not there, I would be gone, you know. I love you!"

She hopped near and hugged me with both arms, kissing my face.

"We aren't out of this yet."

It was one thing to get her out of there, now what in the hell was I going to do with her? Surely the police *and* her husband would come looking for her. What the hell could I be charged with? I wondered. Going to my boat was no good.

"I want to go across the river, Johnny. There is a wonderful woman. Maybe she can save my life. I must go to her. I am dying, truly, Johnny. Something is trying to take me over."

Going to Mexico seemed as safe as anything else right then. If we were going to get across, it was best to try it right away before anyone would be watching for us.

I cut onto the approach to the new international bridge.

It seemed the U.S. border guard took a hell of a long time looking us over before he waved us on. The Mexican guard was less interested.

When we were through the last checkpoint, I sighed aloud and realized I was wringing wet.

"I will never go back to my husband," Lupe then announced firmly. "Never. It is finished. My death coming for me was the warning to go and never go back for nothing. Not even my clothes. Nothing," she added in Spanish.

She slid close to me and put her left hand on my leg in a familiar way I liked when we drove together.

"You don't think I am crazy, do you, Johnny?"

"You are you. Maybe that is more dangerous."

"You think so?"

"I don't know."

"I think you turn this way!" She sprang up to point out a side road off the potholed paved one we were on. "You go out through this part of the town, I think."

"You ever been here?"

"No. My friend Berta was here once when she was pregnant and did not want the baby because she did not know whose it was. She thought maybe it was her father's."

"What?"

She shrugged. "She was young. He was drunk and very mean. Her mother was away then."

"What happened?"

"She lost the baby. Her father was always very good and proper afterward to her. If he was not, he would become a dog no one would like. This woman is wonderful. But she is also a little expensive. You have some money? I don't have any."

"Well, not a hell of a lot. A couple of hundred, I guess."

"Oh, that is plenty."

"That's good."

"Don't worry. Maybe I will pay you back sometime."

"I know."

"This way. There. Turn there."

"You sure?" The place looked like slum in a jungle. No city lights were along there. The road was rutted and muddy.

"I think so."

CHAPTER FOURTEEN

We wandered around all the muddy, dark, mean streets of West Matamoros for an hour, bouncing over deep, muddy ruts, disturbing sleeping citizens by arousing hundreds of hungry, crazed dogs all over that part of town. After an hour I was sure we had set off a square mile of yelping, barking, howling dogs. One beast's complaint fed another's.

"We are going to wake every fucking dog in Mexico," I told Lupe.

"I think it is down this street. Yes! I can feel it."

"You don't have an idea of an address?"

She looked at me as if that was a foolish question.

"I will know when I am there."

"One of these streets looks like another. I don't know where the hell I am."

Lupe cocked her head and stared intently, however blankly, as if listening for subliminal guidance.

"I feel we are very near."

"Everyone is asleep in those houses," I remarked.

"Don't worry. It is OK."

If she said so. I just did not feel comfortable bouncing around the poor streets of the city's working community, setting off their dogs. If they had wanted tourists, they would have put up streetlights and signs tourists could read.

I thought the river was over to my right somewhere. That would put the bullring and the abattoir off to left and ahead

somewhat. The main part of town—the square—would be behind us.

"This is it, Johnny," she whispered.

The short hairs lifted on my neck.

"There is the house."

It was an ordinary little humpty house like all the others on
the tumble-down street. Chickens nested in the trees. Dogs
barked up the street, but no dog barked around the house. It
was eerie. As soon as Lupe said, "This is it, Johnny," everything seemed to become very still. The breeze ruffled the
trees. You could hear the chickens flop about now and then
to keep their balance on a branch in the trees. Yet it was a
peaceful place. Still. I felt entirely at peace, still in myself.

I looked at Lupe and saw her more clearly than I had ever
seen her before. I could see her agony as if it had been drawn
on her face and the skin of her arms and neck with bright red
ink. I could see *through* her! See her soul which was beautiful
and younger even than herself, but shrouded in a cancerous
muck, just shining through.

I did not believe any of what I saw.

I saw her death and my own—neither very pretty, neither
of any importance. I saw the inside of her sexual desire, orgasm, satisfaction, as if I were a clinical spectator. And I loved
her and wanted to kiss her.

She turned her face slowly to look at me, and I nearly broke
out of the truck backwards. Her eyes glowed as if bulb and
batteries had been put behind them, blank, devoid of pupil.
Her lips seemed swollen, dripping wet with something. Her
every feature was exaggerated. Her small teeth seemed
ground to points. I could see through her and into her. She
seemed a foul and rotten thing, yet burning and appealing.

"What is wrong with you?" she was asking me as from a distance. Her voice sounded as voices do when you are return-
ing from unconsciousness.

"What is wrong with you?"

I knew I was shaking my head and had my arms around
her, drawing her close to me, hungering for that obscene,

dangerous mouth. She lowered those inflamed lips over mine, her eyes glowing from within; I felt her body press against my own, seem to absorb me, flow around me like an octopus.

Then I was awake, alert, felt great, as if I'd had the best sleep of my life. I had a hard-on. I saw it, and I laughed. It was the best hard-on I'd had since I was ten years old.

I pulled Lupe against me when we stood outside the truck and poked the great hard-on against her.

"You are crazy. There is no time for such things now, *hombre*. Where did that come from?"

"I don't know. It was just there."

"Put something over it; we can't wait out here all night." There was a light on in this little house. The only light in the block. A silent yellow dog that looked more coyote than dog came to the gate and stood there looking at us.

"He is smiling at me," I whispered to Lupe.

"What is wrong with you—you act drunk."

"I'm not drunk. Nothing. I feel good. I don't know why."

"What did you see in the truck?" she whispered.

"Nothing—you."

"I think you saw something and you almost faint."

As soon as I touched the gate, the dog backed away and stepped aside as a person would. His tail did not wag like a dog's, nor did it curl under his ass like a coyote's. It was the only dog I ever met that I entirely liked.

A lizard slipped up the porch post and hid half behind it, peeking around, though pretending to see nothing. It was a small iguana, I think.

In a six-foot cage on the porch slept a big bird, an eagle or buzzard, its head tucked beneath a wing. It, too, did not seem to be an ordinary bird any more than the dog or lizard seemed like any I had encountered before.

Maybe being told you are going to call on a witch makes you see things differently from the way they are. Or maybe knowing you are calling on a witch makes you see them in another way than the way they are.

The door opened before we knocked on it.

The woman was beautiful, taller than myself—six feet maybe. That was a surprise. The second thought I had was that she was a man. But she had what appeared to be large real breasts and substantial feminine hips. Her voice was both womanly and mocking. She was dressed entirely in black, of course.

"I have been waiting for you for a long time. I thought you would never find the way," she said in Spanish.

She seemed particularly amused at me. She looked directly at my cock and smiled even more. It was, I realized, now quite flaccid and entirely dormant.

"Enter," she said, turning her attention to Lupe, taking her by her right arm, putting her left arm around Lupe as if to steady her. "You have come just in time, you know?"

Lupe stared straight ahead and nodded.

I could not figure the *curandera's* age. She could have been in her late thirties, more than likely older. She was one of those sleek, plump Indian women, with hair as shining black as a crow's wing until they are ancient. I had never seen a Mexican woman that tall. I would have given anything to have seen her naked. I imagined the enormous heavy breasts and soft, smooth, deep skin, the power of her wide lips and heavy thighs, the large fleshiness of her cunt and the muscular strength therein. She was as beautiful as a new nickel and just as true . . . when nickels were Indian heads and silver through and through.

The room was a jungle of dried weeds set in pots, birds, and things in wooden cages, tin votive light holders and mirrors mounted in decorated tin. The floor was clean, bare wood. There was a small fire on the grate in a corner chimney. There was a small stool before the fire and a bowl into which the woman had been shelling ears of multicolored Indian corn.

The *curandera* was leading Lupe directly into the next small room which was mostly filled with an old wooden table that was worn smooth and probably a valuable antique, however, built to last forever of heavy wood. There were the chairs for the table along the wall. Behind the table was an open standing cupboard covered with a fringed shawl thrown across it diagonally, so some of the dishes displayed in the cupboard were visible. They were old, good dishes. The *curandera* was not as poor as her neighborhood.

"You can stay, but you must not speak," she instructed me in Spanish. When she saw I did not understand Spanish too well, she told Lupe to tell me what she had said.

"She also says, if you feel sick or want to faint, to go into the other room. As soon as you get into the other room you will feel well."

"OK." I smiled at the *curandera*. She nodded her head very seriously.

"You brought a fresh egg? An egg fresh today?" she asked Lupe.

"No, No! *Mamacita,* I did not know I was required to bring an egg," she said in Spanish.

"But it is necessary."

"What will we do?"

"Perhaps there is one in the nests. I will go look. In the meantime take off your clothes. You can put them over there on the chair."

"All my clothes?"

"Yes. Everything. I will cleanse you. You came to me just in time, you know."

"Yes."

"I will go look for the egg. If we do not have a fresh brown egg, you will have to go find one and come back another time. It was very stupid for you to come without a fresh brown egg."

"I did not know."

"It is very dangerous. You just got here in time. If we do not have an egg, it is going to be very bad."

The woman ducked through the door at the end of the room and disappeared. The only light was from the fire in the other room, a couple of candles in there, and a couple of candles in the room we were in.

"God, I hope she finds an egg," Lupe whispered, getting out of her clothes as fast as she could.

"You're beautiful, Lupe," I told her when she stood naked in the candlelight, tongues of shadow flicking over the tawny curves and hollows of her body, licking the deep, darker places.

"There is no time for that. This is like a church," she whispered chidingly.

"Do you think she really knew we were coming?" I asked aloud.

"Of course! She is a great *curandera*!"

"Don't you think we should ask what this is going to cost?"

The woman came back into the room bearing in her hand a brown hen's egg.

"We are in luck. There was this lone egg on one of the nests. It is still warm. Here, take it in your hands, but do not drop it. It is the only one." She handed it to Lupe.

"My price is five hundred pesos."

I did some fast calculation. That was about forty-five dollars.

"Ask her if she will take dollars," I told Lupe.

"Yes. She says your dollars will be fine."

"She take American Express?

"*¿Que*"

"Nothing."

"Listen. If you are going to make jokes, please you go wait outside," Lupe scolded me.

"Sorry. I'll behave."

"OK." She turned to the *curandera*. "He is a fool sometimes, but he is not stupid or cruel," she explained in Spanish.

The woman nodded, scowling at me. "I can see what he is and what he is not. He is no longer a puppy, nor is he yet a guardian for you. I can tell you that you and this man will never marry and have children, though you both play with the idea in your hearts. It is not in the stars. Never. But, you will have happiness together for a little while. . . . Now, get up on the table."

Lupe got on the table.

"Lie on your back. Relax. Let me arrange you. Do not resist me. That is good."

She straightened Lupe's body so she lay face up like a corpse, even crossing her hands on her breasts. As she crossed her hands, she slipped something into each of Lupe's palms, closed her hands into fists, and told her to hold what she had put in them very tight.

"What is it?" Lupe asked.

"Herbs. Now don't talk again until I tell you."

The *curandera* placed candles on the table at Lupe's head and feet. She then poured some fragrant oil from a bottle that had once held tequila into her own large hands, warmed it between her palms and began to work it back through Lupe's hair until her thick reddish tresses were fanned around her face on the table. Slowly then she massaged Lupe's face and down over her breasts and body until Lupe gleamed with the oil, all the while chanting some sort of prayer which I could not understand except for the occasional mention of the mother of Jesus. It was in a dialect I had never heard before. It was hypnotic. I thought Lupe had gone to sleep or fallen into a trance. She seemed hardly to breathe. The smell of the oil was that of jasmine mixed with fresh herbs. The room was very warm and close. I felt it hard to breathe, yet I was not so uncomfortable I wanted to leave.

Lupe never looked more beautiful. All the tension had left her face. She looked young. Her body gleamed in the candle-light. Her hair shone. The curly thicket of her bush lifted above her thighs, now oily and glistening.

The old woman—was she old? Was she even a woman?—looked to be in a trance also as she stroked and chanted over Lupe.

I mopped sweat from my brow with the back of my arm. When she stroked Lupe's belly and framed her bush with her strong hands, I was sure she was a man. She massaged Lupe front and back and front again, chanting all the while. The last time she had Lupe hold the egg in her clasped hands on her breast.

Then she took the egg from her and began gently rubbing it

over her, forehead, face, neck, and shoulders and then over the rest of her body. She traced the perimeters of Lupe with the egg as if drawing a pattern of her, coming up between each leg to nestle the egg a second against the lips of Lupe's sex.

She then described a cross on her with the egg from her forehead to her cunt and from the tips of each shoulder. She brought the egg to rest finally on Lupe's navel.

Lupe let out a scream that made me jump to my feet. Her arms were flung outward rigidly; she became quiveringly rigid and seemed to rise off that damned table a few inches. Then she sat bolt upright and screamed again.

The *curandera* placed her palm flat on Lupe's brow, and the scream tailed off to almost a happy note as she sank slowly back to the table and went limp. There was a strange smile on her face I had never seen before nor would ever see again.

The room seemed suddenly cool as if someone had opened a door out back.

The *curandera*'s chant became a kind of song, almost a lullaby. The language, though, was nothing I had heard on this earth. It sounded a little bit like the song Bill Roth had once sang for us when he'd had some wine. It had been a Jewish holiday, I think, when he sang it. But this was not the language Bill had sung.

The *curandera* looked at me and said in Spanish, "She will be well now."

She took another bottle and a cloth and washed her hair and body with the stuff in it. It smelled like witch hazel. Lupe began to come around as the big woman washed her. She turned her head and smiled at me.

I thought it was a smile a happy woman might offer her husband after giving birth. I smiled back and winked.

"You may get dressed now," the *curandera* told her when she had finished.

"I feel so well!" Lupe exclaimed. "I feel pure as if I were newborn."

The witch placed the brown egg directly in the center of the table where Lupe had lain and busied herself with her bottles for a moment, her back to us.

"You look great." I smiled at Lupe.

"I am happy. I am content. It has been so long I had forgotten."

"Maybe I ought to get me one of those massages," I suggested.

Lupe repeated what I said.

"No. Not this night. I am tired now," the *curandera* replied seriously.

I took out my wallet and took out fifty dollars and gave it to Lupe to give to the woman.

She took the money and put it away somewhere in her clothes.

When we were ready to go, the *curandera* took the egg carefully and handed it to Lupe.

"You must take this now to the river immediately and throw it in the water. This is most important. It is the last thing of the cure."

"Yes, I understand," Lupe promised.

"Very well. Go now. Good night." She then looked at me and said something to Lupe which made her laugh.

When we were outside, I asked her what the woman had said.

"You will see, my darling," she told me in Spanish.

The lizard slipped around to the other side of the porch post. The eagle awakened and looked at us. The dog, which looked more like a coyote, silently accompanied us to the gate and stood aside when we went through. I turned to watch him walk back to the porch and lost him in a shadow, or blinked and he was gone. Probably he went under the ramshackle porch. It was a strange place.

Lupe took my arm; she was looking down at me. I had a hard-on as strong as the one I'd had when we got out of the truck. She laughed and squeezed it with the hand that did not hold the egg.

"Did she do that?" I wondered.

Lupe shrugged. "You will see. She has made a little present for you because you are such a good ally."

"I'll put her under contract," I joked.

"Come on, proud one, let's go to the river."

"I have always wished I could have a hard-on like this forever. Do you think . . . ?"

Lupe shrugged. "Who knows? But you will be an embarrassment in public, *hombre.* It could be a curse."

"We should go someplace and use the gift while it lasts," I suggested.

"To the river, *hombre.* I can repeat her gift for you. You think I am without powers?"

"Never have been."

"*Sí.* Now drive," she said.

We cut back toward the main part of town and took the road out along the riverbank. The bank was built high into a levee to keep the annual floods from the city. We followed the road until there were no more levees, until we could see the river on our right side and fields of cotton and corn along the other side. We drove until we could see the glow of McAllen, Texas, across the river ahead. The bank there looked gentle. There was a stand of cane along the other side of the road. I stopped the truck, and we got out.

"Halt!" I heard someone call.

And we were caught in the beams of several flashlights.

I could see the form of some men. The had guns. I thought we had been caught by the Mexican border patrol, the *federales.*

They cut off their lights. We could not see anything then. Someone grabbed both my arms behind my back.

"*¿Que pasa?*" I demanded.

"Shut up, we will ask the questions!" someone in front of me informed me and jabbed in the belly with the muzzle of a submachine gun.

"Tell them what we are doing," I told Lupe.

"Don't break my egg!" she was screaming at someone in Spanish.

"What are you doing out here?" the man with the gun in my belly demanded.

"We have come to effect a cure by throwing this egg into the river," Lupe explained angrily. "There is no law against that."

"We will decide that," the *honcho* informed her.

My eyes were beginning to become accustomed to the dark. Across the river I could see some fellows having a swim near the far bank. They were sporting around, but not too exuberantly.

"Who sent you here?" a taller man, standing back, asked.

"The *curandera*," Lupe said. "I must throw this egg into the river. Are you police?"

"I will ask the questions. Let me see that egg."

"No. You can look at it only."

"Tell us about this *curandera*."

"We should just kill them and be done with it," the one with a gun in my belly suggested in Spanish.

"That is possible," the *honcho* agreed.

"Why do you want to kill us? We have done nothing to you. If you are bandits, we do not care. We have our own business."

"What is your business?"

"I told you. I must throw this egg in the river. It was only by luck that the *curandera* had this last fresh brown egg with which to cleanse me. I was dying. She saved my life."

"If we kill you, woman, she has saved you nothing," the tough ass suggested.

"Let us go. We will cause you no harm. We have not seen you."

"I think that is stupid," the one with the gun on me said.

I knew there were gangs of burglars who swam the river and hit the homes on the other side. They were thought to be young boys, some as young as seven years old, urchins from Matamoros and Reynosa. These guys were not urchins. A Mexican-American deputy sheriff called by everyone the Catcher had shot and killed seven boys on the riverbank the year before as they were "trying to escape" as an example to the others across the river. That had not stopped the break-ins, however. And the people were not happy about his meth-od, as none of the boys had been armed, though there was an old pistol found near one of the boys. They now called the deputy Three-Gun, meaning he carried two guns for himself and an old gun to throw down to prove self-defense.

These bastards were not the kids who robbed homes. I did not know what the hell they were.

"How do we know that egg is not full of poison?" someone of them asked.

"Only the poisons of my spirit," Lupe answered.

"Let's see." The one nearest her cracked the egg in her palm with the barrel of his gun.

The putrid odor of a rotten egg was overwhelming. The young man jumped back.

"Jesus Christ!"

"You said that was a fresh egg!" the *honcho* accused her.

"Yes! Fresh from the nest!"

"It could be a poison," the one prodding me with the gun insisted. "It could be done like that."

The one in the back who ran the show looked at the river. I followed his gaze. The boys who had been swimming had got-ten out. I saw the glint of a car's windshield on the road over there. A little farther along it clipped on its lights.

"Let them go," he suddenly ordered.

"OK. Get in your truck and turn around and go back the way you came. If we see you again, you will be dead," the one with the gun told us.

"It is bad luck if I do not throw the egg in the river," Lupe insisted, trying to cradle the putrid liquid in her two hands.

"If you put that in the water here, you are dead, woman, and so is your *gringo* friend," the *honcho* told her.

"Come on, don't argue," I told her.

"But the cure is broken."

"No. It's OK. Come on."

I led her to the truck. She still tried to keep the stinking stuff from falling through her fingers.

We turned around and drove back the way we had come. The smell of that rotten egg was gagging me.

"She said it was fresh," I observed. I was sure it had been a trick. She had brought a ripe egg to begin with. I wondered what would have happened if Lupe had brought her own fresh egg. The witch would have probably substituted a rotten one.

When we had gone a mile or so, Lupe said, "Please, Johnny, let's stop here and put this in the river." I looked behind us, there was no one following us.

"OK." Anything to get rid of that smell.

I stopped. We got out and went down the bank. I had to help her down to the water where she knelt in the mud and washed her hands in the water.

"OK?"

"I don't know, Johnny. I am worried. We must go back and speak with the *curandera*."

"It's OK. You got most of it in the water." I was tired of the whole damn thing. I did not like getting shot at or having some Mexican punk stick a gun in my stomach and want to kill me.

"No! I must ask her. If you won't take me, let me go by myself."

"All right. I'll take you."

The little house was dark. The dog that had been so quiet barked like hell at us.

Lupe called to the woman inside until there was a light lit.

"Be quiet!" the woman commanded. "What is the trouble? I have gone to bed."

Lupe told her about the egg being broken.

"That is not good," the *curandera* said. "You should have been more careful."

"It was not our fault. Can you do something?"

"Yes, of course. But you were very foolish. You will have to pay two hundred pesos. I will have to work again this night, and I am tired now."

"Give me some money, Johnny."

I thought it was a lot of shit, but I gave her two tens.

The old woman spoke to her dog, and he let Lupe come into the gate. She gave the woman the money. The woman drew her inside. When she came out in about ten minutes, she had a greasy red cross on her forehead and smelled of rosemary and thyme.

"What did she do?" I asked when we were driving away once more.

"She said as I got most of the egg into the river, it will be well. That the evil inside the egg touched me again, she had to clean my hands."

She showed me her palms. There were red crosses in both, like the one on her forehead, and in each were some crushed herbal powder.

"I must sleep Johnny. You must not touch me. If, when I awaken, I feel well, it will be as it was before."

"What do you mean touch you?"

"You must do nothing with me. We must do nothing. She says if you try, you will not be able to do nothing anyway. I must sleep in the bed alone until I feel as well as I did. I can hardly keep my eyes open. Find us a place, Johnny."

I'd had enough of witchcraft for one night and said so.

"Please, Johnny. This is a wonderful woman."

"I don't even think she is a woman," I confessed.

"It does not matter. Do as she says."

"What the hell was that language she was speaking?"

"Nyrait. It is an Indian language of that people. There are not many of them left. They are very old and very mysterious. Very wise. They came from an ancient land before there were great oceans. Maybe they are the people of Moses."

"Moses! He was an Indian?"

"Maybe. Their language is very old. Maybe it is the language of Moses. Maybe he had another name. They say their language comes from another land far across the sea that was once not across the sea, but the land divided."

Who the hell really knew about the Mexicans? Where did the *china poblana* come from—the Chinese shirt that was the national costume of Mexico? There was no record of the Chinese having come there, but they must have, someone earlier that became the Chinese. The Koreans were once the greatest sailors on earth. The clay artifacts on the west coast of Africa were identical in material and often in subject to those of pre-Columbian South America. The same kind of clay. I had read about it. The language the *curandera* had chanted had sounded a lot like the song Bill Roth had sung, not the same, but close.

"Hurry, find us a place for me to sleep," Lupe said.

When we arrived in the square, people were setting up booths for a carnival. Charro Days commenced the next day on both sides of the river, the local Lenten equivalent of Mardi Gras. I parked in front of the hotel just off the square and rented us a room. I went back out and got Lupe and helped her inside. The clerk was curious when he saw she had the red cross on her forehead, but he said nothing.

"She has been to a *curandera*," I explained to him in English.

"We do not want any trouble here," he told me unsympathetically.

"There will be no trouble. She must rest. Bring us a bottle of water."

I had to undress her and help her into the bed lest she drop the herbs she clenched in her fists. There was only the one bed, so I sat up in the chair with my feet in the shuttered window and drank water and smoked and finally fell asleep.

I dreamed of worlds splitting and Jewish Indians and of Chelo Cavazos being an Aztec or Toltec princess in some naked cannibal rite. She was taken to the top of a pyramid and her throat slit on a sacrifical stone. Many throats were slit. I was there, but I could do nothing. Then an old priest came from the temple atop the pyramid dressed in Chelo's flayed skin. It did not fit him well. It was too short, and he had stretched her out of shape, cuts had to be made in her sides for it to fit, yet it was unmistakably Chelo, complete with her hair, breasts, pubes.

There was bright sunlight. A carnival atmosphere. I broke from the crowd as the parade of priests came down the long avenue. People clutched at me and scolded me, but they did not stop me. I ran and embraced the priest in the young girl's skin. Out of the empty eye sockets gleamed a pair of familiar eyes, severe, yet merry. I kissed her dead lips passionately. I was aroused and stronger than the priest, though he was stronger than hell, and bore him down onto the brick street.

The priest laughed and spread his legs. He moved like a woman to receive me. I felt my cock enter the lifeless lips of Chelo's virgin vagina. Then I looked and saw a large dark cock coming from it, sticking out rigidly from her opening.

"*Ai*, fuck me well, my friend," the voice of Ezequiel Cavazos mocked me from inside his daughter's skin.

I jumped up. Ezequiel was *in* there. I hated him and did not understand him.

"It is all right, Johnny. I am in charge here. It is just a parade," he told me.

He took my arm and had me strut along beside him. Chelo's face fitted his own. It was made up with brightly rouged lips and spots of color on her cheeks like a doll, a whore of a doll. From the eye sockets glinted Ezequiel's merry old yellowed eyes.

I awoke in the chair. I must have cried out, for Lupe came from the shower, drying herself with a towel, and asked, "What is it?"

"I had a bad dream," I explained, rubbing the back of my neck where it had hung over the back of the chair.

She began to rub my neck.

It was morning. The heat was trying to invade our shuttered room.

"I feel well, Johnny. I feel really very well."

"That's good."

There was the sound of the carnival getting started outside. Firecrackers were popping all around the square.

"You can touch me now," she offered and lifted her lips to be kissed.

I didn't feel like it. She kissed me.

"You don't have to do nothing. I will do everything."

"What?"

She touched my cock. It was hard as it had been the night before. I hadn't been aware of it. I felt groggy, and my head ached.

"Take off your clothes and lie on the bed. I will make you feel well."

I looked around the room and realized where we were and how we had gotten there.

"Do it."

I wanted to be naked and lie on the bed. It looked cool and inviting, the sheets barely rumpled where Lupe had slept. The bed and the room smelled faintly of herbs and ourselves.

I stretched full length on the bed. It felt wonderful. My cock stood up like a little pole. But it was unimportant to me. I just felt good lying there.

Lupe began to kiss me slowly all over, licking my skin, sucking each of my fingers, licking my cock and balls like a loving cat, making loving sounds in her throat. I felt detached, cool, watching her. She became very aroused. Her face was flushed. I put out my hand to touch her.

"No. Do nothing. Just let me make you feel well. Please."

She sucked me for a long time as if taking sustenance from me. Then she got astride me and carefully introduced my cock into herself. It felt beautiful. I do not think I have ever been so hard. It felt permanent.

She rose and sank on me and told me she loved me and came very big. She continued, working all around on top of me, facing my toes. I stroked her back and buttocks, and she came again. She intensified her movements, fucking like a

crazy woman. The sweat poured from her soft, round body.
Her face looked as it had when she was on the table at the *curandera*'s, as if she were hearing something inside her head.
Facing me, she came again. Still I did not come. She collapsed on my chest, her legs spanning my body, squeezing my
sides.

"You will kill me," she said.

"It feels like it will stay forever," I told her.

"It has never been with no man like this," she said. "It is the
curandera's gift to you because you are so good to me, so
patient with me. Fuck me to death if you like, Johnny. I am
happy."

I rolled her over and fucked her until I was tired but still
could not come. The bed was wet with our sweat.

"No! Don't stop!" she insisted.

I took a new breath and purchase and felt I was losing myself in her. I was blind, or rather could see her only through a
tunnel of vision.

She kissed me as if to suck the breath from me, and I felt
her gripping me inside herself. I had never felt so part of
another in my life.

"Come with me, Johnny. I am going to come. Come with
me!"

"Yes!"

"*GOD!*" I cried as we came.

"Yes! Yes! *OH, YES!*" she cried back.

And I was happy! I was laughing and crying, too. I could
hear her voice saying in my head 'Jes! OH, JES!' It was funny
and beautiful. I loved her, but not even *that* was important.
The main thing was unspeakable, I think. Not unspeakably
bad. Just nothing no one had ever put word to. Nor did I want
to try.

"Oh, Jes!" I mocked her.

We laughed and rolled about the soggy bed happily.

"You like the *curandera*'s gift?"

"Jes."

"You want to hear how you sound when you speak Spanish?"

She gave me a hilarious example of my Spanish.

We kissed and rolled about and stretched and slept an hour or so in each other's arms.

I awoke and kissed her forehead lightly and started to get up to take a shower. She held me fast long enough to tell me, "That is the best love I have ever had, Johnny. In all my life, that is the best. I think it is the best I will ever have."

"Me too," I said.

"It is enough to have that once."

"Every day would kill you," I agreed.

"Once in a while, though, it would be nice," she said thoughtfully.

"Once in a while would be great."

"I will stay with you, if you like," she said.

I did not reply immediately. I studied her. I would like her to stay with me, yet I was not sure. There was something that worried me I could not put my finger on.

She wiped a frown from my brow.

"I said nothing. Do not trouble yourself. I too felt worried when I spoke. If it will be, it will be. I know you love me. I love you. I will not say such a thing again."

We got up and went to the shower, happily, she fooling around, leading me by my cock which now had given up the *curandera*'s gift and seemed the same fellow I had known since I was aware enough to find it with my hand.

We washed each other and were eager to go eat and join the carnival.

I knew we would never stay together. I had known it when we had been as close as we could get. It was all right. It was also a little sad and would always be a little sad, for I would have liked to have been with her always.

I held her close under the shower and kissed her as the water ran into our mouths.

"I love you as much as I can love, Lupe. Maybe I cannot love enough, anyone."

"No! You love more than any man I know. You love me perfect, Johnny. Do not worry about it. Please. You love big, Johnny. If you were not so strong, your love would kill you."

"Why are you crying?"

"I am happy."

She was a little sad, too. It was nothing we could ever talk about.

We were very nice to each other. In everything we did, we liked each other so much each touch, move, look, was a pleasure to make us smile or laugh or just look quietly together at something, holding hands or standing with our arms around each other's waist.

It must be what really being married is like. Probably nothing that could ever last, though. I wonder?

CHAPTER FIFTEEN

It was a little late to be having breakfast and too early to be ordering lunch. The waiter with a red sash wrapped around his negligible middle was anxious to get about whatever else he had to do between breakfast and lunch. I contemplated cracking his snakelike spine across one knee until he agreed to bring us *huevos rancheros,* with a side order of venison for myself, and two beers. We wanted the beers right now.

I was starved. Lupe teased me about my appetite after our prolonged exertions upstairs.

"But, my darling, I do *everything* for you. I am not so hungry."

"*You* say! It's draining for a man," I complained.

"Oh, the poor man," she teased.

The dining room was shuttered and cool. The sounds of the carnival outside in the streets were a muted, yet a quickening insistence to eat and get out into the streets.

In one corner of the room at a large table were eight people dawdling over coffee, oblivious to the carnival atmosphere outside. I recognized Patricia Quinn, the *torera* from Texas, with her retinue.

In the lobby were bullfight posters for the *corrida* the next day. Pat Quinn was on the card for the tourists, but the other two could be good: Jalisco Huerta and his kid brother Jaime.

"You like her?" Lupe asked when I had stared at Pat Quinn a bit too long.

"She sort of fascinates me. I got drunked up one night and

went with Ezequiel's crazy son-in-law, Small Billy Champion, and his gang over across the river to bother the cattle in the stockyards. It takes some kind of *cojones* to get in and torment cattle that have horns on their heads. I mean, even if you are a lousy bullfighter like Small Billy, you can get hooked."

In fact, Small Billy looked as if he would make a career out of getting gored before he picked up enough style to get paid for his work.

"She looks as if she has *muchos cojones*," Lupe said cattily.

"I don't know, she looks pretty good."

She did look a bit leathery. And she had acquired a studied calm and Mexican manner that those serious about troubling bulls all seemed to have. Even sitting at the table, she seemed to believe there was a special beam of light shining from the heavens upon her severely pulled-back brownish hair. There was a pretty, exaggeratedly feminine blond young woman beside her at the table who was both solicitous of the other woman, yet calculatedly aloof of her and of all the others at the table. The others were three young men in cheap light jackets and trousers, each as slender as our waiter, their long hair combed so agonizingly it set your teeth on edge to look at them. There was a pudgy middle-aged man, smoking a cigar who might have been her manager. Beside him sat a very pretty young Mexican woman who looked like a high-class big-city whore, who was bored with the whole thing. She scooched down in her chair with her head on the back of it and closed her eyes at the ceiling. The other man was a fat little *banderillero*, very famous in Mexico, very good, who always wore a white and black suit of lights in the ring. I always wanted to remember his name and never could. Maybe it is Sánchez. I know that at about every bullfight I went to, he was there, doing a good day's work, taking no great risks, but not fucking off either. Maybe his name is González. He was over forty, probably nearer to fifty. He was the real one of the bunch as far as I was concerned.

We decided to get tickets for the bullfight.

The waiter brought our beers. Lupe had a small bottle of Superior Corona, a very light beer in a clear bottle that seemed the favorite of women and *maricones*. I dipped eagerly into a cold glass of Bohemia ale, sharp and clean, with a lot of beer in it. With the *huevos* and venison that soon arrived it was one of the best late breakfasts on earth. After fucking a woman you really like, as much as you really want to fuck her, a breakfast like that could make any old Saturday one of life's last great memories. And there was a carnival waiting just outside. I truly did not want for a thing, or desire to be anywhere else, or desire to be anyone else, not even for a minute.

"I am happy," I told Lupe, taking her hand and squeezing it.

"I am happy too, Juanito." She kissed me, and everyone at the table in the corner of the room turned to look.

I lifted my glass to them all and called, "Good luck," thinking honestly: *I got mine!*

They turned back to their table in a snooty way, so fucking wrapped up in themselves. Only the old *banderillero* dipped his head and lifted his coffee an inch and smiled at us, glancing with appreciation at Lupe's legs beneath the table as well as everything she displayed above it .

"He knows where the good is at," I told Lupe.

"There are some men who do," she said. "most do not. Never."

"That's why you like me?"

"That is why I love you. You really like a woman. That is a rare thing, my darling. I think when you are old, you will still be that way. So, then, you will never really be too old."

"You think I will ever be old, Lupe?"

"I don't know." She turned suddenly said. "I will never be, I don't think."

"Fuck this talk. It is fiesta time down South. And in my heart." I clinked her glass.

She laughed. "To *our* fiesta! Break the clocks!"

I ripped off my old wristwatch, threw it on the floor, and stomped it to death with my heel.

"You are crazy!"

"It wasn't much of a watch. Never was."

She leaned over and grabbed a handful of my hair and shook my head roughly.

"*I love you!*" she hissed as if it were a challenge. "You fill my heart with . . . *todo*! *Todo,* Johnny."

"Eat your eggs. Or I will rape you on this table."

"Do it!"

"I'm bragging. I don't know *when* I can ever screw again."

"Screw? I never like that word." She thought. "Yes. I like it now. This one day. You will screw me again soon. You will see." She leaned very near. Her mouth was against my ear. Her hand stole into my lap. "Screw me, Johnny. I love for you to screw me. Screw me."

I caught her hand under the table.

"You know, I think you are right."

"Of course!" She sat back happily. "Eat your eggs.

"*Mira!* " she said. "There is your friend Bill." She made his name sound like "Beel."

Bill Roth, the editor of the Brownsville *Herald,* a photographer, and the man who translated and edited the paper's Spanish language edition came into the dining room. The Spanish editor was a tiny middle-aged man who wore thick glasses. The photographer was a young Okie-looking kid under a crew cut, wearing a sport shirt. Bill wore a *guayabera* shirt, a Mexican straw hat, a bandanna around his neck, and a *bota* full of red wine slung over one shoulder. He was ready for the carnival. All the men wore small beards. In Brownsville all men who did not grow a beard for the fiesta were put in a jail on the street until they paid a fine. Bill looked like the cartoon character "Gordo," and a lot of Mexicans dubbed him that. I waved, and he stopped at our table.

"I forgot about the fiesta," I said, shaking his pudgy hand, stroking my shaved jaw.

He was looking at me strangely, looked at Lupe, and nodded and said hello.

"You made the morning's paper," he said.

"Um. Seriously?"

He shrugged. "Her old man is charging you with abduction, though no one has absolutely identified you."

Evidently the guys I was at the hospital with had copped a mope.

"He don't abduct me!" Lupe protested. "He save me. I ran away by myself."

"I'm sure. It was a good story, though." He grinned.

"They looking for me?" I asked.

"Not seriously. If her old man finds you, he will shoot you, probably. Otherwise, it's fiesta. No one takes abducted wives very seriously during fiesta. Have a nice time. You too, honey," he told Lupe.

"Thank you. You have a nice time, too."

"I do! I do!" Bill vowed. "Now we have to see Miss Patricia Quinn."

He went over and shook hands with her and the man I took to be her manager. One of the young men ran to fetch drinks for the table. Bill sat next to Pat and asked her questions. She answered the questions in a bored, serious way. She did not seem to have much of a sense of humor.

"You think she and that other one are—" Lupe crossed her first two fingers on her right hand, whispering meaningfully to me.

"I don't know. I heard she likes men."

"I don't think so," Lupe decided, staring hard at the lady bullfighter. "I think she likes that other woman."

"That's slander. You don't know." Lupe always wondered that about other women who seemed a touch less feminine than herself.

"Maybe she likes both," she suggested.

"Looks to me like she likes herself more than either."

"*¡Si!* OK."

After taking a few pictures to loosen the serious young woman up, Bill got her to sit on the front of the table while her manager sent one of the boys to get a poster to pin on the wall behind. She was wearing a man's white silk shirt, open low over nice pert breasts and a wide chamois-colored skirt that buttoned down the front, with her waist cinched in a handmade burro's girth that had been decorated with colorful wooden beads for a belt.

Bill got her to show a bit of leg above her knees. She had strong, pretty legs.

Then she unbuttoned a couple more buttons of her skirt and hiked it up to show him the deep horn wounds on her thighs. There was one deep scar on her inner thigh that ran up into her crotch. She was clinical about the wounds, touching the big one with the tips of her fingers. You could see the leg band of her white panties and a few dark hairs where the scar disappeared upward.

Lupe flinched.

"Jesus, you think a horn went into her?"

I felt a rush of desire watching the young woman detail her wounds. I envied the man who would lie between those scarred thighs. It was a feeling that I felt when watching a good bullfight.

"Would you like to sleep with her?" Lupe asked me softly, but wanting an answer.

"Maybe once," I replied honestly.

"Twice. That would be enough for you," Lupe agreed, knowing more about my honesty than I do.

"Would you like to sleep with her?" it suddenly occurred to me to ask.

"What? *Me*? Are you crazy? What you think I am?

I shrugged.

"Ha! You get drunk on three beers? Let's go now."

We'd had two beers with our food, and Bill had sent another round over. He always did that. I *was* beginning to feel a nice little buzz. I had been empty when I drank the first, and three Mexican beers can just begin to take hold with me.

I think the beers had buzzed Lupe, too. In the lobby she stopped me long enough to ask seriously, "You think I like women?"

"No."

"I never do that, Johnny. You better believe it."

"I believe it." I put my arm around her. But her making such a big deal out of what I had asked depressed me a bit.

"Come on. It's fiesta!" I encouraged.

"OK. I forgive you."

I laughed. Lupe was always forgiving me of things for which I felt no repentence.

"*Mamacita.*" I gave her a slap on her big, bouncing can. When I fucked her from the back, I slapped against her big *nalgas* so it sounded like a seal clapping for a fish. The thought cheered me a lot.

I had to get one of those wine bags full of raw red wine. By the time we were half around the square I could drink from it at arm's length without getting a lot on my shirt.

Fuck the shirt! I bought a handsome light blue *guayabera* from a booth and stuck it under my arm in its cellophane wrapper for later. We bought flat-topped Mexican straw hats that were like the black felt Spanish felt hat Pat Quinn always wore in the bullring and laughed happily at each other under the brims.

There were booths with all kinds of games of chance around the square and spilling up all the side streets. There were several mariachi bands sweating away in heavy wool *charro* suits under enormous sombreros on every corner. Urchins darted about, tossing firecrackers under everyone's feet.

"You like a nice young girl, *gringo?*" an urchin upped to me to inquire.

"What do you think, *hijo?*" I demanded, indicating the full length of Lupe with a gallant sweep of my hand.

The kid shrugged and looked at the woman, making a face of a little old man, bobbing his head crosswise on his dirty little neck—*Si! Si! Si!*—

"OK *Cuánto?* How much you say?" he asked me.

He was only about six or seven.

Lupe roared and tousled his straight Indian hair. He wrapped both arms around her and joggled her ass with his hands, then darted off in the crowd calling back some obscene vow, while offering her his little prick in his faded raggedy blue shorts.

"Some kids." I grinned.

"They are wonderful, you know?"

"Yes."

We stopped to watch a dancing bear in the center of where a street came into the square. He danced to the music of a drum banged by a small boy and the sound of a wooden flute played by his trainer with one hand as the man waltzed around with the bear, which he controlled by strings threaded through the animals' nose and ears.

As we watched, an urchin grabbed the packet containing my new shirt and tried to dodge away in the crowd. I broke after him and snagged him by the tail of his tattered undershirt while a very wide old woman stepped stoically between us, nudging me backward with placid bumps of her broad hips as I struggled to hang onto the kid. It was like holding a wildcat around the trunk of a living, obstructive tree. Finally I slid around the woman and got back my shirt as the little bastard screamed to the world I was a thief and the offspring of a mating between a whore and burro. If he had stopped, I would have given him some change because it was fiesta and I admired his spirit, if not his footwork. The old woman was not pleased I had won back my shirt.

"*Gracias,*" I told her and offered her a drink from the wine skin.

She turned away from me as if I were an object, to watch the bear. That bear would not have been in it with *her.*

"Did you see that?" I asked Lupe when I found her again in the crowd.

"Yes. It was very funny."

"That old woman has an ass like iron."

"Mine is black and blue— *Ai! Cabrón!*" She shouted at a blank-faced man in a lousy suit that matched his silly little mustache and asshole haircut, as he slipped away in the press around us. She rubbed her left buttock. "It is not public property?" she protested. "Walk close behind me," she instructed me.

"This close enough?"

"Yes. Just so I know it is you. *Ai!*"

"What?"

"That old one got me in the front. Let's get out of here."

We went into the New Houston on the other side of the square. People were three deep at the bar. The floor was slick with beer, wine, and tequila. A mariachi band was trapped in one corner with no hope of escaping. To make their captivity more pleasurable, people forced drink upon them and stuffed money in the holes of their instruments. A girl in a wide, flounced, multicolored skirt and off-the-shoulder blouse and a young man were dancing a folk dance on one of the tables, with a red handkerchief held in their teeth.

We squeezed into a booth with the reporter from the *Herald* whose name sounded like Crumbie or Crumpie, his blond German wife, Erica, and the prosperous young owner of a shrimp company and his wife, a tall, handsome, but nervous woman from the East, with very pretty chestnut-colored hair. She did not like our crowding in with them very much. I overlooked that. I knew Crumbie was not going to object to anything. And I knew the snooty woman's husband.

"When you coming to work for us?" he wanted to know. "We are getting a reefer ship in a couple of months. You can make a lot more than you are making, stay out forever if you want."

"I don't want to stay out forever." I smiled. "It feels so good to get back in."

"It's the way it's going to go, Johnny. You guys might as well face it."

"I'll face it when I have to."

Erica was happy to see us.

"I read about you in the paper today. He stole this lady from her husband last night. It is very romantic, yes?" she asked the other woman.

"I didn't steal her from anybody," I protested. "He was trying to have her put away as crazy or something. She didn't want to go."

"I think it is beautiful!" Erica assured us, squeezing both my arm and Lupe's with her tan moist hands.

They'd all had several drinks.

Crumpie, who asked us to call him Bob though everyone else at the table called him Robert, his wife pronouncing it with a very long *O*, had a copy of the morning's *Herald* with him, it turned out.

Lupe and I read of her escape. It was on the front page, but it was not much of a story. My name was not used.

"Someone, reportedly a shrimper and possibly a man the woman knew, raced from the hospital emergency entrance with her and sped away with her in a pickup truck. The woman's husband, a U.S. border patrolman, fired two shots at the fleeing truck from his service revolver." . . . And so on.

"What's he say about me?" Lupe wanted to know.

"Aw, nothing."

"Tell me."

"He says you have been acting strangely for a while, crap like that."

"I *was* crazy!" she told everyone at the table. "I was dying, only no one believes me but Johnny. My husband won't let me see this wonderful *curandera*. She drove away death, and saves my life."

"He mentions about you wanting to see the *curandera*," Crumbie told her.

"Then the Mexican people will understand," Lupe said.

"What was it like?" the other woman, called Susan, asked.

"Oh, it was wonderful. She cleaned me with an egg—" She stopped. "No. I don't want to talk about it now."

The woman shrugged as if she really didn't want to know anyway. She craned around, looking over the heads of everyone in the booth.

Fuck her, I thought.

"Oh! That is a samba! Dance with me," Erica commanded, reaching for my hand.

"I can't dance no samba."

"I will teach you. In Germany, everyone dances the samba."

She hauled me through the crowd onto the tiny area that had never been a dance floor in the New Houston and proceeded with smiles and German assurance to turn it into one for us. When it was clear to all there I was never gaited to samba, she gave up and moved close simply to dance. At that point the spectators lost interest in us. We were left close together, more just moving against each other in the crowd. The blond young woman's breath smelled of sour wine and beer. She had gotten very tanned, tanned down to where the white globes of her breasts peeked from her low-necked crisp little pink and white dress.

"You are very hard," she breathed in my face.

"What?"

She giggled. "I mean your muscles." She said "musscalls." "You must work very hard."

"Not all that hard. You are very tanned."

"I don't work at all. I am so boring. I go to the beach and lie down in the sun . . . alone."

"Alone?"

"Roobert, he works all the time. He works sixty hours a week. And that paper does not pay so much money. I tell him he is crazy."

"When he could be lying in the sun with you? You bet."

"I am alone too much. You come swim with me?"

"Sure."

"I mean it!" she insisted, her mouth close to mine, those blue northern lake eyes drooping seductively as she was able.

She moved her belly gently back and forth against me. "I will do everything with you. You are so *hard*."

"Roobert isn't so hard?"

"He is soft like a big woman. I don't know why I marry him. He was an officer in the American Army, you know? he was with Special Services when I meet him. A first lieutenant. We were better off in the Army. Everyone of my friends tells me not to marry with him. I think I will divorce soon."

"You like to do everything, do you?"

"Yes. I like very much . . . everything. Roobert is not . . . with it!"

"Too bad."

"Yes. I had a lover, hard like you, young, and very cruel with me. He made me do crazy things. I can't tell you such things he made me do."

"But you liked it?"

"I love him. I love what he makes me do, it don't matter how dirty. He own me. I was crazy. So sad. I cry all the time. It was wonderful."

"Maybe I would not be mean enough. I'm a pretty gentle fella."

"Then I would make you crazy so you are not so gentle. Roobert, he is too gentle with me."

She was drunk and not very light on her feet to begin with. When a Mexican hat dance began, I hauled her back to the booth, but not before we had to drink with a bunch of Mexican men who had fallen in love with Erica's blond hair.

We were in the booth which was covered with all sorts of bottles when Pete Gatliff and big Hobie Glass stumbled in. Pete's ear was bound back onto his head under a big, now dirty bandage that went around his head and beneath his chin.

They saw me, and we had company.

Pete was able to squeeze in, but Hobie had to wait until a Mexican got off a chair to take it. No ten Mexicans were going to get Hobie off a chair. They stood back and glowered and said things about us all and looked peeved as hell. I kept one eye on them in case they hit Hobie over the head with something, and the big man ordered another round for us.

"Sonofabitch!" Pete squealed. "You took off and left me and ole Slocum on the operating table. When we came out, Charles told us what you done and we went and got drunk and been out to Boystown all night. They elected Hobie mayor or some damn thing. Show 'em your sash."

Hobie opened his shirt and across his massive hairy chest and belly was a green, yellow and red banner proclaiming THE KING OF TAMAULIPAS , in Spanish.

"Where did you get that?" I asked.

"Off the fucking king himself."

"He didn't want it anymore?"

"Didn't seem like. I carried him around with me for a while. Reckon he thought I'd earned it."

Pete laughed. "Carried is right. He picked up this little fella and stuffed him under one arm and kept petting his head like he was a pup."

"I got right fond of him."

"Wanted to *keep* him. I mean Hobie wouldn't let the guy go! Finally took the sash to let him go."

"Bands followed us around. Took the fella with me in to see the girls. I think he had a real good time in all."

"All except the carrying. I don't think he liked that a whole lot, Hobie."

"He didn't complain a lot, I didn't notice. Real cute little fella."

"Didn't try to escape while you were with a girl?" I wondered.

"Nope. Hung right onto him with one hand."

"My God," the shrimp company man's wife, Susan, said.

"To the King of Tamaulipas!" Erica slurred.

"*El rey!* " Lupe cheered.

We all drank.

Hobie was staring at Erica.

"Ain't she pretty?" Pete asked him.

Hobie had evidently seen nothing in this world prettier, though in his condition he more glowered at her than glowed. She cocked her head at him and smiled, pouted, tried several expressions, yet he continued to glower as if eyes had been set into a boulder. Erica blushed and giggled a little.

"I think that is his way of showing you he likes you," I suggested.

"You are sure?" she asked.

"I hope so," Susan put in. "If those are the eyes of love, I would hate to get him mad at me."

"To the king!" Hobie suddenly bellowed drunkenly. He drank to himself.

I hadn't know he was that drunk.

"He's pretty drunk," Pete told me.

"Looks like," I agreed.

A conga line which had started somewhere snaked into the café and made its way about, hauling recruits into its ranks. Hands offered us wine. Hands sprayed us with ether from spray cans. Hands hauled us up and into the conga line as it snaked its way out the door as the tail was still coming in. We danced out into the street.

The shrimp company man and his wife led our group, followed by Robert and Erica with huge Hobie behind her, his big meat hooks locked firmly onto her wide German hips, Lupe, me, a Mexican woman who kept giggling and trying to tickle me in the ribs and who bounced against me pneumatically every time the line accordioned, Pete, then half the town.

We snaked and danced and drank our way through the carnival booths in the *zocalo*. I took the new shirt from inside the one I wore and changed shirts as we danced. The pneumatic woman behind was very helpful. I left the new shirt open to catch the breeze.

Someone snatched my new hat, so I snatched a huge sombrero off the head of a *charro* in exchange. He did not like that, but he was soon left behind. I would have fought to keep that great new broad-brimmed hat. It was a great hat. Lupe turned and laughed and tried to kiss me.

Whatever they were squirting on us from those cans was making everyone giggle a lot.

The line was broken and re-formed. People stumbled and fell; some lay and were congaed over.

We became entangled with another line or the tail of our own, a couple of fights broke out, but the line absorbed all.

A pretty, natural blond American girl appeared naked on the balcony of a hotel one story up, and a pack of gallants gathered below urging her to leap into their arms. She leaped. And a new line was formed with the naked girl at its head. Someone plunked a beautiful sombrero on her head.

When we snaked past the police station and the nearby cathedral, the large iron-studded doors of which were locked and barred within, I saw Hobie hoist Erica over one shoulder and start to run off with her.

She called, *"Roobert! Roobert!"*

But Robert could not make his way through the crowd as well as Hobie. Hobie made his way like a tank. Then it was carnival, and citizens would impede the course of anyone trying to collect a woman being carried away. I also saw the dirty bandage of Pete's head making its way through the crowd in Hobie's wake. When we could, the remainder of our little band got free of the conga line and formed on the church steps. There were handwritten banns posted on the big doors.

"Where would he go?" Robert wanted to know.

I scanned the crowds that filled all the streets back to where they became dark.

"Does he have a car?" the other man asked.

"He's got a truck," I said, trying to think what Hobie might do.

"Will he do anything to her?" Susan wondered anxiously.

I shrugged. Who knew what Hobie would do? Drunk, I have seen him tip over a small car, eat a Pilsner glass, throw a man through a wooden wall, and boost an old white horse up three flights of stairs in the house of a man against whom he held some nebulous grudge, leaving the animal up there for the police and man to remove. He did thirty days in the county slammer for that one after the owner of the poor animal withdrew his charges of horse theft.

I have seen Hobie eat two entire turkeys and dine on a whole ham as if it were a pig's foot.

"He has curious large appetites," I said.

"Let's report this to the police," she suggested.

"No. No, that is not a good idea," I assured her. "The constabulary isn't going to be interested in it. You are just going to be wasting your time."

"We have to do *something!*"

"We have to start looking for her," the woman's husband suggested.

"But where?" Robert wondered.

"We better split up," the other man suggested.

"That's a good idea," Lupe agreed.

The party had become no fun. She was ready to move on.

So was I.

"Do you think he would take her out to Boystown?" Robert asked. "She has always wanted me to take her there."

"He might then," I suggested.

"We will look there. You try to see if you can find them in town."

"OK."

"If he does anything to her . . ." he told me menacingly, taking hold of my open shirt.

"Tell *him* . . *compadre*. Turn loose my shirt."

"He came over because you were at our table," Susan testified.

"He came to Mexico because it was here. She was looking to be carried off sooner or later. Fuck it."

"What do you mean?" Robert grabbed my shirt again.

"Oh, go to hell, Robert." I removed his hand from my shirt rather forcibly.

"Come on, Robert." Susan tugged him away. "Let's find Erica before that scum hurts her."

"Forget them," Lupe consoled me, though I felt no need of consolation.

But I smiled. It was nice to be consoled anyway. Her hand was on my bare chest, her tousled hair on my shoulder. We kissed passionately on the church steps.

"If I had pencil and paper, I would add our names to those on this door," I told her.

"I love you, Johnny," she told me.

We got invited to a party that took up an entire floor of the hotel. There was most of an orchestera there and mariachis, pretty women and rich men and poor men and hustlers pocketing everything that was loose. Someone had brought a live burro up there. Men dressed as *charros* and revolutionaries wore loaded *pistoles* which they could not resist firing now and then, usually out the window skyward, but they were getting less religious about that as the night wore on. There was the son of a cotton man, an Anglo from Brownsville, dressed as a *peón* carrying a live parrot in a cage, leading a goat which was shitting all over the place. The guy sported two big pistols and a machete, with a belt of bullets over one shoulder. A fat bearded companion appeared. It was Bill Roth, similarly dressed and the owner of the burro, it turned out.

"For the parade tomorrow I am going to be Fidel Castro," Roth told me happily. "I have two of the real armbands of the *Movimiento Veintiséis de Julio* from the prisoners at Fort Brown. We have a jeep and everything."

Bill did resemble Fidel, though about one story shorter.

"Get something to drink. That room down there is the bar."

That room was all bar. Cases of beer and cases of all kinds of liquor were stacked around the walls. Everyone was making his own drinks because the waiters that had been hired had long since joined the party.

Kerpow! Someone set off his revolver, followed by a long Mexican yell.

Pa-zing! someone down below shot back and a bullet thunked into the wall near the ceiling.

"Save me," Lupe demanded.

I hooked a bottle of champagne, then hooked another as an afterthought.

There was dancing in the halls, in the rooms—something in all the rooms.

The men of some orchestra, each in an identical sequin-lapeled jacket, seemed to have been taking turns screwing the naked blond American girl who had led the conga line after jumping from the balcony of her room. The lights in the room were on brightly. She was lying in a tumble of bed clothes, the mattress half off the bed, zonked out of her skull, barely rousing herself to acknowledge she was being mounted by yet another man.

"She has taken twenty men," an awed Mexican woman assured Lupe in Spanish.

Presently, someone had the bright idea of seeing if Bill's burro might enjoy the zonked girl's favors as well. The goat was female, or it might have got firsties. It was placidly eating a lampshade which it abandoned for someone's straw hat.

Two young Mexican men led the burro into the room. That donkey looked drunk to me. Everyone had been plying it with wine and beer and tequila and God knows what.

There was an act out in Boystown like the one the boys were about to try. They enlisted the services of another, chubby, half-naked Anglo girl to play with the donkey until he was aroused, if not eager.

They hauled the girl on the bed over until they held her spread-eagled as others helped the little burro to place his forefeet astraddle her on the bed while standing on the floor. The other girl helped guide the animal's penis into the girl's very soggy cunt and damned if it did not perform. The girl on the bed opened her eyes and muttered something and seemed to suffer some pain and no pleasure at all. Quicker than I would have thought, the spectacle was over.

"Disgusting!" Lupe said.

"Let's get out of here."

"Yes. Let's go to our room. I am tired and disgusted with myself and this fiesta."

We had two bottles of pretty good champagne. I was ready to call it a night.

"Let's get something to eat, Johnny. I feel a little hungry."

"Let's see if the little *cabrito* place is open around the corner."

"OK."

It was open, but packed. I got them to sell us some roast goat to take out. They wrapped it in newspaper.

We threaded our way back through the crowds in the streets and went up to our room to sit out on the small balcony, gnawing on the roast legs of kid and drinking champagne, seeing the fireworks go off from the back streets of the town, listening to the shots and firecrackers and lonely Mexican yells cutting through the noise and music.

I saw Robert and his party come into the square without Erica.

"Too bad," I said.

"It is too late to do anything now, yes?"

"Yes."

"Come to bed with me and screw me well, Johnny," she offered. "You are not too drunk, are you?"

"I don't think so."

I was not too drunk, though I was pretty drunk and kept almost going away while we made sloppy loose love on our bed.

We fell asleep with the doors to the balcony open. I half awoke when a skyrocket went off near by and illuminated the room, turning Lupe's sleeping, naked figure many pretty colors. I kissed her lightly snoring lips and went back to sleep.

It could not have been long before I was awakened by a lot of pounding on our door.

I got groggily out of bed and wrapped the bedspread around me and fumbled the latch of the door open.

I thought it was the police.

It was Bill Roth dressed as Fidel Castro for the parade. It

was morning and the parade was not until that afternoon, but he was ready to go, looking not much different from, or less drunk than, he had been a few hours before.

"Jesus Christ!" I exclaimed. "That *is* you, Bill?"

He pushed into the room. Lupe covered herself.

"Listen, Bob Crumbie is out of his skull. His wife was carried off by Hobie Glass, and they can't find him. They have looked over here and across the river and out at the port. They were out in Boystown for a while where Hobie reportedly paid a whore to let Erica work in one of the sidewalk cribs. But they left."

"Anyone seen Pete Gatliff?"

"He was with them, had a bandage on his head, but no one can find him either."

"I don't know what to tell you, Bill. *We* haven't seen them."

"I just thought you might have some idea where they could have gone."

"A man as big as Hobie can't ever disappear."

"I've got the police on both sides keeping a watch for him, as a personal favor to me. Goddammit! It always happens, doesn't it?"

"Yow. People can't hang onto their property or their wives sometimes."

"Especially during Charro Days. Maybe there should be a license for a fiesta."

"That would kill it."

"Right. If you hear anything, call the paper or get hold of me here or at the hotel in Brownsville."

"I will. That's a pretty real-looking rig you got on there, Fidel."

"They love it. It is almost as if I *am* the sonofabitch. You should see the way the people over here look at me."

"All power corrupts, *compadre*."

"*Campesino*."

"Whatever."

* * *

We were having breakfast downstairs when I realized where Hobie and Erica might be. I tried the floor Bill was on, but there was no answer. It was only about an hour before the parade. The bullfight would begin late that afternoon.

"You want to come with me or wait here?" I asked Lupe.

"I come."

We went to where we had left the truck, rousted a *carnavalisto* from sleep in the bed, or rather simply rolled his drunken ass out onto the ground, where he curled just as contentedly, and headed out of town toward Washington Beach.

We passed Boystown where it sat small and dull out in the mesquite by light of day. Laundry fluttered on lines on the roofs and out back of the buildings.

A couple of miles farther along there was a young boy sleeping in the wheel of a large truck beside the road. The truck had gone. No sign of a truck.

There were tiny shacks out there on small barren plots of ground, the fences made of cactus that had been leaned together. The yards of the shacks were dirt. Bare-assed kids played in the dirt or bothered starving dogs or chickens and an occasional spavined goat. Women squatted in the shade to pat out tortillas, which they cooked on a piece of metal over dried cactus fires, fortified with dried cowchips.

"They look like homestead on the fucking moon," I said to Lupe.

"I would do anything, kill, before I would live like that," Lupe said. "There should be a real revolution. Something!" She looked away so as not to see any more of the shacks. I patted her bare thigh.

"It is too hot. I feel sick."

I took away my hand.

"You should have stayed in the hotel."

"No, it is OK."

Ahead, sitting alongside the road, I saw Pete Gatliff and knew I had guessed right. He sat along the road holding his bandaged head. The bandage was setting loose, I saw when

we drew abreast of him. His clothes were torn, his face
smashed. He had been sick on himself.

"Where are they?" I asked, keeping the motor running.

"Out there somewhere, I think." He waved toward the
beach.

"They leave you?"

"I left. Hobie's crazy. Don't go out there less you got a gun.
I mean it. He's mean. I think he's really gone nuts."

"Get in the back of the truck."

"Hell, no. I think I got some broken ribs. I couldn't walk no
more. I'll just stay here. You got anything to drink? Water?
Anything?"

"No. I'll pick you up when we come back."

"Don't go or you won't come back. I mean it."

I dropped the truck in gear and went on.

I left the road at the beach and drove along it down where
the tide had smoothed the sand.

There were some people, campers and beach rats who had
little lean-tos out there. I stopped and had Lupe ask if they
had seen Hobie and Erica.

They swore they had seen nothing but had heard plenty
during the night. An old man pointed on down the beach.
From the poles of his lean-to were the skins of dried sharks he
had salvaged from the corpses of the hundreds of little dead
sharks that washed up on shore. He would sell the skin for
sandpaper, I guessed.

A few hundred yards along, I saw tracks where a four-
wheel-drive vehicle had climbed up into the dunes. I could
not drive up there, and I parked on the beach.

"What are you going to do?" Lupe asked.

"Go see."

"But if he's crazy? You have no gun."

I did not even have a knife.

"I won't try anything. I'll just go see if they are there."

"If you get killed, I'll never forgive you."

"OK. I'll remember that."

I followed the tracks over a couple of big dunes and saw Hobie's truck dug in up to the hubs in the sand. He sat against the truck naked except for his King of Tamaulipas sash and a party sombrero much too small for him. He seemed passed out, with a bottle of tequila between his legs. Up near the front wheels of the truck Erica was stretched out on her back naked, almost the color of the sand. I could not see if she was breathing or not. Something seemed to be crawling on her. *Christ!* She was covered with fucking little sand crabs. Then I was aware of the buzzards. They were circling high but centering over the place. You see buzzards over all the small shack farms along the route, so you don't think about them much.

I searched around looking for a sturdy club, something. I found a stick, but it broke across my knee. Then I saw a quart tequila bottle half buried in the sand. I pulled it out by the neck and hoped it would do, hoping even more it would not have to do.

I went up over the dune and quietly around the lip toward the woman. She had vomited all over herself. I could smell her when I got downwind. The crabs were busy on her body.

I got down the bank and knelt near her. I touched her bruised face, her lips, feeling for breath. Her sunburned, swollen eyes opened a hair. Her lips moved, but she could not speak. There seemed to be excrement on her face. I noticed beneath a buzz of flies around her head, two large human turds. He had shit on her face. I brushed the little crabs off her and bent to pick her up, thought better of it and began to drag her by the arms up the dune. She whimpered aloud in pain.

She said something. I bent near. She said, "Leave me. I do not want to live. Leave me." I could barely hear her. She was still very drunk. I dragged her a bit more.

"*Leave that alone!*" Hobie growled from where he sat.

I had the bottle securely under my left arm. I kept dragging the woman.

"I said leave that whore here! She's mine. She said she's mine forever. For better or worse," he slurred, but did not get up. "*LEAVE HER!* She's a dirty pig, a filthy cunt. She's *mine!* I can kill her if I want to. She told me. *I OWN HER, GOD- DAMMIT!* " He tried to get up. He tried very hard to get up, got up to his hands and knees and pitched forward on his face.

I picked her up then and put her over one shoulder and humped out of the dunes. It was hard going, and I felt very out of shape and bad of head myself.

Lupe saw us coming and got the door of the truck open.

"*Ai!* She smells like a toilet." She held her noise. "Is she alive?"

"At least."

"And the man?"

"Drunk."

"Can't we wash her in the sea?"

"Let's get her out of here first."

"Leave me. Let me die," Erica moaned feebly.

"If there was a vote, you would get mine," Lupe told her in Spanish.

Up past where we had spoken to the old man, we stopped the truck and carried Erica down to the water to lay her in the surf.

"If we don't hurry, Johnny, I think she will die," Lupe de- cided. "She does not look well. Something inside her is bro- ken. She is bleeding." Blood flowed thickly in the water be- tween her legs.

The old man had come along to observe in Spanish, "If I had known there was such treasure to be found on this beach, I would have had that woman for myself for as long as she would last."

"Go play with yourself, old man," Lupe told him, in his tongue. "It cannot hurt your brain more."

We picked up Pete along the road on the way in.

We saw a jeep with four *federales* in it ahead. It also had a radio aboard. I sped up until we were abreast of them and Lupe yelled over to them to tell them we had a woman with us who might die. They inspected the woman collapsed on our seat, heard our story, and finally radioed ahead for an ambulance and told whoever they talked to to try to find her husband at the hotel.

They did not have a siren on the jeep, but with much honking of the horn and shouting and menacing gestures, they escorted us fast as possible through the streets to a hospital.

We waited until Robert arrived with the shrimp company executive and his wife. I told them how we had found her.

"She likes the beach," I explained.

The police assured him they were on their way to arrest the man who had taken her out there.

The doctors thought she would live but she should be taken to the hospital in Brownsville immediately. An ambulance was on the way.

I tried to explain about Pete, whom they now found in the back of my truck, but nothing I could say could keep them from arresting him as a witness, if not a participant in whatever happened.

"He didn't rape her or nothing," Pete insisted pathetically, hardly able to stand. "She wanted it. Everything. I swear. She just went wild. Hobie couldn't handle her. I think he fell in love with her or something. I think he killed somebody out in Boystown. Some pimp, I think. I heard what sounded like a back broke. He almost killed me. He went crazy."

"Get him out of here before I—" Robert Crumbie threatened.

Lupe and I left.

"I think she asked for it," was Lupe's opinion.

"Those people who play at being mean just don't know what the fuck they are fooling with. They have seen too much TV. Too many heroic movie fights. They don't know what can really happen to a person," was my thinking. "There's a whole generation or two going to grow up like that. God help us, Lupe."

"They are more dangerous than the really dangerous ones, yes?"

"Yes. They might get us all killed, fucking around, trying to be *bad*. Shit, baby."

"I say so, too. Get me a little drunk. Make me happy.

It is still fiesta. It will be awful to be unhappy these days."

"We won't be unhappy. We are in love. We are fine. I like you. We are happy when we are not bothered by fools."

"I like you, too. But look, our clothes are ruined. We look like bums."

"Then we will go buy new clothes."

We bought new clothes from the stalls along the side streets off the square. Lupe picked out an off the shoulder peasant blouse with some embroidery on it and a wide, multicolored, flounced skirt. At another stall she found a black mantilla. She said it was a good one, handmade. It had been in a heap of used clothes an old woman smoking a black Mexican cigarette offered for sale.

"It is a bargain!" Lupe exclaimed, swirling the shawl around her shoulders expertly, lofting it over her head. I got a pair of khakis that Lupe said fitted my ass like those of the Mexican boys. Then she selected a blue T-shirt with a picture of a fighting bull and the word *TORO* stenciled on it.

With my stolen great sombrero, I looked like a Mexican dude from Dudesville, like one of those *pachucos* who lounged on corners and clicked their tongues at passing asses. Pants too tight to put your hand in the pockets.

I studied myself in the mirror in our room.

"Shows my cock and balls."

"Yes, I *like*. You have nothing to be ashamed of, my darling." She gave me a couple of strokes.

She had pulled back her hair under her mantilla and stuck a red paper rose behind her left ear.

"You look beautiful."

She was bare-legged beneath the long, wide skirt. I reached beneath and ran my hand up between her legs and thought, later, I would like to throw that skirt up and take her with her clothes on.

We found a café up a cool side street where they had moved three tables out on to the sidewalk. We sat down and ate fresh oysters, which we opened with the stubby *puntilla* that came on the plate and squirted them with lime juice and saw them

wrinkle when the juice hit them. They were the best oysters I
have ever eaten. Then we had a whole cold lobster between
us and drank three cold beers with the meal. The tables took
up the entire narrow sidewalk. Most people who passed did
not mind stepping off into the street. A few had objections.
Some insulted Lupe for being with a *gringo*. A typical holiday
crowd.

"You have the tickets for the *corrida*?" Lupe asked, as it
drew near the time to think about following the parade we
could hear in the distance over at the bullring.

I beat myself about the pockets.

"Hell, I left them in the hotel."

"What would you do without me anyway?" She had the
tickets in her purse.

We filled up the wine skin at a bar and shouldered our way
back to the square to see the parade. We should have gone
back to the hotel and watched from the balcony, but that was
impossible now. I saw some urchins up on a statue of some fat
hero and dragged Lupe over and hoisted her up to where she
could stand on the base of the thing and cling to the monu-
ment and see the parade. A little boy below was more intent
on positioning himself to see up Lupe's skirt than he was in
seeing the parade.

The parade had started on the U.S. side of the border and
came across the bridge .

There were hundreds of mounted *charros*, high school and
military bands, floats covered with fresh flowers and pretty
waving girls, and hundreds of citizens in costume.

There was Bill Roth and his crony, the young cotton man,
dressed as Fidel and Raul Castro in a military jeep, looking
very authentic. The crowd cheered them as if they were the
real articles. Castro could have been *presidente* of Mexico by
a landslide and of the lower Rio Grande Valley of Texas as
well. I reminded myself I had to speak to Lupe about those
boys who wanted something shipped to Cuba.

People in the parade threw change and candy kisses to the
crowd, and urchins broke through the line of constabulary to

scramble for the riches from the street, dodging beneath the hooves of horses and around the fenders of open cars.

In three open cars, the principals of that afternoon's bullfight rode dressed for the arena, their left arms tightly wrapped in capes, their right free to wave at the people. Patricia Quinn wore the flat Spanish hat, short black jacket and tight, striped trousers rolled up over boots of a Spanish rancher, rather than a suit of lights like the men. Jalisco Huerta had a great rugged face and rather blondish hair and smoked a big, black cigar. I liked him. He was Mexican, there was no doubt about that. He was also as brave as hell. He seemed a happy man. His brother, Jaime, was young, had a rather baby face, serious, and wore a dark purple suit. He looked very young, as if he hadn't really begun to shave yet.

When the parade had passed and turned to where it would park, we inched our way along with the crowd that would ultimately find its way to the bullring. We walked in the street with the crowd. Cars honked continuously, trying to inch through the pedestrians and got a load of passengers on their hoods and atop and hanging off the rear bumpers for their trouble until they were down on their axles.

A boy of nine or ten pressed close on my left side and held out a watch in his hand.

"You wanta buy a good watch, mister? Twenty dollars."

It was a good watch, a chronometer with an expansion band and obviously still warm from someone's wrist.

"You need a watch," he observed, noting my now bare left wrist, where the cheap watch I had stomped to death had been on my wrist was whiter than the rest of my arm.

"Only twenty dollars," he pleaded, glancing quickly over his shoulder as if expecting someone to be coming after him.

"I don't have twenty," I said. I had twenty, but I was running out of money.

"What you give?"

"Ten."

"More."

"Give you ten." I took the bill from my pocket.

"OK." He snatched the ten, and I grabbed the watch and stuck it in my tight pants pocket as he melted away in the crowd.

"It's a good watch," I assured Lupe. "Worth a hundred easy."

"So now you have a good watch."

Our seats were in the *barrera*—but in the sun. With my big sombrero, the sun did not matter. We were right above the door and chute where the bulls came out. The crowd was about half tourists. It did not promise to be a really serious bullfight. Some drunken Anglo woman in a man's hat began cheering for the bulls and promising the *toreros* what she hoped the beasts would do to them while they were parading in the ring. We had missed most of the exhibition by the *charros* and the folk dancing of the children which had preceded the bullfight. They had dragged the sand in the ring with mules decorated for the occasion and began the parade.

Jalisco Huerta had the first bull.

It came boiling out beneath us and charged around the ring, hooking the boards of the *barrera,* and finally jumped over the *barrera* into the alley behind, sending the men back there scrambling out into the ring until it could be chased back around and out at the gate at the chute from which it had entered the ring.

The crowd catcalled and hooted and whistled. Huerta finally came out, took his bull, and worked it methodically along the wall in the shade.

It was not a lot of bull, barely more than a big calf. The guy next to me told me the horns had also been shaved. Yet it was a genuine little bull, which Huerta quickly controlled and worked better than he had to for that crowd.

Just before the *picadores,* the blond that led the conga and had been gang-banged by half the young men in the hotel and a burro arrived on the arms of two spiffy Mexican gents. Half the crowd turned to look and whistle at her. She wore dark glasses and waved as if she were some sort of star. I guess perhaps she was. Amazing what a woman could take and survive, I thought. Then a drunken college boy in Bermuda shorts got up on the wall behind the *barrera* and demonstrated his skill at drinking from a wine skin to resounding cheers.

With the *muleta* Huerta worked his bull virtually with his back to the wood, no place to go, and the crowd finally became his.

Huerta then screwed up on the kill. He is a good killer but went out away from the horns before going in and stabbed the beast in bone and butchered it with three swords to get it down long enough to stab it with a dagger. The little fat *banderillero* did that.

Yet Jalisco's work was not shameful and the *presidente* awarded him an ear which he marched once around the ring.

The lady behind us in the man's hat yelled: "I wish he'd ripped your nuts off, you little showoff!"

Patricia Quinn had the second animal and scrambled around after it rather than controlled it, except for some good work with the cape and some good *banderillas*, but the performance was not of a piece as was Huerta's. The crowd liked her, however. She made it seem that the bull was totally at fault for its lack of ability to be killed with style and grace. The harridan in the man's hat shut up. I guess she could not boo a woman.

Pat put the sword in through the little bull's neck rather than down into it by coming over the horns, so the end of the blade stuck out below and behind its left front leg. It did not look nice as she and the *banderilleros* spun the animal around with their capes to bring it to its knees, so they could put it away with the *puntilla*. The little bull coughed up foamy blood. She had got it in a lung, obviously, rather than in the heart or by severing the aorta.

Bullfighting then seemed a very ugly, senseless, and graceless spectacle, and you feel very sorry for everyone involved, as well as for yourself, for being there.

Jaime waited for his bull in the center of the ring on his knees with his cape spread before him, much to the pleasure of the crowd.

The bull boiled out of the gate, head down as if on a track. Jaime swung up his cape, but a hair too late; the bull barreled over the *matador,* tumbling him brave ass over surprised baby face. The crowd thought he had been killed. But the bull had been coming too hard to hook the young man.

Jaime jumped up madder than hell, his face red, and went after the bull as if he would fight him hand and tooth. He became sensational, rooting his feet in the sand, doing every pass and trick pass in the book, spinning between the horns, working the cape behind his back with his body exposed between it and the bull. He broke the *banderillas* in half and placed them all himself. With the *muleta,* he was a little more cautious, moving, leaning, in close after the horns had passed to get his belly bloody and look as if he had worked closer than he had. But they all know how to do that. He was very good. He was awarded both ears.

After Jalisco Huerta' second bull we should have all gone home.

The animal was larger than the others that day and had a pair of horns you would put up on your wall, if you would do that sort of thing. It favored his right side, which Huerta corrected with the sticks, but not before breaking them down to about four inches long before placing them. Then he had the *picadores* each give the animal one lance before taking it away. He so dominated the animal with his cape that he had the crowd cheering as a single voice. It was as a bullfight should be. It lifted the heart and cleared the mind. It was not a contest by any means. It was an exhibition, a drama, a religious rite for men who kept their hats on and smoked cigars and for women who still understood that as long as the world is the way it is, there is a difference in the sexes that's important to both. It was an art, a living, moving sculpture in which there were real, not figurative, risks, honest danger. Would you do it? Could you ever do it beautifully? You screamed your appreciation because you could not.

Huerta was not without tricks. He sat on the step of the *barrera* and worked the bull. He did the *telefono,* placing the tip of dazzled animals' horn in one ear. But also he did everything else he was supposed to do, as well as I have ever seen it done. He stood stock-still for the kill and received the bull on the tip of his sword, drove in over the horns to shove the blade to the goddammed hilt right where it should go, and that bull dropped in its tracks as if someone had pulled its plug.

The crowd went wild. Hats, flowers, shirts, jewelry, every damned thing came sailing out of the crowd into the ring. Bottles of booze, skins of wine. I let go of my great sombrero, much to Lupe's surprise, and it sailed magnificently out into the ring.

Huerta was given both ears, the tail and a hoof. I had never seen that. He carried the grisly objects around the ring, then threw them up into the crowd. A girl climbed over the walls to be kissed. Huerta picked up my big hat and put it on his head. He found a cigar and stopped to light it. He drank from the wine skins and threw them back into the crowd. He threw the jewelry back into the crowd, the clothing. He threw my sombrero to someone on the other side of the ring and put on a woman's hat, strutting happily around, puffing on the big cigar.

"If I have a son, I will name him Jalisco," I decided and told Lupe.

"And if it is a girl?"

"Jalisca."

"OK," she said. "But that is not something you should attempt by yourself. You should have a woman. She will have the baby."

"Yes, I'll try to do it like that."

"Good."

We left in the middle of Patricia Quinn's second bull. She was just going through the motions entirely now. I didn't blame her. No one was going to do better than Huerta that day.

We walked back in the early evening with our arms around each other's waist, not talking much. We both were aware, I'm sure, we would have to leave the next morning. I was really about out of money. I could have found Bill Roth and borrowed a hundred with no trouble, but I didn't really consider it. I'd had enough fiesta. But I was also worried about what would happen when we went back across the river. What would Lupe do?

In the room I did not throw Lupe's skirt over her head and fuck her as I had considered doing. We undressed and took a shower together and made love very gently and for a long while on the bed without talking at all.

We lay blowing smoke up at the ceiling.

"Lupe, I need some money pretty quick."

"How much money, *querido mio?*"

"As much as I can get. Are those guys who wanted me to take a trip to Cuba still around?"

"I see them around, yes."

"They still interested?"

"I don't know."

"Can you find out?"

"I can find out."

"Do it, will you, Lupe? Five or six thousand bucks could get me out of a hole and back up to scratch."

"OK. I will find out."

"You're a sweetheart."

"It is nothing for me to do. Ask me something hard."

"Marry me."

She took the cigarette and drew on it deeply and blew the smoke at the ceiling.

"You feel like that now maybe. If you feel like that later . . . I will think about it." She laughed. "You don't want to marry. You just want to make me feel good. I know." She placed her fingers on my lips to stifle any protest. "You feel much love for me. I too for you. We want to say something. There are no more words to say, we have said everything, done everything, so we think about to be married."

I did not mention it again.

"If you go to Cuba, will you take me with you?"

I thought for a long time.

"It might be dangerous."

She just looked at me.

"You said if you went, I could go."

"You can go."

I had planned to take one man, and I had already decided on my man. I did not plan on taking Lupe even as I promised.

The hotel dining room was full of bullfighters and their crowd. We went out and down the street around the corner and ate roast goat, then went and danced, got a little drunk and went back to our room.

I fucked Lupe in the ass for the second time since I had known her, and this time she became very giving and fucked back and cried and wanted to kiss when I came, though she had to twist her neck around with difficulty to do so.

"I never like that with no one but you," she said. "I like everything with you."

"I like everything with you too, Lupe."

"Maybe we could live in Cuba," she suggested suddenly. "Maybe we could join the revolution and be somebody in Cuba when Castro wins the revolution."

"If he wins."

"He will win."

"I joined the Army once. I didn't like it a lot."

"It is not so cold in Cuba."

I had told her how cold it had been in Korea.

"What would they pay?"

"Pay! That is all you think of. *How much does it pay?*"

"Just a good ole American boy, Lupe. Anyway, it's their quarrel. It was the Koreans' quarrel too, and it never became mine. I'm tired of being shot at for nothing. Next time I want the fuckers to come to me, or I want *mucho dinero,* enough to live on the rest of my life, or I don't want to go. I want it to make some goddamned changes. For *me.*"

"The world stinks, Johnny. It is OK like this." She stroked my chest with her palm. "But when you look around, it stinks."

"Happy fiesta."

She snuggled on my shoulder. "I love you, Johnny."

Before I fell asleep, she said, "I think my death does not go
so far away."

I held her close, my left hand on the flare of her hip.

During the carnival people could pass freely back and forth
over the bridge between the United States and Mexico, un-
hindered by immigration or customs controls. The guards on
either side stopped no one. Mexicans came back across the
river with things they could only get on the U.S. side, and Anglos came back with things they could only get on the Mexican side.

We crossed at a time when we knew Lupe's husband would
not be on duty. Still, we stopped and loaded the truck with
people preparing to walk across the bridge.

Once across, we bid the passengers *adiós* and skirted the
carnival doings in the center of the city to make our way toward the port by the back streets.

Lupe said she had a girlfriend where she could stay and her
husband could never find her. She wrote a telephone number
where I could call her. She promised to find out about the
guys who wanted to move something to Cuba. She said we
could meet at her girlfriend's house whenever we wished.

"She will never say nothing. Never!"

I knew we could not meet on the boat.

I kissed her good-bye and watched her get out of the truck.

Her girlfriend was a nurse. She lived in the best section of
the old part of the city. Many of the large houses had been
converted into apartments and rooming houses as the money
moved out into the new homes on the *resacas*. Her girlfriend
had a small apartment in what had once been a studio behind
a large, white Moorish type of house where one of the last
surviving members of a grand local family lived alone and occasionally gave someone a piano lesson. It was near the new
hospital. The street had been widened into a boulevard. It
was not where anyone would be looking for her without being
sent.

"Call me tomorrow."

"I will."

"Thank you, Johnny."

"Thank you."

"Buenos noches."

I did love Lupe. I liked her a lot. But I was glad to be away from her for a while. I was glad to be rolling back to my boat. Yet that made me anxious too. I really needed five or six thousand. If I could get that, I could get back at least to even. Otherwise I would just dig myself into a hole. Another busted trip like the last, and I would likely have to sell my boat to one of the companies to keep my job.

I wanted to move anything I could move to Cuba anyway. One load, in and out, and I could get well.

I thought of everything that had happened that weekend. I thought of Chelo and her beautiful sister *la Encanta,* who was in jail; of their father Ezequiel dead and gone in the Gulf. It hadn't been so long. It seemed years ago. I thought of Shea, my buddy, dead and in some frozen ground in Korea—a lifetime ago.

"The world stinks"— I heard Lupe say in my mind.

"Sometimes," I said aloud.

CHAPTER SIXTEEN

I stopped at Mendoza's store on the way to the port to buy a few groceries. Half of the place was devoted to bait and tackle and a gun counter, the other half to groceries. I got a quart of milk, bacon, bread, a dozen eggs, sandwich stuff, a pie. While Mendoza was totaling up the stuff, I went over and looked at the handguns in the glass case. I hadn't owned a pistol since the Army. I still had the Thompson submachine gun wrapped up down in the engine room on the boat, the shotgun and the carbine from the shrimp war. I had plenty of .45 caliber bullets for the Thompson. There was a used Army .45 pistol in the case with a tag on it. Fifty bucks.

"What do you want for that forty-five automatic?" I asked Mendoza.

He went and brought the gun.

"Fifty dollars."

"Give you thirty," I bargained.

"It is a good gun." He locked back the slide. "Look at the bore. It is perfect. It was hardly ever used."

The bore was excellent, the lands sharp as a new; there were no pits.

"Thirty-five," I offered.

"I tell you. Forty dollars, and I will give you three extra clips. OK?"

"OK."

He wrapped up the gun and put it with my groceries.

"You need some bullets?"

"No thanks."

"If you don't like it, bring it back. I will give you credit on any other gun you like."

"Thanks. Listen, I'm a little short of cash. Put it on my bill, OK?"

"Sure. Oh, you gotta fill out the paper for the Cops."

He got out the form required for the purchase of the pistol, and I filled it out and gave it back.

No one in Texas ever asked you what you wanted with a pistol.

If Lupe's husband came looking for her, he would be packing a gun. If it came to trouble, I wanted the equalizer and work out the legalities later. It isn't a bad system—truly. The world being what it is.

I went to the boat and made some bacon and eggs, turned on the radio for a while, and read. It began to rain. Big drops fell on the deck making spots the size of half dollars, riveting the water in the channel, sending up little hourglass-shaped geysers until the channel was completely pocked by them. The wind began to blow hard. I went off and checked my lines. The boat was riding up and down against the dock; the old tires I had over for fenders between the dock and the boat squeaked against the wood.

Up at the head of the dock the melon man's stick and canvas stall came apart. The canvas cover cartwheeled down the street and flattened against the Good Eats Café. Two young girls were blown along the road, soaked by the rain, fighting to keep their carnival dresses down in the wind. Up in the cities on both sides of the river, I knew the carnival booths would be coming apart, people scurrying for cover. Great forks of lightning sizzled out of the sky, one fork out over the Gulf, the other touching ground near Brownsville. The cracks of thunder split the sky, took my breath away. My hair felt electrified. You could see the storm all across the Gulf. Though it was not yet dark, it was like evening. A truck crept along the street with its lights on, pushing about a foot of water in front of it. The rain was cold then. The temperature had dropped at least forty degrees in less than an hour. I hurried back into the snug of the cabin.

I put on lights and stripped off my wet clothes. I put on clean soft Levi's and a Levi jumper with a rough blanket lining. The rough plaid felt good against my bare skin. I pulled on warm wool socks and rubber deck boots. I poured myself a cup of strong sweet coffee and had a shot of Fundador with it. The sound of the storm was so good to hear when I was warm and dry, that I did not bother with music. I felt fine, clean, content.

I cleaned and lightly oiled the new pistol while sitting in the nook in the galley. It looked like a pre-World War II model. The machining was superior to those I had carried in the Army. The metal around the grip had been worn until the bluing was about gone. The grips were real wood and felt good in my hand. The story goes that the U.S. government adopted the pistol for us in the Philippines to stop hopped-up Moros who could not be stopped by the service pistols before the .45. It also used the same bullets as the Thompson submachine gun. I loaded the clips and snapped one in the butt of the pistol.

I had fallen asleep reading in my bunk and was awakened by someone knocking loudly on the door of the cabin. I had drawn all the curtains. Only the light over the bunk was lit. I did not bother to turn it off. Reaching under my pillow, I got up, slipping the pistol into my waistband beneath my jumper, and went to open the door.

There were two deputies in slickers, the rain running off their Texas hats. I knew them both: Deputies Shaw and Hinajosa.

"We heard you were back," Shaw said.

"Been having a little fiesta," I said.

They nodded.

"Come in out of the rain," I invited them. "What's the trouble?"

They came and stood making puddles on my deck.

"They say you grabbed Lupe Contreras away from her

husband and ran away with her?" Shaw explained his mission.

"Haven't seen her. Want some coffee?"

"That would be good."

"Hinajosa?"

"Sure. Black for me."

I poured them coffee and held up the brandy. "A little sweetening?"

They nodded yes.

I laced the coffee generously.

"Her old man claims you abducted her," Shaw said, sipping the strong coffee appreciatively.

"I haven't seen her. Honest." I raised a hand to swear. "Who said that?"

They did not answer.

"We'd like to look around your boat."

"Sure. I haven't seen her."

"You fit the description of the one who took her out of the hospital. He had a truck like you," Hinajosa said.

"They get the license number?" I asked. "Should be easy to check a license number."

Shaw smiled the least bit. They knew I was lying. I knew they had no witnesses. I didn't think what I had done was a very serious crime anyway.

They finished their coffee and set the cups on the table.

"If you see her, you tell her her husband is looking for her."

"I'll do that," I promised.

They didn't want to search the boat.

"Her old man is pretty upset," Shaw warned me.

"I guess he would be."

"Thanks for the coffee. Pretty good coffee."

"Anytime."

They went down the plank and got in their car. I saw Shaw pick up the handset in the car and call in as they drove off.

I locked the door after them, put out the light in my bunk, the pistol back under the pillow, and went to sleep in my clothes.

The next morning was like awakening in a steam bath. I had to get out on deck to breathe.

Great fluffy white clouds billowed up over the Gulf for thousands of feet. The clouds and the sky looked washed clean. The smell in the air was like that of a bright laundry day with a line of clean white sheets flapping on a line. Steam lifted from the deck and the dock. Everything stood out brightly, sharp against the blue sky in the sparkling air.

God! The Gulf can be impressive. So beautiful. It made your blood feel clean almost instantly. It made you glad to be alive—happy.

I dragged out my bedding to sun and air on deck and went up to the café for breakfast. I had to go into the bank, no joke. I had about three bucks on me.

Babe Cayce flashed a little bit of a diamond ring under my nose between it and my eggs and potatoes.

"It's an engagement ring, dope," she informed me.

"Very pretty. Who's the lucky fellow?"

"Charles."

"Charles?" I thought *What Charles?*

"Charles Principal!"

"No hell!" That was a surprise. I knew Charles was sweet on the young Babe, but I never thought he had a chance, being so slow and quiet. Hell, he was about twenty years older than Babe, losing his hair already.

"Well, I sure wish you luck. I just saw him the other day, he never mentioned it to me."

"Last night. He just came to the house and showed me this ring and popped the question. He's going to take over Pop's boat."

I looked at her old man sitting at the end of the counter trying to read the newspaper without the glasses he needed but would never go buy.

"Going to quit it, huh, Pop?" I said.

"Well, we'll see how the boy does. Gotta quit sometime."

"How old are you, Pop?"

"Be eighty years old this year."

"Time to retire and start living."

The old man smiled. "That's what I figure. Think I'll get me and Mama one of them little trailers and just take off and go show her some of this great country before I die. Hell, I haven't seen the big mountains since I was your age."

"Ought to do it."

"Think we will."

Babe was about fifteen. That would have made Pop sixty-five when she was born. Mother Cayce would be some thirty years younger than the old man then. He was some old man.

"He has been promisin me that trip for twenty years," Mother Cayce said from over the grill behind the counter.

"Blew down the carnival, I see," the old man said.

"God's wrath," the old woman claimed. "That's the Catholics for you. Got to have this Satan's holiday, then not eat nothin and go repent for it."

"You'll come to the wedding, won't you?" Babe asked.

"Wouldn't miss it!"

"Then you can kiss the bride."

I looked up at her and thought Charles and she would get along just fine. She would settle down in a few years. In the meantime, Charles would be so happy to be married to her, and he was not the jealous type. I felt it would work out.

"OK," I said.

"About damned time." She pouted.

I asked her to put my breakfast on my tab.

I called the number Lupe had given me from the booth along the street.

"Are you all right?" I asked.

"Yes. You too?"

"Fine. Can I see you?"

"You can come over. Nobody is here. But give me some time. I just get up and look ugly."

"OK. I'll be there in about an hour."

"I miss you last night."

"I missed you, too," I lied.

I'd had bad dreams all night.

I had to shift the pistol in my waistband around toward one hip to sit comfortably in the truck. I had put on a T-shirt beneath the jumper but had to wear the jumper to cover the pistol. I wished then I had bought a smaller gun.

Palm trees were down here and there, the streets and gutters decorated with fallen palm fronds. The roof of a Latino's shed had blown off and was sitting near the road. Chickens were blown into the wire of the yard at another place. A woman was out salvaging the dead birds and putting them in a basket. Dogs, looking cleaner than they had in a long while, loped around being nosey.

A big semi-reefer truck had gone off the road and lay on its side in the water-filled ditch. The thawed shrimp were already getting high. It would stay there for a few days, and every time anyone passed it and got a whiff of the rotting shrimp they would say, "Hello, girls!"

In Brownsville people were busy in the streets trying to salvage and repair what they could of the carnival booths. Others were down to look at the waters of the Rio Grande rising on the levee at Fort Brown.

I stopped at the bank and cashed a check and saw an officer I knew to promise that I would have a check for the payment on my boat in a couple of weeks.

"That's all right, Captain. We understand." He winked at me, the bastard. "Thanks for stopping in."

There would be a penalty, of course. Hell, no, they weren't worried. They had the paper on a damned good boat. To be fair, they would carry you for a couple of busted trips without ragging you. All those young officers in their chump suits, sporting around town in their Plymouth G.T.s or some such shit. This guy kept a Chris Craft runabout with a couple of bunks on it at the marina. He wore a skipper's cap with an owner's device on it when he took the boat out for a runabout.

Maybe I was beginning to dislike people. Out on the street in the glare I wondered about that. I'd read Mark Twain once said only about two percent of the people on earth were worth knowing. Misanthrope—a pretty word, like a pungent flower—a hater of mankind; a cynic; one who believes that human conduct is motivated by self-interest. Be a good name for a boat—the *Misanthrope*.

Maybe I am getting old? I wondered. Be washed up at thirty, old and bitter. A hater of mankind.

Two Latino girls passed in colorful carnival blouses and long swinging skirts. They looked like plump pretty brids. That flawless creamy Mexican skin is as addictive as milk chocolate candy bars. You wish it were a foot deep so that you could sink your head into it, your whole self. I could understand those old Aztecs flaying the skin off some beautiful virgin and getting inside her to lead the annual parade. Whew! Man, that's crazy, isn't it? I mean they actually *did* that!

I shook my head to stop the talk with myself inside it. Sometimes I got so goddamned fed up with solo conversations in my head. You should just be able to cut that stuff off, just walk around seeing and breathing and verbalizing nothing. Pure experience. You could probably live twice as long.

I went into the newspaper office and straight on back to the newsroom.

Bill Roth was behind his editor's desk, bearded, wearing a *guayabera* shirt and *huaraches*.

"How's Crumbie's wife?" I asked.

"She'll live," he said. "Had a punctured uterus and bowel. He must have stuck a stick or something up her. They found sand up in there."

"Hell."

"They got her over here to the hospital just in time."

"What about Hobie and Gatliff?"

He shrugged. "There are no charges on them over there. García told me when they sobered up they would be escorted to the bridge and let go."

"Um."

"Yep . . . Listen, I have to get over to the federal office. Big doings. Looks there may be a federal order coming down on the revolutionaries we got out at Fort Brown. Something's happened. Looks like they may be let out."

"Something's changed?"

"Looks like. A couple of hoods from Dallas are around, too. Something's happening. If you hear anything, let me know."

"I will."

"You making any money?"

"That's a problem."

"I understand." He folded some blank paper to fit into his pocket and prepared to go see if he could find out what was happening. "Oh . . . steer clear of Bob, huh. He's upset."

"Right."

"No need to hurt the bastard more."

"Right."

"And if you see Hobie and Gatiff, you might encourage them to go fishing for a long time."

"I don't want to see them."

I walked out onto the street with him. We said so long.

I parked the truck in an alley a block from where Lupe was staying and walked there through the alleys and came in through the backyard.

She asked, "Who is it?" before opening the door.

She was wearing one of her friend's black slips. It was too small for her. She also wore a blond wig which made her look like someone trying to took like Marilyn Monroe. From the back there was a definite resemblance. I wrapped my arms around her and kissed her. There was nothing but a brassiere under the cool silky slip.

"I must go away," she said as I nudged her toward the bed in the one-room kitchenette apartment. The place smelled of women, their perfumes.

"You like me blond?" she asked, letting herself be lowered to the bed.

"It's different."

"That why you want to make love to me?"

"No."

We fucked. She did not come. Her mind was elsewhere.

As we lay smoking, I told her about the police coming to my boat. I told her about Crumbie's wife.

"I must go someplace, Johnny."

"Where?"

"I don't know. I don't want to go anywhere. I feel very sad." She looked about the room. "My girlfriend is wonderful. But I can't stay here. I don't have no place to go. I don't have no home." She said it as if she had just realized that. "I want to go away to a new place. I am tired of everyting. Of old things."

"Me too?"

She looked annoyed. "No. Stupid. But we can't be as we were here. I am worried, Johnny. I feel old."

"I felt like that too this morning. I understand. I know how you feel."

"Yes. You always know about me. But there is one little part no one can know, ever. Everyone is like that, yes?"

"Yow."

"Now I am pushed into that little part and I feel alone."

"I know . . . Let's go to Florida."

"*¿Que?*"

"Florida. We can take the boat to Florida, fish out of there."

"You would do that for me?"

"Yes."

"I love you, Johnny. You make me happy to hear that." There were tears in her eyes. I kissed them away. "But could you live with me? I am a crazy girl, Johnny."

"You aren't crazy."

"Yes! You don't know me. When I see you, I am happy, ready to be happy with you. There is other times, you would not like me. I don't like me those times."

"Yes, I would."

"Oh, Johnny. You make me happy, even now. But you say you have not so much money."

"I'm broke. I'm in trouble if I don't get up some money pretty quick."

"How much money?"

"Five or six thousand would get me out of the hole. Even a good trip would hardly do it now. Time! Man, Lupe, time can fuck you. Can you see those guys who wanted something taken to Cuba?"

"I will try. Tonight, OK?"

"But be careful."

"Sure. Don't you like my disguise?"

"You should wear that wig on your ass. Everyone knows there is only one like it in town."

"I will wear a big skirt and flat shoes and sunglasses."

She hopped up and clipped on a large pair of inpenetrable sunglasses.

"You recognize me?"

"No, I wouldn't."

She came back and lay down, still wearing the sunglasses.

"You love me?"

"Love you."

"More this way?"

"More the way you were that last time you came down to the boat."

"Yes!" She whipped off the glasses and wig. Her hair was pinned tightly to her head underneath.

I kissed her mouth. It was so soft and wet and giving.

"I would like to knock you up," I told her. "Really do it some time."

She took my limp cock gently in her hand. "Fuck me, Johnny. With love."

"With love, Lupe."

"I feel much love for you."

CHAPTER SEVENTEEN

When I called Lupe the next morning, she said, "They will talk to you, but they are very cautious after the last time. They will meet you across the river."

"OK."

"Something has happened, *querido mío*. I don't know what. But I could feel something. They act big or something."

"OK. You didn't tell them I was broke, did you?"

"You think I am stupid? I told them you were interested because of me, that you were going to take me away from my husband. I tell them we are in love."

I did not like her telling them that, but I understood her thinking.

"They said you are a fool, but they will talk with you. Also, then I don't have to sleep with nobody."

"That's good."

"Sure. I think so."

She told me where to meet them: a small café on a side street into which tourists only ever peeked before going on. The meeting was for eleven that night, after everyone had dinner.

The carnival across the river was even more tattered by the storm than it had been on the U.S. side. The people with booths around the plaza were trying to get them set up and open. A few were going. Workers were restringing colored

lights. It was a cool night. The people strolling about wore
jackets and sweaters. The wind had come up after dark and
promised more rain. A few were trying to have fun, but the
gaiety of the fiesta was gone. It was really all over.

The café was lit by three large yellow bulbs hanging beneath reflectors from the ceiling. The tables were against the
walls out of the puddles of the lights. It was more bar than
café. I did not like it that the two I was to meet were the only
patrons. A fat bartender in a dirty shirt was reading a Mexican
paper at the head of the bar. He looked up when I came in
and then back at his paper when I went on back to pull out a
chair at the table where the two Lupe had brought to my boat
waited with their backs against the windowless rear wall.

The one I knew as Raimundo called to the bartender, who
stirred himself and brought me a bottle of beer. No one had
asked my brand.

I told them I was ready to make the trip.

"When?"

"Immediately. I would have to take on ice and stores, look
as if I am going fishing."

"When?"

"Day after tomorrow."

"Santiago will go with you," Raimundo said, indicating the
dark little young man with him. "How many will you take?"

"Just me and another man."

"This other man?"

"He will be no problem."

"You understand. Santiago will be in charge."

I looked at Santiago. I did not like him, and he did not like
me. I nodded my assent.

"The money?"

"It is as we discussed. When you have loaded the cargo
where Santiago will show you, you will be given half. When
you unload it, you will be given the other half."

"OK."

We agreed when Santiago should come down to the boat
the next night.

"We like Santiago," Raimundo explained. "He is our brother. If anything goes wrong, we will find you."

"I understand."

"That is good," he said in Spanish.

We shook hands, and I left.

I called Lupe. She said to come over and bring her something to eat. Fried chicken. She was hungry for fried chicken. Her girlfriend was out on a date and would not be back until morning, she thought.

I bought a sack of chicken and some beers at the drive-in.

Lupe had on one of her friend's nightgowns. I had never seen her in a nighgown. I thought how it would be to come home to her for the rest of my life. It felt pretty good.

She was hungry and put a newspaper on the bed and spread out her feast. She sat cross-legged on the bed to eat it while I told her about the meeting across the river.

When she had finished eating, she sucked her greasy fingers and kissed me with greasy lips.

"When do we go?"

"I told them I would ice up tomorrow and leave early the next morning."

"Good! I am a prisoner here."

"I'm not taking you on this."

"¿Que? Si! I go!"

"It's too fucking dangerous, Lupe."

"Fuck, Fuck! *I* go! I am not going to sit in this room for weeks! No! I go! You tell me if you go, I go. *I go!*"

"I told them I would only take one man."

"Fuck you! Fuck what you tell them! *I go!*"

I tried to take her in my arms. She would not have it.

"If you don't take me, I will kill myself."

"Lupe. . . ."

"I am serious. You think I will sit here in this room. You are crazy. You say I can go."

"Lupe. . . ."

"*No!* You think this is not dangerous? Stupid! If you leave me, I will hate you and kill myself. That is my last word."

She got off the bed and went to stand with her arms folded, her back to me, staring at the shade pulled down on the window.

"I trust you," she said softly. "You tell me if you go, I go."

"I just don't want to risk your getting hurt."

"You hurt me already. I am not afraid!" She spun around to face me. "You are are more afraid than me."

"That's true."

"You think I want to be with some man who is more afraid than me?"

"I'm afraid for you."

"Let me be afraid for me. If you really love me, you will take me. You rather see me dead in this room?"

"Lupe. . . . Come here. Let me talk to you."

"*No!* There is nothing to talk about. I go or you will never see me alive again."

"Come here . . . please."

"Say I go and I will come to you."

"You go."

She came sulkily to the bed.

"You promise?"

"Yow."

"On every good thing that is between us?"

"On every good thing that is between us."

"OK." She got onto the bed and let me take her in my arms. "I am glad. Now I don't have to kill myself."

I grinned.

"I am serious, so don't make a mistake, *cabrón.*"

"OK."

I touched her breast beneath the filmy nightgown.

"I don't know if I can trust you," she said.

"I'll take you.."

I believed she would kill herself. She had more courage than anyone I have known. She had more courage than myself. And she was not stupid. Her world still had real witches in it. She believed people could be literally hexed into animals. Nor was she afraid of what came after death. Nothing could be worse than life itself. Yet she gave herself to life.

She gave herself to me.

I felt young, a boy, and she a woman. I told her this. I told her she was more brave than myself. She became very maternal, gave me her breast to suck as might a child, stroked my head and crooned to me in Spanish.

"So many worries for such a young man," she soothed. "I will take care of you. I will be your friend, your lover, your mother, your whore," she promised in Spanish. "Sometimes it is good for you to be a little boy," she explained in English. "Yes, suck well." She rocked my head against her breast and sang me a soft Mexican song.

When I got between her buttery warm thighs, she was still being "mother."

"Love your *mamacita, hijo.* She gives you everything."

"*Mamacita,*" I repeated.

"*Sí. Sí, hijo.* My sweet little boy," she said in Spanish.

Her girlfriend came home before I was out of the bed to change her clothes to go to the hospital. I awakened to the sound of Lupe and the girl chattering in Spanish and laughing together in the kitchen where there was a table on which to eat.

The girl came into the other room in her slip and put on her nurse's uniform. In the mirror as she bent close to put on lipstick, she saw I was awake and said, "Hello. Sleep well in my bed?"

"Very well."

"In the arms of love. Ah! Life is so romantic."

Lupe said something rapidly in Spanish, and the nurse laughed.

She replied in Spanish, "I like him. If you throw him out, throw him my way."

She put her cap on her head and a sweater over her shoulders.

"Bye, It was nice meeting you. Don't you two wear out my

bed," she called to Lupe in Spanish. "Don't do nothing I wouldn't do," she told me again and went out the door.

"Berta likes you," Lupe said as I got up and went to the toilet. "She would like to sleep with you."

"Um."

"She is very good, I think. You can sleep with her if you like."

I came up behind Lupe as she scrambled eggs at the stove and put my arms around her. She leaned back to let me kiss her. I covered her belly with my hands.

"You want to sleep with her?"

"No."

"It is OK. I am not jealous."

"I *know*. Maybe I would like for you to be a little jealous."

"You sleep with her, and I will kill you." She turned around and placed a kitchen knife across my windpipe. "Kiss me . . . again . . . again . . . . That's enough. I am making you a good breakfast. Besides, I get my period last night."

"Oh."

"*Si*. You see what you will have to put up with if we are not just lovers."

"There are ways and ways, pretty lady."

"Of course. But I want you to know I am human. See. My belly is fat and ugly now. I have much gas." To illustrate, she farted. She raised her eyebrows at the look on my face.

I laughed. God, I felt I hadn't laughed in so long I thought I would crack my face.

"So. If that is all it takes to make you happy. . . ."

I bent down and kissed her belly.

"I like you every way you are."

"Don't squeeze me, or I make you die laughing. Sit down. Now the eggs are too dry."

She sat toast and jam before me and sat down to watch me eat.

"You don't have any."

"I am not hungry."

"I don't know how to get you on the boat," I said, thinking aloud.

"I can wear my disguise."

"Yow. . . ." I had to think about it. "I will have to call you when I work it out."

"I was serious yesterday when I said those things. You know that?"

"Yes."

She came and sat on my lap for a few minutes after I had finished eating. There were things I had to do, people I had to see.

She kissed me at the door and told me she loved me.

The sunlight hurt my eyes after the continually shade-drawn room.

First, I had to go see Eli and tell him what I was doing.

His wife called him to the door. I drew him outside, and we talked on the porch.

He wanted to go.

"Don't be nuts. You got your wife and the kid on the way to think about. I just want to get us even, so we can start thinking about making some money again."

Finally he agreed.

"My asshole brother-in-law thinks he can get me that job with the park board. My wife wants me to take it if he can do something for me. I don't know. What do you think?"

"I'd think about taking it, Eli. You got to keep the wife happy."

"Yeah. That's true. . . . Anyway, have a good trip, man. What about Chelo?"

"Make something up for me, will you?"

"Sure. Be careful, man."

"I'll try, *compadre*."

We shook hands.

"Watch your ass, hunh?"

"I'll try."

Next I had to go see Pop Cayce and see if he would lend me

some money for ice, fuel, and stores. He lent me some but not enough.

I went and found Charles Principal at the room where he stayed. He had some money in the bank. His bed was unmade. I wondered if Babe Cayce had been there. It's funny how your mind works. Here I was trying to borrow some money to take my boat out to run some guns and shit to Cuba and I was wondering how Charles and Babe fucked, if they did. He reluctantly let me have enough to get what I needed. He wrote me a check. I looked at his balding dome bent over his checkbook—he had to sit down to write his check—and wondered what made him tick, what it was like to be Charles Principal. I then suddenly wondered what it was like to be me.

Finally, I had to find Frank Smith. No one had seen him.

I went back to Brownsville and found him in jail. He had been picked up for being "plain drunk" and thrown in the tank overnight and hadn't any money with which to bail himself out the next morning. I paid him out.

He did not look good. He had pissed his pants and been hosed down by the jailers. He was shaking, just this side of DTs.

"I need a hand," I explained to him.

"You can count on me, Johnny," he babbled.

"Yow. That's why I came for you."

"I can straighten out, quick."

He could hardly walk. The light outside was like a bat across his eyes.

"You need a drink?"

"Christ, Johnny, it would save my life."

"I got a pint in the truck."

He tipped the bottle up and would have drunk half of it if I hadn't held onto it and pulled it away when he had taken a good belt.

"I *needed* that," he breathed, his eyes still on the pint. "Whew!" He shook himself. "Maybe just another and I'll be all right." I gave him another belt. When that one hit bottom

and he had grimaced and shaken himself out again, I offered
him a cigarette and started the truck.

About a mile down the road he was looking better.

"I'll be all right, Johnny. I want you to know I sure appreciate this. You can count on me."

"When you need a drink, you come ask me and I will give
you one. I catch you taking one on your own and I will feed
your miserable ass to the sharks."

"You can count on me, Johnny. Just give me a chance and
I can straighten up and fly right."

"Yow. You just ask me when you really need one, OK?"

"This is damned good of you, Johnny."

"Maybe and maybe not. I need a hand. That's all."

"Anyway, I want you to know I sure as hell appreciate it."

"Right."

I got him on the boat and gave him some clothes and made
him eat something before I would give him another little belt.
With his hair combed back and cleaned up and enough booze
in him to raise his spirits, he worked OK, getting the ice
aboard. I left him while I went to buy groceries.

"Where's Eli?" he wondered.

"He's taking a job in town."

Then Frank worked the harder to show me he could be a
hand, perhaps dreaming of the first steady employment he'd
had since hitting the skids years before back in Chicago. It
was hard to believe he had been a pretty successful lawyer
anywhere.

When we were loaded, I let Frank have enough liquor to
help him sleep. He was worn out.

Around midnight, when the port was alseep, I took some
clothes and went in the truck to get Lupe. I had been carrying
the .45 in my belt since the day I got it. I had left it in the
truck only when going in to meet Raimundo and Santiago
and when I got Frank out of jail.

Lupe pinned her hair up tight to her head and washed off
her makeup. She put on the clothes I brought for her. She

was lost in them. I rolled up her pants legs and put a cap on her head and zipped her into a windbreaker.

"What is my name?"

"Jesús Christo."

"Don't borrow trouble," she warned.

"Pedro Gonzáles."

"I knew such a one. No good."

"Pick a name you like."

"Emiliano Zapata."

"You are a little short."

"Emilio Zapata."

"OK."

She snuggled up to me. "You like a nice young boy, *señor?*"

I squeezed her ass. "Um, a nice fat one. Are you a virgin, *hijo?*"

"Almost, *señor.*"

"That's close enough."

"Kiss me."

I kissed her.

She went back and wrote on the mirror in Spanish with lipstick: "Thanks for everything. I love you. See you again sometime. Good-bye—Emilio."

"I don't tell her nothing," she explained.

In the truck I made her hold her cigarette the way a man would hold it. She sprawled on the seat with her legs apart.

"This the way, *señor?*"

I pinched her twat and she squealed.

"Poor little fella, someone's cut your cock off."

"All the better for you, *cabrón,*" she said in a gruff, low voice.

Frank was awake. Lupe went into the cabin and closed the door to the galley behind her.

Frank looked at me, but he said nothing.

"I didn't eat anything," he reported.

"If you were hungry, you should have eaten. The icebox is open."

"Well, I thought I ought to wait."

Pathetic bastard.

"Fix yourself something."

"Johnny, you said to ask if I needed a little pick-me-up."

"Eat; then I'll give you one."

He busied himself making a sandwich. His hands shook. It was a very unimaginative sandwich.

"Have another," I told him when he had skarfed the first.

He made and ate another to get the drink he really wanted.

There was only a little more than an inch in the pint I had been keeping for him. I gave him the whole thing.

"Nothing more until breakfast," I warned, knowing if he needed one later, I would have to give it to him.

Smoking a cigarette, he felt bold enough to observe, "I heard you were working with a girl aboard."

"That's right."

"I'd heard."

Santiago came aboard around three in the morning. I had Frank bedded down in the galley. I figured to put Santiago in the pilothouse. He came in a car in which there were two other men. He came aboard and began looking around while the car waited. He found Lupe in my bunk, though the curtain was drawn. He searched everywhere a person could be.

"I don't like this. You said one man."

"She isn't a man." I tried to make a joke of it.

He was not amused.

"Her old man is looking for her. She has to come. I am responsible for her. She will be all right. Besides, she can cook good. The other man can't."

"We are not going for our pleasure," he reminded me.

"Nevertheless, an army travels on its stomach," I reminded *him.*

"What is below here?"

I took him out and down to into the hold and engine room.

"What is the ice for?"

"To look like we are fishing."

He seemed to think that was a good idea.

"It will have to go over when we are outside."

I nodded that I understood.

He went back down to the car and talked with the others. Then he brought his bag aboard. The car turned around and left.

"How soon can we leave?"

"As soon as it starts getting light."

"You have some coffee?"

"Sure, a big pot." I got him a cup of coffee.

He didn't like it, but he drank it.

"You can bunk in the pilothouse," I told him. "It is comfortable."

"I won't sleep now."

"Well, it's a good place to keep watch from."

He would go along with that.

From his bag he pointedly took a Thompson submachine gun without the stock and snapped a loaded clip into it. Another clip was taped to the first upside down so he could quickly reverse it.

"I would keep that out of sight until we get out," I suggested.

He just looked at me as if I were stupid. He also let me know he was packing a pistol.

Then he had an idea.

"You have some guns on this boat?"

"Some."

"Bring them to me. I will have the only guns."

I got him the carbine and the shotgun, then realizing he had probably seen the pistol in my belt, I handed it over too.

"That's all?"

"All."

"Why you need so many guns?"

"This one is for sharks," I said touching the sawed-off twelve-guage. "The rifle is for general use. The pistol is for the woman's husband."

That made sense to him too.

I did not mention the Thompson gun hidden down in the engine room. Sometime, when he was more relaxed, I would get down there and get it together and load it. I just did not like him having all the guns aboard.

I got a cup of coffee and joined him. I figured I might as well sit up with him until it was light.

At first he was reluctant to talk.

Then I asked him, "What is your interest in this revolution anyway, Santiago?"

"I am Cuban. My father is a Negro. I am a Negro too. I never have the advantages in my country. My people, my *compadres*, never have the advantages. I will tell you something, and you will understand:

"My father, he works on the docks, you understand, unloading the ships?"

"Yow."

"So. He supports Batista when he makes the sergeants revolt and takes the country, when I was a little boy. But your country, it owns Batista. He is a gangster. I could tell you stories what his gangsters do to little girls, everything. But my father supports him. In Cuba there is good unions for a long time. Under Batista. OK. A boss can't fire nobody and hire a friend in their place in Cuba. If he fire someone, he must ask the union to give him another man. Cuba has the highest income for each person in all of South America, under Batista. But Batista, he lets the gangsters from your country come into Cuba. They screw everything. In my father's union there came men from your country to run that union, milk it of its money and take the power. They are gangsters. Your government sent them. They talk a lot about how bad it is to be a Communist. If you want your job, you don't say some things no more. You don't say the things Batista said when he led the revolt of the sergeants. Now bosses can hire their brothers and fire men they don't like and the unions will send them their brother. And the *communistas* support Batista. It is true. They fire my father. He makes a protest to his union.

My father is a big man. Twice me. He is black as this." He showed me the metal of his pistol.

"Someone say something bad to him at the union, and he knock the man down and go away. One night some men catch him on the road and beat him up. He lose one eye, many teeth. They break his legs. But he don't die. Some people bring him to our house. He lives. When he can walk again with sticks, he goes to the government with a young lawyer who is now with the *movimiento,* but then he has—what you call it?—consciousness. He goes with my father. They sit for three days outside an office before they can make their complaint. The laywer, he has made papers. My father will sue the union and these men who beat him up. My father knows one of these men. He knows him from when they were boys.

"We hear nothing. Then the men come back and take my father from beside my mother in the bed and take him away. They beat him up again. And this time they shoot him full of holes and leave him hanging on a fence for all to see the next day. The lawyer, he is arrested for something and goes to jail. There he meets some men in the *movimiento.* When he gets out, he goes to join Castro in the hills.

"When I hear of the *movimiento,* I go and join with them also."

"You do any fighting?"

He looked at me narrowly.

"Sure. I fight. When we fight, we do not just kill the soldiers. We talk with the people. The people help us. They do not want the Yankee gangsters in the country.

"They work and grow *tomates* for Yankees. The Yankees take the *tomates* to your country and put them in cans and bring them back and no one can pay the price for them. It is stupid. Anyone can see that. You don't have to read or write to understand such things. When I go to the hills, I cannot read much. Now I can read. When we don't fight, we have school. When we win everyone will have school."

"You love Cuba?"

He looked puzzled.

"*Sí.* . . . I want to see all the people get the advantages. You understand? Love? *Amor?* It is not that. Not so *romántico.* It is something else, hunh? . . . You love your country?"

"Yow."

"But it does many bad things. It is a gangster country. Why you love it?"

"It's the only one I've got."

"If there is a revolution in your country, do you join it?"

"I don't know. Would depend. I guess if they shot up my father and left him on a fence, I sure as hell wouldn't go with those who did it. I never knew my father much and didn't like him much. He was a rummy. But I know how you feel."

"That is one thing wrong with your country. Your fathers are made fat and stupid. You have no fathers, no brothers, no *compadres.* They must do too many bad things to pay for their comforts and they become bad . . . and stupid." He used a Spanish word that meant silly, clownish, as best as I understood it.

Santiago did not have much English, and most of what he said was in Spanish, but I think I understood it. He learned his English as a shoeshine boy on the streets of Havana. He had also sold newspapers. I told him I had done both of those things.

"But you do this now for the money. You help us for the dollars," he accused.

I tried to tell him why I needed the money. I told him about the insurance that isn't any security, how I got the boat in the first place, the payments that were due. The story about Lupe's husband was true, but it was not the main thing. I would do what we were doing for the money anyway.

He nodded his head wisely.

"You are not so stupid as I thought," he told me in Spanish.

I put out my hand. He looked at it; then he took it.

It was almost time to cast off.

I went back and checked on Frank. He was snoring like a rummy, fitfully, tossing on his bunk.

I slid the curtain on my bunk open a bit and sat down to look at Lupe. One hand was curled under her cheek. Her hair was pinned tightly to her head. She had a very round head. My head and the heads of my family were long and oval. I gently cradled the back of her head in my palm. If we had a kid, would it have a round head or an oval one, was a thought, or half and half?

She stirred and opened her eyes.

"*¿Qué pasa?*"

"Nothing. It's all right."

She closed her eyes and made little kissing movements with her pale lips. I bent and kissed her as you would a child and slid the curtain closed.

"We don't need to awaken them," I told Santiago. "You can take off the lines and come haul them in, OK?"

He was a bit suspicious of being left on the dock, I think, but realized I had nothing in the world to gain by leaving him and went to do as I said.

When we were going out the channel, I asked, "You get seasick, Santiago?"

When he understood what I meant, he looked very concerned.

"I do not know," he replied in Spanish. "I have never been on a boat before."

Some revolution.

CHAPTER EIGHTEEN

Santiago got seasick. Lupe got seasick. I knew Frank was going to be seasick.

At first Santiago was suspicious about taking the Dramamine. I had to show him that Lupe and Frank were taking the same thing from the same bottle and popped one myself before he would take the tablets.

"Tell him if I wanted to harm him, I would catch him bending over the side and toss him to the fish." I asked Lupe to translate. "Tell him to relax."

Before she could repeat everything I said, Santiago clapped a hand over his mouth and bolted outside toward the rail. Lupe soon followed.

I looked at Frank until he must have figured "what the hell" and got up to hand his way out with the others.

When they came back, I gave them all more pills and a shot of brandy with lime juice in it.

Santiago had not told me yet where we were going, but we were headed south, not far off the Mexican coast. If I were loading guns down there, I would do it around Twenty-fourten. In spite of the danger of the hidden rocks, it was a desolate place where you were not likely to be troubled by *federales*. It was a wreckers' place, an old smugglers' place, and before that a pirates' place.

When Santiago was straightened up enough to show me where he wanted me to go on the map, I was gratified by my guess. He pointed to The Rocks.

"We can't run in too close there," I had Lupe explain to him for me. I wanted no misunderstanding. "How are you handling the cargo?"

"It is arranged," he said. "You go in close, and I will make a signal, and we wait."

"OK."

"If everything is all right, they will bring everything out to us."

"That is how I would have done it," I had Lupe tell him.

He had loosened up a bit more. Lupe brought us some frijoles and meat and bread for our lunch.

"I will stay in Cuba now," he said. "We are finished here. I will go back into the hills to fight now for our victory." Good beans make people confident.

"Someone else will take over the supply!" I wondered.

He nodded. He smiled.

"Fidel has made a deal with your country. He was just in your country."

"I didn't hear anything about it."

He laughed. "He don't come in no big airplane. He swim." He made swimming motions. "He swim the Rio Grande. He cut off his beard and swim over and come up with some boys in the river. He go meet with an old ex-*presidente*, Prio Soccoras, in a motel in McAllen, Texas. I know. I was in the river. Prio is your man. Now you will help us too. Soon all the men in the prison at Fort Brown is let go. Just three days ago an airplane takes off with many good guns for us from a little airfield in Tamaulipas. Your country knows we will win and now tries to be our friend, to get what you can from us when we win, to try to buy Fidel. Some people in the *movimiento* are afraid Fidel will sell out to you. He will not. He is smart, mister. He will let you give us the guns we need. He will let you send your agents, your mercenaries to open a new front near Havana. But you will see what happens when we win. Fidel is not like the others you have bought. You don't buy him. You think he would do a deal with Prio and let men like him back to get rich and fat? You will see."

I looked at Lupe and we remembered the night we had gone to the *curandera* and been stopped on the road along the river by the men with guns. There had been boys swimming down there that night. Maybe what Santiago said was true.

"Good beans, Santiago?"

"*Sí, bueno.* Maybe you are not so dumb to steal this one from her husband," he added in Spanish.

I had forgotten how she looked with makeup on her face. She wore jeans too large for her, gathered at the waist with a piece of line. One of my sweat shirts, with the sleeves rolled up, hung loosely from her shoulders. She wrapped her head in a big bandanna. And she was barefoot for want of proper shoes to wear on the boat. If her feet got cold, she could wear the sea boots Chelo had worn.

We had spent less than an hour together in the bunk since we cast off, and then I had just held her awhile.

I put the boat on autopilot and went back with her to the galley. I had to get Frank his ration of whiskey. I took her in my arms and held her close and kissed her mouth.

"When we get to Florida, we are going to get some really good clothes and put them on and go to the best place in town."

"I like to be like this, Johnny," she said, plucking out her big sweat shirt. "I like it. I get tired trying to be beautiful. I am happy, even if you don't think I am so beautiful."

"I think you are beautiful. Your nose is getting sunburned."

"I don't care. I feel good now. I want to go with you always, OK. Work with you, yes?"

"Sure."

"I don't want to stay home and wait. You leave me home, and I will get into trouble, I promise you."

"Never leave you home."

She kissed me. "I am the same inside and underneath. The rest, it washes off me."

"I'm glad you are here, Lupe."

"I am glad too."

* * *

When Frank Smith was through being sick, he realized we were not just going fishing.

I gave him his booze ration.

"Looks like we are going to be carrying something to somebody, Johnny," he said.

"That's right. When I got you, I didn't think it was necessary to tell you, the shape you were in. I didn't figure you would mind. It's easier than fishing so far."

"It's OK with me, Johnny."

"I reckoned to pay you five hundred or twenty-five a day, which ever worked out to more."

I figured if we got in there and got out it wouldn't matter what a rummy like Frank might say later on when he was plastered. There would be no proof.

"What we have to do, Frank, is get all that ice overboard now. You scoop, and Santiago and I will haul up and dump it."

I had only taken on enough ice for a short trip, but it was going to be a job getting it out nevertheless. When it was off the boat, I would hose down the rest and pump out and leave the hatch open to dry as much as it would. If the stuff we were going to haul was packed properly, there would be no problem.

When the ice was off, the boat picked up a little speed, but the motion was more apparent. Someone who really knew what they were looking at would know we were light.

The radio made Santiago nervous. Though we did not see any other boats on the course I was running, we could hear them on the radio. Santiago was not sure they could not hear us as well, so I shut the radio down and put on music.

There was a news broadcast in Spanish reporting that loyal Cuban troops had trapped Castro in the mountains again. They were making an all-out push with air support. Batista himself promised Fidel Castro would be dead or captured within the next forty-eight hours.

"They are lying," Santiago assured us. "You know how many times in one year they have said that?"

"How many?"

"Plenty! Every week. They say that on Friday. On Monday there will be many empty cots in the soldiers' barracks. We do not lose one battle with them. Not one. They never win nothing. Now the soldiers do not want to go into the hills. It is all over. You don't have to do this again. One year, more or less, we will be in Havana, and all the people from the country will come with us. You will see."

"I'll remember you said it, Santiago."

"OK. . . . How long now?"

"Not long. We will be there tonight. It looks like it's going to be a little rough though. We might have to lay out until it gets better."

"They will be looking for us now."

"Well, maybe it won't be so rough later."

I had shown Santiago how to keep on the course. He took some pride in being able to steer the boat. I told him I wanted to go check the engine and left him and Frank in the pilot-house.

I took Lupe's hand in the galley and motioned for her to come with me.

"I still have my period, *querido.*"

"That all you think about?"

I led her with me down below. It was cool and dark and damp down there with the wooden bins where we stored the catch. You could see the great frames of the boat's hull, smell the wood that had held shrimp.

In the engine room she put her arms around my neck and kissed me.

I took her hand off my cock.

"Lupe, I want to show you something."

"I know what he looks like."

"Be serious."

I got down and took the submachine gun from where I had it hidden beneath the tool bench. I unwrapped it and took off the stock so it would be smaller to hide. I showed her how to use it.

"Just pull back on this and squeeze the trigger. It will keep firing until it is empty."

I loaded a long clip, then another and taped them together with electrician's tape. I showed her how to reverse the clips when the first was empty.

I put the clips in her loose jean pocket and the gun down the other leg and covered the bulges with her sweat shirt.

"Give me five minutes to get back to the pilothouse, then come up and lie down in the bunk, pull the curtain to take a nap. Put the gun down between the mattress and the wall with the clips right beside it. If anything happens and I can't get to it, you try to get it and shoot everyone you can except me. OK?"

"OK. I will try, but I am afraid I will forget what you showed me."

"Think about it in your head until you remember it."

"You think anything will happen?"

"No."

"I don't either. I like him now, Santiago. He is so *cándido*."

"Yow. Just remember. Just in case."

"OK. I try not to shoot you."

The way that gun climbed and hopped around, I did not think my odds on surviving her help were long. I hoped I would get to the thing first.

I really did not think there would be any trouble. You read in books about all the shooting and shit around smuggling something. If what you read represented par for the course, no one would ever smuggle anything.

We were almost off The Rocks at suppertime. I decided to run on in while we had light and anchor even though the sea was running a little heavier than I would have liked. If they brought the stuff out in small boats, which was about the only way they could bring it out, it might be a bit tough transferring it. I discussed this with Santiago, and he agreed we go in and see.

I put Frank up on the bow to look for rocks and went in

slow on the rising tide. If this worked just right, we ought to be able to come out on the ebb and never scratch our bottom.

Inside the water was bit quieter, but still choppy.

Lupe made us some canned soup and sandwiches, and we drank beer. I gave Frank his shot, I was feeding him my Fundador now, so we all had a good belt to wait for dark.

When it was dark enough to show a light, Santiago took a lantern and went out and flashed some prearranged signal with it. There was no light on the shore.

"Maybe they are not there yet," he decided.

We waited a half hour and he flashed again. He did this a third time before he got he light he was looking for.

"Is it OK?" I asked him.

"It is OK. We wait now."

An hour later a rubber boat propelled by a small outboard came out. Santiago was up at the rail with his tommy gun. The men in the boat were unarmed as far as I could see. They were dressed like native fishermen. I put over a ladder, and one climbed up to speak with Santiago earnestly, too far away for me to hear a word.

Santiago came back.

"It is OK. He wants to know if you have some good cigarettes."

"Cigarettes?"

"*¡Si!*"

"Sure."

I went and got a carton of smokes and gave them to Santiago, who gave them to the man. He tore open the carton, got himself a few packs, opened one of these and lit up before he went back down to the rubber boat.

"They run out of everything there waiting for someone to come."

It was another hour before they began bringing the stuff out. They had every kind of little boat that would float, each almost awash with boxes of rifles, hand grenades, some .30 caliber machine guns, and boxes of ammunition.

There were copies of Thompson submachine guns from gunshops in Brooklyn, New York, ostensibly made to fire only one shot at a time, but all you had to do was a few things with the sear and some other parts to have yourself a machine gun. Most of the stuff was in Army boxes that had been painted over. The grenades had once been dummies, reloaded and primed. We took on enough stuff to outfit a light infantry regiment. I hadn't expected so much. They were still coming alongside when I had to tell Santiago, "We are getting heavy, *compadre*. If we don't go soon, we will miss the high water and we could get stuck in here."

"We are about finished," he announced after speaking to one of the others.

"How long?"

"One half an hour."

"OK. But then we must go whether you are finished or not."

"OK. I tell them."

He told them.

When the thirty minutes were up, I kicked over the engines and told Frank to handle the anchor.

"One little bit more," Santiago pleaded.

"No can do, Santiago. We have to go now."

"Five minutes. There is someone who must come with us?"

"What?"

"Yes. These three and one other."

"You didn't say anything about men, just cargo."

"These men must go with us. They have their orders. They are finished here. What is the difference?"

I didn't know. I just did not like the agreement being changed.

"When the anchor is up, we are leaving," I said.

"We will wait for this comrade," he said in Spanish and leveled his fucking gun at me.

"If he doesn't hurry, we will wait until tomorrow a sitting duck out here."

"He will be here."

The anchor was up and I was starting to move a bit when the rubber boat came alongside. It too was loaded with guns and two men.

Santiago told one of the men to get up the ladder.

"Forget the rifles," he told him. "We must go now."

The man was on the ladder, and I goosed open the throttle a little.

Frank ran a lead line on the bow, shouting out the depth to me as we crept out of there.

At one point the number Frank called was equal to our calculated draft and I prepared to hear a bad nosie. We scraped a bit. I held my breath. Lupe looked at me until Frank called out a better depth and I knew we were going to get out of there. On the rocks in the moonlight, we could see the picked bones of a shrimp boat that had piled up a few months back.

Once we were out in the Gulf, I put Frank on the wheel and went back to check our cargo and see how the revolution was coming.

The cargo was well enough loaded. The revolution was having a snack and drinking all my beer. Lupe was making them feel at home. The four we had taken aboard had short dark beards. They now all carried guns.

They were happy to be going back.

They told each other how well things were going and assured each other it was only a matter of a little time now and they would all be riding victoriously into Havana.

I heard Lupe tell one of them in no uncertain terms, "That is *my* bed, *hombre*. Only me and my man sleep in this bed."

They were not disagreeable and were generally more polite than Santiago. Three were very young; the fourth, who obviously outranked our man, was about forty. When we were in the open Gulf, he came to me and asked me in English if I had something for his stomach. He was feeling a bit sick. I got out the Dramamine again for the new passengers. There was very little left. The Gulf was rougher than it had been the day before.

By breakfast it was raining and blowing. The sea was breaking over our bow.

I was glad. I hoped it would stay that way until we were near Cuba. Those guys were going to be sick and off our necks as long as it lasted.

We were three days from Cuba before the weather cleared.

The boat stank. Lupe had moved our stuff, including the gun, into the pilothouse. I stowed the gun under the seat. She had quit trying to cook anything but canned soup. We ate soup, bread, canned fruit, and fresh oranges.

The one they called the major had given me three thousand U.S. dollars, all in twenties. Three days away lived their twin brothers.

I felt confident in my navigation as we approached Cuba but dead reckoning across so much open water was chancy. I did not know for sure where I was. I had a chart of the coast I wanted to come up on. They had a hand-drawn map of the cove where they wished to off load.

The major assured me it was perfectly safe, entirely in the control of the revolutionaries.

"If we had a dock, you could go in and tie up the boat with complete safety," he vowed.

He was a tall man, very thin, with a broken nose and the kind of eyes you like to see on an officer if you are in a combat unit. He was as sick as the others, but he yet kept control between the necessity of excusing himself and going to the rail.

"I was with Fidel on the *Granma* when we first came to Cuba and made our little invasion. We were all sick. It was terrible. The motor quit. There was nothing to eat but rotting oranges. This is paradise by comparison."

"Santiago says you are going to win."

"We will win. Soon. There is work to do yet in the country. We are in no hurry now. We own the countryside."

I told him what Santiago had told me about Castro swimming in the Rio Grande and all that.

"Santiago talks too much in his enthusiasm. But when this history is written truly, it will be very interesting. Very surprising. And you will have been a little part of it, Captain," he teased.

"I'd just as soon get this over with and forget about it," I told him honestly.

We had to run along the coast in daylight while the major looked for the landmarks to guide me in. When we found the hills he was looking for, he congratulated me. I hadn't been two miles off in my calculations.

"Come to Cuba when this is over and we will give you a job," he said. "We will want to develop our fishing industry."

"Maybe I will do that." I grinned.

Though the revolutionaries controlled that place, the major said we would unload after it got dark, so I turned and ran out of the sight of the coast and put my nets over as if I were fishing.

When it became dark, I hauled the nets. We had some nice fish and even a few shrimp. We shared out the fish. The men put up some in a box to take with them.

We ran into where we could anchor. We showed no lights. No smoking.

Small signal lights were exchanged.

The men waited with loaded weapons along the rail until the first boat came out.

It was a twenty-five-foot fishing boat. With all the hands to help, the stuff went off faster than it had come on. But there was only the one boat. We had to wait for it to go in and unload and come back out.

"There was to be another boat, but the motor is no good now," the major apologized.

We were still working and waiting when it began to get light. There was still a couple of boat loads to get off. When the sun came up, I expressed my worry.

"Only one more, maybe two. We are safe," the major told me. "Then you can be on your way."

The plane was a U.S. A-20 attack bomber with no markings on it. It came over the hill at low level and began strafing while we had the last of the stuff on deck and were loading into the other boat. I saw the pocks of the shells from the nose cannons kick up the water as they raced toward us, before I heard the scream of the plane's engines. I could see the fuckers in the plane. They did not look Cuban. The looked like Anglos.

The Cubans on deck were firing their tommy guns at the plane.

"Fuck that!" I yelled. *"Get that shit off of here!"* I ran to cut loose the anchor.

Lupe ran after me to help.

I heard the big shells slam into the boat.

Shit! Shit! I yelled in my heart. *"Get that boat off of us!"* I yelled back at Frank.

He was scared, but he was pretty good. He was getting the lines from the boat loose, yelling at the Cubans to get in their boat and go.

The major was ordering his men to get into the other boat when I came back from cutting loose from our anchor.

The plane had banked and made a circle and was coming back.

It dropped two bombs, both of which missed and exploded off the port fantail, rocking us pretty hard. It climbed and turned to come back on a strafing run. Two of the Cubans were down on the deck already. One looked like Santiago.

The big slugs came across the water like twin zippers, climbed up the side of the boat and across the cabin. I heard Lupe grunt and sort of cry out behind me. I looked back and saw her down on the deck with a large bloody hole in her middle which she covered with her hands.

I grabbed her up in my arms and lunged into the pilothouse. I laid her on the seat and told her it would be all right.

I got the engine running and opened the throttle and ran it up to the most efficient rpms. It would turn faster, but the screw would be just flailing water.

I ran first one way, then the other, trying to give the plane a less good target to shoot at, make us look injured.

Frank crawled in on his hands and knees.

"I think they are dead back there." He was shaking. "Johnny, I need a drink in the worst way."

Jesus Christ! I took the bottle from the drawer by the wheel and handed it to him.

He was guzzling when the plane made another run at us, and bullets tore through the pilothouse ceiling and deck, shattered our windshield. I punched the broken glass out so I could see.

"Take care of her, you son of a bitch!" I yelled at Frank, knocking the bottle away from him.

"Johnny," Lupe husked. "I love you." Blood bubbled from her lips.

Oh, goddamn! "Please!" I cried aloud.

"She's going," Frank said.

"Take this fucking wheel and keep laying her back and forth as that bastard comes in."

I dropped on my knees beside Lupe. I put my ear to her chest. I looked up at her face. Just her lips moved as her eyes went blind forever. Her right hand fell away and smacked the deck.

The plane made another run and splintered us up some more.

The fucker will shoot us apart, I thought. I could hardly see and then realized I was crying, that there were tears clouding my vision.

I saw Frank retrieve the bottle and take a hell of a long drink.

What did it matter?

I went back into the cabin and gathered up everything that would burn: bedding, towels, everything. I got cooking oils, alcohol, paint, thinner, lard, everything I could find and got out on deck.

The plane was heading up into the sun and going to make its turn.

The little fishing boat was on fire and sinking behind us. The bodies of two Cubans were on the deck along the rail. One was Santiago. I strung the blankets and stuff along the rail beside the bodies. I doused the stuff and the bodies with the oil, thinner, paint and alcohol, tore chunks of lard and threw it on the mess. I threw some heavy rope on there and got down to light it with my lighter as I heard the plane make its turn to start its diving, strafing run. I lay on the deck as if I were dead and flicked my lighter until the thinner caught, and fire raced along over the bodies of the Cubans and the other stuff I had heaped along the rail. It caught just as the slugs were chewing into the deck. Something stung me in my right thigh. I looked and saw a splinter of wood like a ragged lance head driven through my thigh. I knew it touched the bone, hit it, and glanced off. The damn thing was about a foot long.

I thought I might faint and cursed myself aloud until the feeling passed. The slugs raked us again.

Black smoke from my fire was now billowing over the fantail of the boat.

We had traveled about five miles since the attack began.

The plane made two more runs and went off toward the direction from which it came.

I hopped into the pilothouse and told Frank to go back and watch the fire. To get the hose ready and, if it got out of hand, to start putting it out. Otherwise let it smoke in case another plane came out.

He kept looking at the big splinter through my thigh, but said nothing.

After a while he put out the fire and came back into the pilothouse.

I sat down on the seat across from where Lupe lay dead.

"Them Cubans are still smoldering," Frank said.

There was vomit on his shirt.

"Have a drink."

He took one and offered me the bottle. I took it and drank.

That piece of wood had to come out. Every movement of the boat nearly knocked me out.

"Frank, you got to pull this thing out."

He looked at it, and I could see he didn't want to do it.

"You got to do it, Frank. I won't make it with it in there."

I took my knife and held the wood where it broke through my leg and trousers and tried to cut it off just above where I held it. Every time I touched it pain almost knocked me out. That was not going to work.

"Get the big cutters from the tool box." I had a pair of cable and bolt cutters in there. "Put it on auto and get them."

He did as he was told and came back with the cutters.

"Cut that thing off right against my leg. One fucking snap."

I yelled when he did it and came up off the seat and fell back, trying to suck air.

"Give me a drink, Frank."

He gave me a drink.

I turned over.

"Get it with both hands and pull it out. Don't fucking yank, but just pull steady no matter what until it is out."

I got a grip with both hands on the sill of the shattered windows.

"When I say now, do it."

"Now."

I heard myself scream, came up off the bench, thought my brain would explode, then I went out.

I felt whiskey in my throat and coughed and came to.

Frank had the first-aid box and had it open but did not seem to know how to proceed.

I took a drink of the brandy and got myself straightened out.

While I tore my pants open to get at the wound, I knew how I was going to work the rest of the trip. It became crystal clear and definite. It was the only way to try to handle it.

There were sulfa packets in there. I opened one and doused it in the exit side of the wound and had Frank pour another into the entry. I put on heavy gauze pads and wrapped it tightly to stop the bleeding. I had some penicillin tablets in there and took four, washed down with brandy.

"What are we going to do?" Frank asked.

He was getting slurry.

"We'll be all right Frank."

"I don't know. The boat's pretty much a mess, Johnny. They are going to want to know about this."

"Don't worry, Frank."

"I sure think this is worth a lot more than five hundred, Johnny. I sure do."

"I'll take care of you, Frank."

"You got any more of this?" He showed me the empty bottle. "Sure, Frank. Here's the key to my locker. Go get us a bottle."

He took my keys and went back to the cabin.

I hopped over and lifted Lupe off the seat where she lay and put her on the floor. I closed her eyes. From beneath the seat, I took the Thompson and waited for Frank to come back.

He had opened the bottle and helped himself before he brought it into the pilothouse.

"Hey, where did you find that thing?" he asked, eyeing the gun.

"Take a big drink, Frank."

He started to drink, then lowered the bottle.

"You want one?"

"Go ahead. I'll catch up."

"Sure." He looked at the gun and took another drink.

"Stand over there in the door."

"What are you going to do?"

"Stand over there, Frank, and turn around."

"Listen, you aren't going to shoot me, are you? You wouldn't do that."

"Get over there, Frank. Drink all that you want."

"What the hell, Johnny?" He moved though. "What is this? It don't make any sense to shoot me. You need me. You'll never get in alone."

"Turn around, Frank, and drink."

"Aw, hell, Johnny. Don't do this to me."

He was crying, just a little.

"Turn around, you fucking rummy! *Turn around!* I can't stand your goddamn face!"

"Please, Johnny."

He turned around, facing the Gulf. I could see the sun shining through the thin, lank hair on his head.

"Take a big one, Frank."

"Please. . . ."

"DRINK!"

He tipped the bottle up, looking into the sun, and I could see the back of his scrawny wrinkled neck working to get down the booze.

I had switched the change lever to single fire. I raised the gun and touched the trigger, and Frank's head exploded. He jerked, the bottle went flying, and he fell. His feet kicked a couple of kicks, and he was still.

It was very quiet then out there.

I sat awhile, smoked a cigarette, looked at Lupe.

In death she did not look as I remembered her. I took my jacket from a peg, knelt down and kissed her bloody, lifeless lips and put the jacket over her face.

I peeked at Frank. The front of his face was gone. Brains were leaking out. They should have been pickled. They looked just like any kind of brains.

I went back and put on the radio and gave a May Day. I switched to the Coast Guard channel and tried to raise them. I was too far away, I guess.

I finally picked up a shrimp boat out of Tampa and told them I had a man go berserk and shoot up my boat and set it on fire before I was able to kill him. I said I was burning badly and was sinking fast. I gave them my position again and told them to raise the Coast Guard if they could. I said I would stay with the boat awhile longer but would have soon to take to the raft. I told them I was injured. They said they were over an hour away.

I then went down and opened the sea cocks, threw some thinner around in the engine room, and set it on fire.

I got together some supplies and water and a six-pack of beer and got the raft over on a line. I checked the fire again. It was going good down there. I had to close the hatch against the flames. A can of something blew up down there and rocked the boat.

I put out the ladder, climbed down it into the raft, and cut the line with my knife. I paddled off about a hundred yards or so and watched the *Sgt. William T. Shea* burn. It was about an hour before the fuel tanks got hot enough to blow. After that she went down pretty fast.

I could not have taken her in shot all to hell like that. Now I had a chance to collect the insurance, get started again. That was all I really thought about.

I felt sad and empty, as if everything in my life that had gone before had ended, had been canceled out. I was still me, but everything now began from that raft in open water. I would remember Lupe and everything else, my childhood, things I had done, places I had been, but it was only that—memories. My name could be anything. I had crossed some barrier. Every feeling, every thing I did now would be qualified, something I had felt and done before. Nothing would be new again.

The boat went down with a sucking rush that surprised me.

When she turned on her end, she was a big damned thing. I noted how clean the freshly painted bottom looked.

In a while Frank's body bobbed up on the surface, face down. I expected the Cubans to come up, then figured maybe they were stuck to the deck by the fire.

It was not long before the sharks came to hit Frank. At first there was a big bull shark, then others. It took them only a minute to divide Frank between them. One bumped my raft on the way out and nearly tossed me out. It circled me awhile, then came in to bump with its nose. A bull or mako about nine feet long. A shark will bump its target first usually and then come take a chomp. I held the raft's little oar like a spear in both hands, and when it came to bump, I jabbed it hard on the snout. It dove beneath the raft and never came up again. I was scared then. Really scared.

I kept scanning the bright horizon for the shrimper from Tampa. If he missed me before dark, I could be lost.

The sun was hot on my leg. Blood had darkened the bandage. I tore the cardboard off the six-pack of beer and shaded my leg with that. I opened a beer and drank it. I bobbed up and down, lost in the bottom of a low swell, then lifted to where I could see the horizon.

I had been in the raft a couple of hours when it lifted and I saw the white high-nosed shrimper on the horizon.

I tied my shirt by the sleeves to an oar, and every time I lifted I waved the hell out of my flag.

I saw the shrimper seem to be going past and swore.

"Over here, you dumb bastards! Here! Over here! Look over here, you shitbrained fuckers!"

Then it turned toward me, and I loved them, whoever they were.

They came alongside. Three black faces peered over at me from the rail, two men and a boy. One threw me a line and made the raft fast alongside. They put over a Jacob's ladder and helped me aboard.

The man who helped me into the cabin was tall and handsome with gleaming black skin and a strong face. His short nappy hair was just graying at the temples. He helped me onto a bunk.

The older black man and the boy got my raft aboard and came in to see how I was.

I knew there were some black shrimpers who ran their own boats out of Florida. Those were the first I had met.

"How's the fishing?" I asked.

"Been pretty good lately," the man said softly. "How bad you hurt there?"

"Piece of wood splintered through my leg. Don't know how the hell it happened. We were on fire. I opened the engine room door and an explosion knocked me on my ass and drove this big splinter through me."

"You say you had a man go nuts?"

"Yow. A rummy I got out of jail for the trip. He was all I had with me. Had him sipping along, you know, but it didn't hold him. He broke into some liquor and went crazy and started shooting up the boat and raising hell."

"Well, I guess you was lucky."

"I had to kill him."

"Um. . . . Well, you rest. We fix you something to eat pretty soon. Lester, you get that first-aid kit and see can you help this man." He put out his hand. "I'm Jeremiah Fellows. This is my dad, and my son, Lester."

"I'm sure much obliged, Captain." I nodded to the other two.

The old man hopped away.

The boy brought the first-aid box. He stood right there being helpful and watchful as I unwrapped the bloody bandage and redressed the now ugly and swollen wound in my leg.

"Mérida is about the closest place to run you in," Captain Jeremiah told me. "I'll do that. There's a hospital there. And you can catch a plane home when you're able. You got any money?"

"I'm all right."

"You got any insurance on that boat?"

"Yow. Still paying on her."

"Well, you be all right then."

"I hope."

"Worries me. I let my insurance drop when I had this boat paid for. Couldn't afford it. Kept going up every time you turn around. No sense in workin if you gotta pay it all away on insurance. But if I lose her, I lost everything."

"I was going to let my insurance go as soon as she was paid for," I empathized.

"Well, it beats workin, right?"

"Shit, I reckon."

He laughed.

"There's a bottle if you want a little drink."

"This coffee is fine. About as good as my own. There's chicory in there."

"You bet. Ain't coffee without a little chicory in there."

I slept awhile. I awoke when they were eating supper. The boy brought me a plate of shrimp gumbo on rice and a big chunk of cornbread. The old man was the cook and a good one.

They ran me into Progreso, the port for Mérida. The captain had radioed the port, and there was an ambulance on the dock to take me to the hospital.

The leg was really swollen and throbbed all the time now.

The doctors in the hospital were very interested in the wound. An older, doctor, bald and lean, examined it and told me:

"It is like a *cornada* from a bull. We will open it up and clean it out, and you will live."

That is what he did. They gave me a spinal block, and I watched them work on the wound. It took about two hours for the doctor to do what he had to do. There was a nurse with very beautiful eyes above her surgical mask who assisted him. Her name was Rita, and I asked her for a date while they were working on me.

"She is happily married, *señor,* with three beautiful children," the doctor informed me without missing a beat. "I am fortunate enough to be her husband."

"Don't let what I said influence you now," I begged off.

He laughed. The nurse's eyes smiled. They were pretty · good.

I was in the hospital two weeks with a drain in the wound.

The little Indians who came each morning to give me my coffee and a bath were giggling, yet unembarrassed. Unlike their Anglo counterparts, they whipped the sheet off me, stripped me and scrubbed me as I lay stark naked, as they would the floor, singing softly some popular tune. I got to like them a lot.

I used the phone a lot. I called Eli and told him the story I wanted told back in town. I told him to go to the bank and to see the insurance agent.

The American consul came and brought me some cigarettes and took a statement from me, which I signed.

The Mexican authorities came and also took a statement.

When I was able to leave, the doctor came to tell me goodbye. The little Indians came to giggle and say *adiós.*

The bill only came to about four hundred dollars. I paid it and took the receipt and caught a taxi out to the little airport.

The plane flew over the pyramids in the jungle at Chichén Itzá, banking to give the tourists on both sides a good look.

I sat beside an American woman about thirty who said she was studying for a master's degree in archaeology at the University of Wisconsin. She had a little portable typewriter in a case under her seat.

We had a couple of drinks, and she told me she had just split from her husband who was a psychologist who had started messing around with some sort of hallucinogenic drug and gone nuts. She'd had him put away. They had two children. She showed me their pictures. They were cute kids. She asked what I did. I told her. Then she asked about my leg. I told her what had happened the way I wanted it remembered. She asked if I were married. I told her no.

Later she suggested, "Why don't we stop in Mexico City for a couple of days? I would like to let my hair down. I haven't really had any fun on this trip. The men I've met are all such nerds."

I did not ask what a nerd was. I told her I would like to make the stop but I had to get back as soon as I could and tend to business.

She wanted to exchange addresses. I told her to write me care of General Delivery, Port Isabel.

We put our chairs back to sleep. The back of her hand brushed mine, then stole into it. So we held hands.

I felt pretty good. Empty, but pretty good.

The world was nuts. People were just trying to make it, you know. We were all in some fix or another.

CHAPTER NINETEEN

I had missed the wedding of Charles Principal and Babe Cayce. She said she would never forgive me. Charles had lost a lot more hair.

Pop sat his cup down beside mine and got on the stool. There were not many people in the café.

"You make any money, Johnny?" he asked out of the corner of his mouth.

"Not enough, Pop. Wasn't worth it."

"You know, the only time I ever got shot at except during the shrimp war was by some other fellows who were looking to hijack me. No profit in it now. Some fellas are around from San Antone and Dallas. Fat, bad types. They're doin it all now. It's a regular freight line, I hear. The FBI and the other government men are looking the other way. All them Cubans been let out of Fort Brown. Had some come around here looking for jobs. I'd stay out of it, son."

"Don't worry, Pop."

"Well, listen, Hobie Glass' boat is for sale. He went crazy, you know."

I hadn't heard.

"Yep. Took five deputy sheriffs to get that fella down and chained. Came back a little after you left and just kept drinkin. Hurt someone's wife bad, they say. They took him away. If you got any money or some way to get some, you ought to put something down on it. There going to be any trouble about your insurance?"

"The agent says there shouldn't be any trouble. But can you imagine what its going to cost me next time around?"

"You can't win. If it was winning that kept me goin, I'd of been dead long ago."

I went to see the people about Hobie's boat. I gave them a thousand for the option on it. It was a good boat, bigger than the *Shea*, newer, steel hull.

Eli was willing to wait for what I owed him. He had taken the job with the parks department his brother-in-law had gotten for him. His wife was beginning to put on a pregnant belly. Eli looked as if he were already getting fat.

I spoke to the people at the bank and told them what I was trying to do, about the option on Hobie's boat. They were encouraging but suggested I go with one of the companies and let them help with the boat. I told them I would like to try it once more on my own. They were nice enough but looked at me as if I were crazy or stupid.

In the end, I signed with a company. I would own the boat, get another in a couple of years with luck—one boat pays for another—but I signed with a company. It was all right, I guess.

I had rented Charles Principal's old room. He and Babe had rented a little house.

Chelo came to see me in the family's old Studebaker. I invited her in and had nothing to offer her. There was only one chair and the bed. She sat in the chair.

I told her the story as I had schemed it.

"Why you don't take me?" she asked. "Don't I work for you no more?"

I looked at her.

"Someday maybe I will tell you the true story. I couldn't take you this time. "

I told her I was getting another boat. I had an option on it and was just waiting for the insurance money. I told her I signed with a company. "I can work the boat as soon as I get a crew together, they said."

"I will be your crew."

"I will need another man. And I don't know how they will feel about me taking a girl along."

"You know I work good."

"I know."

"It is hot in this room."

"Yow."

There was only one window next to the bed. It was open, but there was no breeze.

"I have been thinking," she said.

"Yes?"

"Do you have a woman?"

"Well, no special one."

"An almost special one?"

"No one."

"Everyone says you run off with Lupe Contreras."

"No."

"I want to sleep with you."

I looked at her in the chair. She sat on her tail, with her slender legs stretched out before her, her ankles crossed.

"Why?"

"Because I think about it and I know I want to sleep with you. You do not have to make me no promises, nothing. You don't have to say you love me. No bullshit."

"Jesus, Chelo. It sounds pretty cold-blooded."

"What I think and feel is not cold-blooded. I just don't know any other words to tell you."

"Are you a virgin?"

"Almost, I think."

I laughed.

"That's close enough," I said and remembered when I had said that last.

"Uh, when do you want to do this?" I teased.

"Now, if you don't mind."

"Here?"

"Is it all right?"

I shrugged. "I guess so."

She stood up and pulled her shirt over her head. Her small breasts were held in a white cotton brassiere.

I took off my shirt and eased my trousers over my still stiff leg.

She stepped out of jeans and left them on the floor, unsnapped her bra and dropped it on the chair, stepped out of her white underpants and stood facing me, naked, not quite sure what to do with her hands. She was slender, yet womanly. Her breasts were small and pert and pink-tipped.

I limped over and drew her naked body against mine. Around her neck was a gold chain with a cruxifix and the shark's tooth on it.

I kissed her. She did not know how to kiss. I taught her a little with my lips. There is more to it than simply opening your mouth. She learned and began to like it a lot, it seemed.

We lay down on the bed.

I stroked her body for a long time, kissing her mouth, her breasts, her body.

"You smell good. Clean."

"I am clean," she said. "I took a bath before I came here."

I looked at her face and felt very tender.

"Lupe is dead," I told her.

"No!"

"Yes. I will tell you everything one day maybe. You must not mention it to anyone."

"I won't. Did you love her very much?"

"Yes. I think so."

"You love her still?"

"I don't think you ever stop loving someone. I don't know. She's dead. That whole life of mine is dead. You are the only thing that has come through it, and I feel like I hardly know you now. You are different."

"Maybe you are different also."

I kissed her mouth.

"Show me how you loved Lupe," she requested.

I took her hand and placed my cock in it and showed her how to stroke me gently and drifted my fingers down to the top of her tight little slit.

I was gentle with her. She was right, she was almost a virgin. She liked fucking. It was as natural for her as laughing and crying. Before I came, I thought she might get pregnant, probably would get pregnant. I did not care, I came until my balls ached.

When we lay side by side, I lit a cigarette and offered her a puff. She did not smoke, but she took a draw, then another.

"How do you like it so far?" I wondered.

Her small hand stole over and held my soft cock.

"I like it."

She fingered the red, puckered scar on my thigh gently.

"Tell me what happened truly."

"Not now. I will one day."

"Promise?"

"Promise."

"OK."

She lay close with her head on my shoulder in the circle of my arm. I stroked the small of her back, her waist. She held my cock in her hand while she slept.

She stayed that night and every night thereafter.

One morning I told Chelo I had promised myself I would one day name a boat the *Lupe Contreras.*

"But I don't want to now. I don't want to name the new boat that. Why don't you name it?"

"I don't care what you name the boat. The name means nothing to me."

We called her the *Caldo Largo.*

A cousin of hers showed up and became a permanent member of the crew. Luis, he was a good man. We also took her brothers with us a lot.

We were getting by.
She was pregnant. I told her I would like to get married.
"If you wish," she said. But she was pleased.

Chelo's sister was tried in another county too far away for
the family to go attend the trial. She was found guilty of murder and given ten years suspended. She was at work in a week
in the window of a cotton company in Brownsville, and people would walk by and look at her.

We had the wedding then. There was a barbecue in the
port, and everyone got a little drunk. Chelo and Babe Cayce,
who was also pregnant, measured nonexistent bellies. I
danced with Chelo's sister, still called Encanta, and told her
she was the most beautiful woman in the world. I found her
out back of things later and kissed her mouth. She kissed me
back and said it had been so long since she had kissed someone and felt such a way. She felt to me the way Lupe had,
only more beautiful, yet softer and sort of rotten. Her eyes
fluttered back under her lids when she kissed in a spooky way.
We had both calculatedly killed someone, was a thought, she
and I.

"Can I come see you?" I whispered.
"What of my sister?"
I said nothing.
"Yes," she said.
"Soon."
"Yes." She kissed me again.

That night, I took Chelo to the house I had rented without
telling her. Her sisters and mother had cleaned it and decorated it for us.

"I will still go with you often," she said.
"Sure. But we need a house now."

We lay in the bed with the fan blowing on us. I cradled
Chelo's belly in my hand, an erection between her legs and
thought of her sister.

Nothing is ever perfect. People are how they are. It is like Lupe once said: "There is some little part no one can ever know."

For that part there are no words.